A VARIABLE DARKNESS

Thirteen Tales

by
John McIlveen

Haverhill House Publishing LLC

Eve first appeared in *Wicked Tales* (2015 NEHW Press)
In Agatha Craggins's Defense first appeared in *Wicked Witches* (2016 NEHW Press)
Got Your Back first appeared in *Anthology III: Dying Distant Ember* (2014 Four Horsemen)
Eye of the Beholder first appeared in *Borderlands 6* (2016 Borderlands Press)
A Trunk Story first appeared in *A Sharp Stick to the Eye* (2018 Books & Boos Press)
Yankee Swap first appeared in *Hark the Herald Angels Scream* (2018 Random House)
Teacher's Pet first appeared in *Northern Frights* (2017 Grinning Skull Press)
Frontrunners first appeared in *Dystopian States of America* (2020 Haverhill House)
Triggers first appeared as a limited-edition chapbook (2017 Twisted Publishing)

A VARIABLE DARKNESS © 2021 John M. McIlveen
Hardcover - 978-1-949140-26-2
Paperback - 978-1-949140-25-5

Cover illustration and design © 2021 David Dodd

For more information, address:

Haverhill House Publishing
643 E Broadway
Haverhill MA 01830-2420
www.haverhillhouse.com

For my mother-in-law, **Geraldine Colasanti**, whose gentle
spirit and love for the written word are an inspiration.
Grazie mille

ACKNOWLEDGEMENTS

Very special, heartfelt thank you to:

Chris & Connie Golden, Tony Tremblay, and John & Dianne
Buja -- true friends through and through.

Maverick and Walker -- for making us smile.

Linda Nagel, and again, Dianne Buja -- for your editorial skills
and for kicking me in shape where needed.

David Dodd -- for your consistently brilliant cover art and
uncanny editor's eye.

And, as always, my Roberta. The reasons are beyond measure.

INDEX

"*A Variable Darkness* is a veritable feast of darkness, in infinitely varied shades. Great stories, great variety. Don't miss it!"
> --F. Paul Wilson, bestselling author of *The Adversary Cycle* and The Repairman Jack Series

"With *A Variable Darkness*, John McIlveen has leveled up. These stories are the perfect blend of heartache and heartless, somehow simultaneously unflinching and brutal, with a trademark thread of dark humor. This collection deserves your attention. I can't wait to see what he does next!"
> --Christopher Golden, New York Times bestselling author of *Red Hands*

"John McIlveen's *A Variable Darkness* is a breathtaking collection. Its stories run the gamut from wise, lushly written prose to modern, witty tales. Each story dives beneath the surface and contains fathoms. I thought about "Nobody's Daughter" for days."
> --Mercedes M. Yardley, Bram Stoker Award-winning author of *Little Dead Red*

"Reading John M. McIlveen's stories feels like listening to a seasoned storyteller weave words into magic around a campfire. The stories in this collection are scary, sad, funny, heartwarming, and make you think a little more deeply about the people we see around us every day. He gives us witches, goddesses, aliens, smelly ghosts, and so much more to make you laugh, cry, or send a shiver down your spine."
> --Michelle Renee Lane, Bram Stoker Award nominated author of *Invisible Chains*

Praise for his Bram stoker award nominated novel
HANNAHWHERE

"*Hannahwhere* is a revelation. This constantly surprising novel has some very dark moments, but John McIlveen's clean, clear prose carries you through them and back into the light of the good, decent people who fuel this story with their desperate efforts to do the right thing. Hannah herself is a joy. If she were up for adoption, I'd be the first in line."
> --F. Paul Wilson, New York Times bestselling author of *the Repairman Jack series*

"From the very first line of *Hannahwhere*, you know you're in good hands. John McIlveen raises a compelling new voice with a story that is at once playful and frightening, thrilling and heartbreaking. Highly recommended."
> --Jonathan Maberry, New York Times bestselling author

"Love it, love it, LOVE IT!"
> --Rick Hautala, bestselling author of *The Demon's Wife*

"Hannahwhere is everything a book should be--filled with unforgettable characters, fast-paced, and a page-turner. I loved it!"
--Heather Graham, New York Times bestselling author

"*Hannahwhere* is a thrilling, emotionally complex paranormal mystery. The little girls at the center of the story will touch your heart and unsettle you, all at the same time. A wonderful first novel from an exciting new voice in genre fiction."
--Christopher Golden, New York Times bestselling author of *Red Hands*

Praise for INFLICTIONS

"McIlveen paints with a broad palette of colors, and he blends them and highlights them with a master's touch. Tragedy and comedy, vengeance and salvation, hope and horror, the absurd and the sublime, all skillfully worked into the same pages and presented here for our enjoyment."
--James A. Moore, author of *The Seven Forges* series

"Shocking, moving, and always surprising, John McIlveen's Inflictions will delight and terrify the reader in equal measures. A solid collection from a talented writer."
-- Tim Lebbon, author of *Coldbrook*

"John's not afraid...he pulls no punches."
--Christopher Golden, New York Times bestselling author

"A disturbing and thoroughly entertaining creepfest. So much wicked fun."
--Jonathan Maberry, New York Times bestselling author

"The writing is so strong, and the stories so expertly crafted, that their unflinching nature is all the more visceral. *Inflictions* is as fine a collection of horror stories as I've read in the past ten years."
--Rio Youers, author of WESTLAKE SOUL.

"No matter the subject or narrative, in *Inflictions*, McIlveen never fails to engage the reader. *Inflictions* is highly recommended."
--Tony Tremblay, Stoker nominated author of *The Moore House*

"McIlveen's writing wraps around you like tentacles from a fog, and drags you into the ferocious mists kicking and screaming."
-- Dr. Alex Scully – *Hellnotes*

A VARIABLE DARKNESS

INTRODUCTION

Tony Tremblay

John McIlveen and I first crossed paths in 2010, our introduction facilitated by friend and publisher Nanci Kalanta at a horror convention called Necon. John was busy selling books and taking time to talk to everyone who stopped by his table, so our meeting was short. Despite the brevity of the encounter, my first impression of the man was more than favorable; his sense of humor won me over immediately.

Two years later, Nanci, Chris Jones, and I were putting together an anthology called *Eulogies II*, and Nanci suggested we ask John to contribute. He sent in two stories, both of which were so explicitly outrageous and dark Nanci balked at accepting them. Chris and I loved both stories and convinced Nanci to accept the tamer of the two. While discussing those stories with John, between our laughter and a shared morbid sense of humor, a friendship was born—as was a name change. He told me all his friends call him "Mac."

Soon afterward, I picked up Mac's first collection of short stories titled *JERKS and Other Tales from a Perfect Man*. The stories were hilarious, weird, and heartwarming. I craved more. When his second collection, *INFLICTIONS* was released, I jumped on it. The breath of the stories stunned me. These tales highlighted Mac's ability to terrorize, his unique sense of humor, a prowess at pulling heartstrings, and shone a spotlight on his literary aptitude. The collection also hinted at a bent toward existentialism, which would fully manifest itself in *HANNAHWHERE,* his bestselling, *Drunken Druid Award* winning and *Bram Stoker Award* nominated novel. Those stories in *INFLICTIONS* stayed with me for years and, fortunately for me, Mac never tires of discussing them over dinner or a top-shelf margarita.

My friendship with Mac blossomed over the years. I beamed with pride when the aforementioned *HANNAHWHERE* (Crossroads Press) was published to universal praise. I was awed when he started his own award-winning publishing company (Haverhill House) that publishes both high profile and first-time authors. His part in co-producing our affordable horror convention called NoCon allowed me to work side by side with him. Despite stretching himself to the limit with these projects, not to mention the pressure of his day job, Mac continued to compose novels and short stories. Many of those short stories found their way into this collection.

The stories chosen for *A VARIABLE DARKNESS* plays to Mac's strengths and they are among the strongest he's written. These tales are stunning, achingly beautiful, mind-blowing, and on occasion sidesplitting.

The collection starts strong with *Eve*, a soul-searching story about death, redemption, and second chances. The theme of second chances comes up often in *A VARIABLE DARKNESS*. *Got Your Back* is a novella length tale about a police detective who wakes up one morning with an unusual medical condition and the only cure might be to confesses his involvement in a fatal incident. *Frontrunners* puts us in the head of a female soldier during a make or break training exercise when things go horrifically wrong. *Triggers* takes us for one hell of a ride with a man named Ray who has blocked out a traumatic experience when he was a child. We travel along with Ray as various triggers bring those memories to the forefront.

When it comes to the horrors of love gone wrong, there are

few authors who can match Mac's penchant for titillation and the resulting bad karma that ensues. *The Making of Monsters* is a detailed study of a man's steamy affair with a younger woman and the depth he falls as a result. *Teacher's Pet* is a story we've all read in the news concerning teachers who have trysts with their students, only the climax in this tale is decidedly unusual.

While all of Mac's stories deal with some type of horror, when it comes to classic tales of gore, scares, and thrills, Mac is at his best in *A VARIABLE DARKNESS*. In *The Eye of the Beholder,* a father goes to great lengths to save his son from creatures in the darkness surrounding his home. *Yankee Swap* delivers us the tale of a demented man who tortures those who have annoyed him in the past. Mac also takes on the witch trope with *In Agatha Cragginse's Defense*, with a conclusion that is delightfully fiendish.

For those that adore Mac's offbeat, often profane sense of humor, it doesn't get any better than *A Trunk Story*, a laugh-out-loud tale of a husband and wife purchasing a car with an "extra" in the trunk. Be prepared to lose it all over again with *From a Purr to a Roar*, a tale about a telepathic cat who delights in telling things like they really are.

I mentioned heartbreak as one of Mac's strong suits, his tale *Nobody's Daughter* is soul crushing. It's the strongest story in the collection—maybe the best story he has ever written. In Nobody's Daughter we are introduced to Ammar Sardell, and we follow along with his discovery of a young woman living in the boiler room of his apartment building. The young woman, a drug addict, is not happy her crash pad has been discovered. Initially, she is not fond of Ammar's attempts at assistance, however he is not deterred. What follows is a tale that will empty your soul and have you mourning the state of humanity.

As true to its title, *A VARIABLE DARKNESS* contains stories that cover the spectrum of terror. Though no two tales are alike, when considered as a whole, this collection has a cohesiveness rarely found in anthologies of dark tales. If you're previewing this introduction, I hope I've made a strong enough impression on you to purchase it. If you've bought the book and started it here, you are about to begin one hell of a dark journey. As for me, I'm looking forward to many more dinners and margaritas with Mac to discuss these brilliant stories.

Tony Tremblay
Goffstown, NH
August 2020

EVE

Guy read the text message. One simple word—not actually a word, but what had become the usual expression of boredom between him and his friends.

Whazzupp?!

He had just toggled the send button, responding with the same nonsensical expression, when he felt an impact that spun the vehicle, tearing the steering wheel from his left hand and sending his iPhone hurtling to the rear of the vehicle. Before he could make sense of what was occurring, the Escalade hit the guardrail with enough force to catapult over it and land on its roof on the opposite side. The SUV slid another fifty feet, toppled over the embankment, and rolled four times before coming to rest on the leafy forest floor, one hundred fifty feet away and sixty feet below the highway. He lay on the hillside, halfway between the roadway and his Escalade, having been launched through the shattered side window to collide against a large spruce with jarring force.

He opened his eyes but didn't move ... not before assessing

his condition. He felt no pain, which he found peculiar because he recalled the force with which his body had hit the tree, and he could see the mangled scrap that moments earlier had been a late-model Cadillac Escalade, only months off the showroom floor. He licked his lips and inhaled; no blood or difficulty breathing, only the earthy musk of fallen leaves in the early stages of autumnal decay, mingled with the smell of steam and antifreeze from the vehicle's fractured engine, which clicked and pinged as it cooled.

He wiggled his extremities, flexed his arms and legs, and moved his head around. All seemed well, so he gingerly pushed himself into a sitting position, stood up, and bounced on the balls of his feet. He felt a momentary elation that quickly dissolved into dread with the realization of just how deep a pile of shit he'd gotten himself into. He had made only three payments on the seventy-thousand-dollar vehicle. Insurance would most likely contest it once they found out he was texting … and they would find out. They routinely checked phone records nowadays, since texting accidents had become an epidemic. He considered reporting the truck stolen, but just as quickly dismissed it. He'd be caught in that, as well. *At least I'm sober,* he thought, but it was a small victory … he was screwed any way he looked at it. *May as well call 911, tell the truth, and face the music.*

The tumble down the embankment had jammed the doors of his SUV shut except for the rear tailgate, which had folded onto the roof. Searching through the smashed windows, he looked for his phone, but couldn't find it, and reaching beneath the seats only turned up remnants of shattered glass and other strewn items. He'd have to backtrack up the embankment and look for the phone there. If he couldn't find it, he could flag someone down from the roadway.

… If he could only find the embankment.

Around him lay only forest, flat and dense with trees—

endless oaks, birches, locusts and maples in every direction, rising skyward on thick trunks … and one smashed-up Escalade.

Guy knew this wasn't possible, but denial dampened his reaction. Hills don't simply disappear. There had to be a logical explanation, like shock, or maybe delusions from hitting his head. That had to be it, because he thought he could also see a young girl moving among the trees, about a hundred yards deeper into the woods. He refocused, and sure enough, there she was, dressed in light blue overall shorts, long strawberry-blond hair falling halfway down her back. She appeared to be writing or scraping something onto the trunk of the tree, but it was difficult to tell from such a distance. He took a few hesitant steps toward the child and stopped.

"Hey, little girl!" He called. "Hey!"

She looked over at him with indifference and dutifully returned her attention to whatever it was she was doing. He started to walk toward the girl and when he had cut the distance in half, she moved to a tall elm about a dozen trees away from him. She deftly climbed the tree and propped herself at the crux of a branch some sixty feet overhead. There was nothing natural in it, the way she had ascended with the dexterity of a squirrel; Guy had never seen anything quite like it from a human. He watched her for a few moments, wondering if she were avoiding him, but she just as deftly climbed back down and headed in another direction.

"Wait a minute!" Guy said.

The little girl stopped and watched him expectantly. She looked about nine years old, thin-limbed, and fawn-like, with vibrant blue eyes. Under closer observation, he realized her hair was dark brown, not strawberry-blond as he had first thought, and attributed it to the play of sun through the trees.

"I got in an accident," he told her. "I can't find my way out of the woods."

"I know," the girl responded, her tone neutral. She resumed walking.

Guy followed, equally concerned for him and her. He asked himself why such a young child would be alone in the deep woods. "Are *you* lost?" he asked.

"You're lost," she said, in the same impartial manner. She looked at him, her alert brown eyes reflecting him and the surroundings, and walked over to another tree.

Brown eyes?

Guy felt prickles of unease run through him. There was no question that her eyes had been a striking blue before she'd climbed the tree. He looked back at his Escalade, trying to get his bearings so he could get the hell out of there, but the SUV was no longer in sight. He ran a few steps in the direction he thought he had come from, but stopped, uncomfortable with the idea of letting the girl out of sight. Everything else he had looked away from had disappeared.

He returned to where the girl stood. She now had rich ebony skin, but the same light-blue overall shorts, which he found more disconcerting.

Isn't it the clothes that are changed, not the child inside them?

She seemed unconcerned, giving him the impression that *she* wasn't lost, which meant she was faring better than he was. Again, she scribed something onto the tree.

He stepped beside her, feeling as if he'd fallen into the rabbit hole. "Something's going on here that I don't understand."

"Something's always going on," she replied, matter-of-factly.

He couldn't tell if she was being disparaging or just answering him the way most children her age would, but she was making him feel dense. Frustrated, he asked, "Can't you give me a direct answer?"

"I can," she said, pinning him with glimmering green eyes. She skittered up the tree, spent five minutes up above, moving from branch to branch, then climbed down.

He followed her thirty yards to a huge, majestic oak. "What are you doing?"

The girl, now with shiny, waist-length coal-black hair, started writing on the tree with what looked like a simple wooden stick, but as she moved it, the name Joey Wilkerson appeared as if engraved. "Writing," she said.

"Writing what?"

"Names."

"Who is Joey Wilkerson?" Guy asked, understanding that his questions would have to be precise if he wanted precise answers.

"A broken heart," she said, but offered no explanation.

She climbed the tree again and moved from branch to branch. Meanwhile, he inspected a number of trees and saw that most of them had names engraved: Dedrick Aaldenberg, Luis Rosios, Peter Craig, Hirohito Ishushima, Glenn Levesque—and hundreds, maybe thousands more. She descended, now wearing a mane of tight auburn ringlets.

"Are these all broken hearts?"

"Yup," she said, the simplistic word making her, for the first time, sound her age.

"Why are they all men?" he asked, as he followed her to another tree.

"Boys, too ... mostly boys," she said. "There aren't enough trees for girls and women; their names are on the leaves."

Guy thought about this for a while and asked, "Why so many females?"

She looked at him and smiled sadly. "Thirty-one years," she said.

"How do you know how old I am?"

"That's how long your eyes have been closed."

"I don't know what you mean."

"I know. You will when you have to," she said, rubbing an

almond-shaped eye with the back of her hand.

"Who are you, Confucius?" he blurted with frustration. "What little girl talks in circles like this?"

"Me," she answered. "You are angry with the wrong person." She engraved the name Abubakar Kwabena.

"You've already written his name," Guy said, noticing the name was already on the trunk once, and again. "Twice."

"A heart can break more than once. His has broken three times." She looked around and held out a pale arm. "Girls, women, they grow another leaf. Some trees have many names; some names have *her* own branch."

He followed her gesture and looked back at the pale-skinned girl with Afro hair and Asian eyes. "Speaking of names, what is yours?"

"I was never named," she said. "What would you have named me?" She seemed so sincere that he seriously considered it.

"Eve," he said.

"Then, for you, I am Eve."

"Okay, Eve, why are you writing the names of all the broken hearts?"

"Broken hearts deserve recognition."

He chuckled and said, "My name should be written here somewhere a dozen or two times."

"You are here…once," said Eve.

"Once! How is my name here only once? I've been trashed by more women than…" Guy quieted when he noticed the way she looked at him. Her smile was much too knowing for the Samoan child's face that wore it.

"A wounded pride is not a broken heart."

Guy's indignation was defused when Eve took his hand. She led him a long way into the woods, during which her features changed numerous times.

"Why do you keep changing?"

"Is there a specific way a girl is supposed to be?" she asked.

He felt the question was layers and ages thick, and any answer he gave would be insulting to her and condemning to him. He didn't answer. Eve smiled.

They stopped alongside a heavy oak. Eve pointed to Guy's name on the trunk and met his eyes. "This is your heartbreak," she said.

"And which one was that?" he asked, feeling diminished, like a child trying to defend himself.

"When your mother died."

"I was four!"

"Four-year-old hearts break."

"I know! I mean…" he sputtered. "That was the last time my heart broke?"

"That was the last time anyone could reach it," Eve said. "You locked it away."

He wondered if he was unconscious, or hallucinating from the accident, and if that were so, would he be this coherent or even have these thoughts? "How do you know about my mother?" he asked.

Eve gestured to the surrounding trees with her sun-weathered Cherokee arms. "It's what I do," she said.

"But how would you know? You're what… nine years old?"

"I'm what you need me to be," said Eve.

"There you go again with your befuddling comments, confusing me even more," Guy complained. "Why are there no evergreens here…where are we?"

"Here is also what you need it to be," she said. "To understand."

He blew out an exasperated breath. "Understand what?"

"Your accountability. You have broken hearts."

"Okay, so whose heart did I break?"

"Many."

"Many? How? I don't remember being such a bad guy."

"*Bad* is an assessment, as is inconsiderate, neglectful, and unconscious." Eve said. She pushed a strand of her platinum-blond hair behind her ear. "Some hearts you broke intentionally, some out of spite. Some were unintentional, yet still they were broken."

"Who?"

Eve moved to a nearby oak and climbed to a low branch. She quickly returned with a single leaf and handed it to him. He read the name inscribed on it.

"Marlene Rinaldi? I didn't break her heart!"

"Really?" asked Eve.

"Okay, I was sort of a dick, but she was whacked. We dated in college for about a year, but we agreed we were better off going our separate ways, and then she started stalking me."

"Odd behavior for someone who'd agreed to separate," Eve said.

"Well, okay... she didn't exactly agree, but we were better off apart."

"Absolutely," Eve granted. "You can't make someone love you, although she loved you immensely, as you knew."

"All right, if you're trying to make me feel guilty, you succeeded. She had serious problems. I heard she killed herself."

"She did."

"I wasn't with her then. At least *that* wasn't my doing."

Eve held his gaze but didn't answer.

"Now wait a minute! You're saying that I broke her heart and caused her to commit suicide?"

"I didn't say anything... you did," Eve said. She started for another tree. "You broke her heart, but you weren't the direct cause of her suicide—you weren't *that* influential. A far more painful heartbreak caused her to take her own life, although you did play a part in it."

"How was I responsible for that?" Guy asked, flustered.

"The baby died," Eve said. Her skin darkened to a warm Brazilian bronze as quickly as if someone had dimmed a light inside of her. It was the first time he had actually witnessed her face change.

"She had a baby?"

"Stillborn. She was in her ninth month," Eve explained.

"It was mine?" Guy cried.

"It's simple math," Eve said. "Marlene was already alone and depressed, the death left her utterly heartbroken."

"I had no idea," Guy said, shifting to a new level of surreal. He felt sick to his stomach.

"You threw her letters away unread, ignored all the calls, and deleted the texts. Marlene didn't want you back as a mate— you're no prize." She crinkled her nose in effect. "She *was* hoping you, the father, would acknowledge his own child so she wouldn't go through life feeling her father had abandoned her."

"It was a girl?"

"Yeah, she would have been nine now—if she had lived." Eve engraved the name Kenneth Mossiman on a tree trunk. She turned to Guy and met his eyes, her stare direct. "Her name would have been Eve."

He stared back, unable to speak for a long time. "Are you…?"

"As I said, I'm what you need me to be for your situation," Eve said.

"What do you mean by my *situation?*" he asked, but Eve simply smiled.

"I didn't want this to happen," he said.

"Is that a comfort to you? What kind of monster would you be if you did?" Eve asked. "Most consequences of most heartbreaks are not fully intentional, and many are unknown by those who cause them," Eve pointed at the name she had just engraved on the tree. "Like him," she said.

"Kenneth Mossiman?" he read aloud. "Well, I know I didn't break his heart."

Eve held his gaze but said nothing.

"Oh, come on!"

"As I said, most broken hearts are not intentional. Those who cause them, directly or indirectly, are unconscious of the pain inflicted." Eve's hair transformed to a fiery copper as if to stress her words. "Bethany, Kenneth's wife, was the driver of the car you hit while you were texting. Her pain was intense, but fortunately it didn't last long. She had just dropped her three-year-old son off at daycare."

He reeled and had to use a tree for support.

"Kenneth's heartbreak will last another forty-seven years. It will fade gradually with time, but it will never leave him," Eve said.

"Are there more?" Guy asked. Feeling disoriented and very old, he rubbed a hand over his face.

"Yes," said Eve. "But for heartbreaks, these are the worst."

How can this be? Guy wondered. He was having a conversation with a child who ethnically fluctuated and could be the nine-year-old spirit of a stillborn child he might or might not have conceived with an erratic ex. It was nonsense, and regardless as to why he was having this episode—be it a head-knock, nightmare, or daydream—it was just a matter of time before he came to. He opened his eyes and looked at a Korean Eve, still with fiery copper hair. She offered him a sweet, understanding smile, but said nothing.

"Alright, I'll play along," he said. "We've already established that I'm inconsiderate, unconscious, and despicable beyond the norm."

Eve laughed and said, "Don't give yourself so much credit. On the grand scale of things, you're pretty common. Everyone plays a part in heartbreaks somewhere along their lifeline, deliberate or not, and some thrive on purposely causing it. On the bad-guy-good-guy scale, you're as usual as salt... but you have a decision to make."

"And what would that be?"

"Your situation," Eve said. "Haven't you figured out why you're here?"

"I'm either dreaming or hallucinating."

"You're dead, Guy," Eve said. Guy gave a harsh, derisive laugh, but Eve silenced him with serious, hazel eyes. "Bethany Mossiman wasn't the only fatality in your accident. Right now, your body—your shell—is lying forty feet from your vehicle. You are suspended in the In-between. I am your guide."

He felt a sudden inrush of pain. He fell to the ground, writhing as scorching blades of agony stabbed and twisted throughout his body, in both of his legs, down his right arm, the right side of his chest, and his head—dear *God,* his head! Lying on his back on the forest floor, the pain became so complete he couldn't move. Eve knelt down beside him and took hold of his left hand. The pain in his chest intensified and he cried out. He tried to focus on Eve through the hurt, but his vision kept shifting from light to dark and back. Shadows and a stir of voices swelled and ebbed around him. *Blunt trauma head... tree. Compound fracture... leg... arm... need backboard.*

"Can you hear me?" came a voice, close. "Stay with us, buddy. Talk to me."

Guy focused on the face of a man... friendly looking, wearing some kind of uniform. The man gradually diminished as Eve returned.

"It's time for you to choose, Guy. You have to choose between returning to your present life or moving on to your next," Eve said to him, but her voice was deeper and satiny—soothing and alluring—a woman's voice.

She still held his hand, and gently moved it onto his chest, over his heart. He could see the flesh of her arm was now black like onyx, as was her face and her hair... everything. She was no longer a child, but a woman, draped in robes made of the darkest shadows. She had become the night—terrifying, yet beautiful... so beautiful.

"In a few minutes, the window will close," Eve said. "You will default into death and move to your next life, unless you choose to remain in this one."

An intense stab brought the paramedic back into view as he maneuvered Guy's shattered arm. "Can you tell me your name?" the paramedic asked.

"But, before you decide," Eve was saying, fading back, "there needs to be balance in whichever choice you make."

"Balance..." Guy muttered.

"That's good! That's good! Talk to us..." said a hopeful EMT with large, compassionate eyes. She opened a large package of gauze and handed it to an unseen person near Guy's head.

"If you return to your present life, you must resolve your past," Eve continued, tugging him back to the In-between. "You will live with a new resolve." Something moved behind her— something large, dark, with feathers. *Eve has wings,* Guy realized through his gauzy consciousness. Her hand gently touched his cheek and she coaxed him to meet her eyes, which were black opals, hypnotic pools of oil with fire flashing within.

"You will live to rectify your life by avoiding the thoughtlessness and neglectfulness that dictated your old way of living. You will retain the knowledge that each person you encounter is like a well. If you only glance inside, what you see is only the surface. Below the surface, there may be treasures, danger, horrors, or beauty as you've never witnessed before, but you will never truly know that person, or what is below their surface, until you make the effort to explore. In your present life, there will be times of happiness, though much loneliness."

Guy's body exploded with agony as the paramedic and EMT carefully maneuvered him onto the backboard.

"If you choose to move into your next life, there must still be balance," Eve said, her voice somehow weaving through the torment. "While you will create little heartbreak, you will experience much, though there will also be much love. You cannot experience heartbreak without love." The black angel leaned forward as if to kiss him. "Now," she whispered, "decide."

Guy's whole existence became agony, and with his last coherent thought, before the blackness swallowed him, he chose.

He opened his eyes to a chaos of motion and light.

IN AGATHA CRAGGINS'S DEFENSE

Gloucester Massachusetts
June 1693

Agatha Craggins was a witch—or so many townsfolk thought—but I wasn't convinced.

It wasn't that she didn't look the part—she did, with her coarse, straggly hair as gray as bog mists, and her nose long, crooked, and arrow sharp with one perfectly grotesque wart just to the right of its tip. From it sprouted five crooked, black hairs, much resembling a spider, be it absent a leg or three.

Short and stout of body, she displayed anonymity of gender beneath her correspondingly formless wraps, which fell to her feet like ethereal drapes. To say Agatha Craggins was unattractive was a gross understatement.

She lived in a cabin along a swamp-lined path bordering one of the inland ponds, deep in the woods on the western part of town. Stagnant, insect-ridden, and festering with lichen, none traveled there without reason, and when reason existed, most formed even stronger reasons to avoid it.

Rather the recluse, Agatha kept mostly to herself, but on Tuesdays would waddle two miles into town to buy provisions, and then waddle the two miles back, for she had neither horse nor mule. Each time, she would lug a wicker basket for her goods, her shoulders draped in a heavy shawl and a dark kerchief on her head, regardless of the weather. As she shuffled, she would mumble, murmur, ramble, and curse, but always under her breath and to herself, paying no heed to the stares, jeers, and jitters of the townsfolk, who would point and laugh. They would gossip and whisper in hushed tones—yet conspicuously—of the "withered old shrew" or the "wizened hag," who—unbeknownst to all—was only four years into her sixth decade.

From the markets she would purchase roots, herbs, spices, and tonics, most by special order. With exotic names like elder, cassia, mandrake root, and linden leaf—not your average soup fixings, perhaps—her selections branded her, for the people embraced these as evidence.

"Nightshade!" they'd allege, knowing little of which they spoke.

Although no one could prove any misconduct on Agatha's part, the accusers remained smugly righteous in their allegations and self-important in their religiosity. *For these are troubled times,* they would profess, *when demons walk the day-lit streets in the guise of common womenfolk, seducing and deceiving with the spells they cast.*

Agatha was the bane of the faint-hearted, the source of all illnesses, the root of misfortune, and a justification for iniquities. For her unattractiveness, she carried the blame for those enchantresses who were far guiltier than she, yet exonerated by the imbursement of beauty.

Parents would keep their children in check, threatening them and promising them the sufferings of Agatha's spells. Children would chase each other, brandishing crooked branches like wands, cackling and shrieking of the same woes.

And although many mocked her and participated in her denouncement, they let her be for fear of befalling the unseen terrors of which she mumbled...or of which they imagined she mumbled. Therefore, Agatha lived in peace—until the Tuesday that little Thomas Dobbins went missing.

At sixteen years, I was older than Thomas by a decade, but I would often see him playing near his home. Fair of hair and skin and handsome to the point of beautiful, he was a loveable and spirited child, pleasant and easily engaged. His mother said he was a reservoir of endearment and adventure; his father affectionately quipped that he was full of the devil. It struck me how wide-ranging that allegation was, for he said the same of Agatha.

Thomas disappeared in full daylight, two houses away from his home, and a mere four blocks from the center of town. On that evening, a crowd had gathered on the waterfront of Fort Point to voice their outrage and conspire to destroy what they feared, which was usually anything they didn't understand. Our home faced the cold waters of the Atlantic Ocean and was the focus of those who gathered. The townsfolk raised their fists in protest and brandished their words like weapons. In their eyes burned the fires of sadness, fear, and excitement; in their hearts, the resolve to find reason or restitution. Some just hungered for the thrill of the hunt.

Randolph Fenton let the curtain fall back into place and shook his head. He was Gloucester's Marshal Deputy by title, and the simple fact that no other desired the post. He was also my father.

"What are they doing?" I asked.

"They want answers. They gather like gulls to form strength in numbers," he said. "Unfortunately, ignorance and rage in numbers often begets a lynch mob."

We pulled on our coats and I followed him outside to face the writhing throng of perhaps fifty strong, among which were Minister Burles, Judge Bernard Stern, and the child's parents, Henry and Abigail Dobbins.

"It was the Craggins hag!" charged the persnickety matron Fields. "I saw her near the harbor with my own eyes, not a block from the Dobbins's' home." The very eyes of which she had spoken roiled with outrage from her equine spinster's face, gaunt and etched deep by her own acidity.

"And how might she have abducted him? In her little wicker basket?" my father asked her.

"If she hacked him to bits, then yes," sniffed the unpleasant old busybody, casting the child's mother into racking sobs.

"Would have made a bit of a mess, I'd fathom, the likes of which I have not seen in my investigations," said Father.

"Search the old crone's house! Surely she carried him off there!" demanded another voice in the mass.

"We have no grounds. Besides, the old sort can hardly carry herself, never mind a healthy child," said Father.

"Be aware, Randolph, you underestimate the power of the Devil and his acolytes," said Judge Stern, whose granite-hard voice and surly countenance aptly depicted his name. "It is this brand of negligence that will be your folly."

"And it is this form of assumption that persecutes the innocent," my father responded, his indifference to Judge Stern's station bringing forth gasps from many of those present.

"What proof have you of her innocence?" challenged the judge.

"And what proof have you of her guilt?" replied my father.

"Be that as it may, it is your exact calling that requires you to differentiate between the two," Judge Stern said, haughtily.

"And I shall, lest we become the theater of blood the good city of Salem has."

Of Agatha Craggins's innocence I had no doubt, for I had known her for nearly a year. On a late spring eve of our previous year, 1692, I had followed the biddy home, impelled by curiosity of this peculiar old bag, for I had heard the stories and presumptions. I tracked her progress, taking precautions to remain from her sight, and I was certain I had done so until she paused on the narrow path to her house.

"Why do you stalk me, child?" she calmly inquired, not turning to confront me.

The power of her voice and her thick Gaelic brogue were disconcerting; I had only heard murmuring and mumblings prior. I was befuddled not so much by her acknowledgment of my following her, since she may have heard my movements, but by her regarding me as a child. Not once during her travels had she turned or even looked in my direction. I remained silent and still, veiled by the girth of a large oak and some low-lying brush.

"Come now, lass, what is your purpose?" she persisted.

Again, I said nothing.

"Very well," she said with a shrug and then turned in my direction.

Through the obstructed view of the brush, I saw her raise a hand toward where I hid and conduct the smallest of gestures with her index finger. A queer sensation, cool, but not unpleasant, traced up my spine and down into my legs, which then, of their own accord, carried me onto the path before her. A fear as I had never experienced before gripped me. My entire being longed to flee in terror, yet I could not move; I was bound as surely as if I were wrapped in burial sheets.

"My, what a lovely sight you are. What is your name, hen?"

Still in shock, I could form no words. The ancient ogress impatiently grimaced, rolled her eyes, and quickly flicked a finger my way. My name spilled from my open mouth like water.

"Evangeline Fenton," I said, despite my knowing that to give a witch your name gave her power over you.

"Aye, daughter to Deputy Marshal Fenton," she said. It was not a question.

"Witch," I managed. The single word sounded more an

allegation than the precursor to the endless string of questions I ached to ask her.

"Some do accuse me of being such, ignorant clodpates they are, but I prefer *sorceress*," she said. Her eyes gleamed, looking youthful and wise within the confines of her otherwise repulsive face. "How old are you, kitten?"

"Fifteen," I said, accepting the futility of resistance.

She studied me for a moment and I felt uncomfortable under her scrutiny. Her suspicion seemed to ease, but not expire.

"You surpass your years. You have the face of a woman, the body of a siren, and the eyes of a temptress. Men will be wise to take heed—you have your own sorcery."

How can she distinguish my body under the many layers of loose-fitting clothing? Can she see through to my naked form beneath? I wondered, not at all entertained by such thoughts.

"You have not answered me," she said.

"I do not recall a question."

"Why do you stalk me?"

Again, I paused under the truth of my answer, and then spoke before she could pin yet another hex on me and loosen my tongue.

"To see if it is true," I said. "What they say about you...that you are a witch."

"And now you know. I'm sure *they* will, too, once you report back," she said.

There was disdain and tired acceptance in her voice that told of a history of similar troubles, but her suggestion that I would "report back" opened a narrow window of hope. She stared at me expectantly and I kept an eye on her hand, waiting for the finger-flick that would permanently still my tongue or seal my lips. Maybe she was toying with me, as a cat torments a mouse. She would use that binding hex again and drag me into the depths of the pond, leaving me to be feasted upon by whatever resided in its dank waters.

"Are you going to kill me?" I asked, assuming that was the only way she could guarantee my silence.

Her eyes met mine, and when she saw my question was serious, she shook her head and released a loud cackle, a grating shriek like a rusted wheel hub.

"Your mind festers with the same absurdity as the rest of your people," she said. It was mockery, yet it contained profound sadness. "Because you are beautiful, you are not vilified; you are seen in a positive light. But since I am disagreeable to the eye, I am considered guilty of hideousness. Because I live a different style of life and reside in solitude, I am regarded with suspicion and am even assumed evil. Do you think I prefer loneliness? Do you think I enjoy such an existence?"

I had no answers for her. She lifted her basket and turned from me dismissively. *She's leaving*, I realized. She had no interest in me. I took a reflexive step toward her and was surprised the binds no longer held me. *How long had I been free? I wondered. Why hadn't I felt their release?*

"Wait!" I said. Agatha paused but didn't turn back. "Can you teach me...the things you do?"

The question startled me more than it did the old woman, but I remembered the feeling of immobility and the uncontrolled spill of words from my lips, and I couldn't deny the lure of having that kind of ability. *What other things could she teach me?* Agatha turned to me.

"Now, why would I do that?" she asked. "I have lived in Gloucester for all of my fifty-four years, and have never been accepted as a daughter of this town. I ask nothing of anybody except to trade with the markets. I have been mocked, scorned, and at best, shunned by those who live here. Yet you, the daughter of the Deputy Marshal, expect such a gift from me?"

I was speechless for a while, astonished by her confession of her age. I had assumed her to be in her eighties and had even entertained twice that, with her having been branded as a witch. I knew I would have to appeal to her, or at least paint myself as worthy of her "gift."

"I have never done you harm," I said.

"You have never done me charity."

This was a truth I could not deny, but since she hadn't turned away or terminated our conversation, I took it as a victory.

"Maybe we can make a trade, my companionship for your knowledge."

"You consider that a fair exchange?"

"You confessed just a moment ago that you do not prefer loneliness, and I sense in you that you would enjoy the company or you would have already dismissed me."

A wistful look crossed her face. "I've been alone since my mother died twenty years yore. She was the last person to show me love, empathy, or humor."

"And your father?"

"Never knew the sod," she scoffed. "Nothing but a wayward roustabout, thick with the clap. He took advantage of my mother, who was excessively compassionate and desperately naive. He promised her the world and left her with an ugly disease, and an even uglier child in the womb. She could have hated me, but she showed me only love—and a knack for hexes and spells." She considered me for a moment. "You are a fascinating lass. Come back in two days, after your studies. Bring me something convincing. An object that confirms that you perceive me as others do not."

I searched for hours, clueless about what I was looking for, until I considered I was looking from the wrong perspective. If I were to appeal to Agatha's sense of self, I should be assessing with her eyes. Two days later, I returned to her cabin with a carving by one of the artisans on the wharf. Created from a whale's tooth, it depicted a heart engraved within a larger carved heart, and due to a flaw in the ivory, a ragged hole had collapsed within the inner heart. Because of this unsightly blemish, the artist had given it to me in trade for nothing more than my prettiest smile. I felt it was right, as did Agatha Craggins, who studied the perfectly imperfect gift with inquisitive eyes, and then wept.

From that day, Agatha painstakingly shared with me the gifts her mother had given her, all the while conversing with me and asking me questions I answered conscientiously. She taught me that there was not a black magic and white magic, as many believed, but only one neutral magic; the darkness or light within magic came from the intentions of those who practiced it.

"We must never undermine the free will of another soul," she stressed. "There within lies the darkness."

She tutored me in incantations, prayers, meditation, and the use of incense smoke, oils, charms, amulets, and talismans. I was a quick study, both attentive and sympathetic.

Of course, at Agatha's insistence, we kept our gatherings secret. "No sense both of us burning at the stake," she would joke, though her message was severe and resolute. "Those not enchanted see all magic as evil. Fear and ignorance make people irrational and act rashly," she explained, which was the primary reason she avoided the people of Gloucester instead of trying to meld with them.

I saw the magical arts as freedom and as a confirmation of my being. I adopted them, lived them, breathed them, perfected them, and made them my own.

Agatha's teachings proceeded nicely for nearly a year, until little Thomas Dobbins went missing.

On *that* night, when Judge Stern and my father stood face-to-face and challenged each other to prove her innocence or her guilt, I knew it was my time to speak up about Agatha Craggins. As I have mentioned, of her innocence I had no doubt, for she had never harmed a soul; her nature made it impossible.

"Instead of debating whether she is guilty or innocent, why not visit her home and ask for a look around?" I suggested to the quarreling men. "Why, if I were suspected of such a heinous act, but was innocent, I would surely give you a grand tour from the top of my loft to my root cellar floor."

I took special attention to emphasize *root cellar floor,* because that was precisely where little Thomas Dobbins's' body lay. It was quite easy, really. A little spell of attraction and little Thomas Dobbins would have followed me to the ends of our Earth. And follow me is exactly what he did on that Tuesday afternoon as an oblivious Agatha Craggins walked to the market.

"Why, that's a splendid idea," said Judge Stern.

"Indeed," said father. "I cannot see why she would deny us such, if she is truly blameless."

I reached into my dress pocket and felt the contents, which sifted like pearls between my fingers. I shivered with pleasure at the potential there, for what was better than a child's tooth for a witch's cause but *twenty* teeth?

Agatha might have said there was no white magic or dark magic, only intent, but all would come to learn there is no intent darker than mine.

GOT YOUR BACK

Wednesday

Ricky Briggs awoke to an urgent bladder, but when he tried to get up, he realized that pissing was the least of his concerns. He had slept badly on many occasions, often arising to lower back pain or his legs so entirely asleep that his ass felt like a block of wood. A few times, he woke up with such severe cricks in his neck that it took five minutes to move his head at all, but never had he experienced a feeling like the one he felt now. It wasn't pain that worried him, but the absence of pain and the difficulty to move. He knew he was in some serious shit.

He lay prone on the mattress with his face turned to his wife's vacant pillow. His pillow most likely lay on the floor beside his bed, flung aside during his usual tossing and turning.

Ricky moved his right foot, which responded splendidly, eliciting a resounding snap as he rotated his ankle. His lower legs moved freely, but when he tried to move his whole leg there was a lot of resistance. He wriggled his fingers without difficulty, but his upper arms resisted in a similar way to his legs, and when he tried to move his shoulders... that's when things got really wonky. His ribs felt as if they were traveling with his shoulder blades, swimming around loosely beneath his flesh, and even though it was painless, it was thoroughly disconcerting—but not nearly as troubling as the fact that he couldn't move his head at all. He tried to maneuver his elbows beneath himself in order to lift his torso, but little happened. He was stranded and helpless, which, added together, equaled scared.

"Melanie!" Ricky hollered. His words were muffled by the press of his cheek against the mattress. He waited a few moments and then called again, "Melanie!"

He thought he could hear her talking somewhere downstairs... probably in the kitchen.

"Melanie! For fuck's sake! I need help!"

A few moments later he heard her angry pounding as she ascended the stairs to the second floor.

"Jesus Christ, Ricky. I was on the phone with my mother," Melanie complained. "What's so important, already?"

Melanie was twenty years out of Jersey, but the nasally accent still held firm and her penchant for whining only made it worse. Ricky had once considered it cute and endearing, but after fourteen years of marriage it now affected him like a dental drill scraping at his eardrum.

"I can't move," he said, trying to maintain a sense of bravado, but his fear was too strong and it seeped through in his words.

"Whaddya mean you can't move?"

"Just what I said! I can't move! Well, I can move my arms and legs a little, but I can't move my head at all."

"How come?"

"I don't know," Ricky said. "Maybe my neck fell asleep or

something. Help me turn my head your way. Maybe that'll wake it up."

Melanie slid a hand under his cheek and started to turn her husband's head, but recoiled when she felt the lack of support. Ricky's head rolled on his neck, and then settled at an impossible angle almost directly facing the headboard.

"Oh my God, Ricky! What's wrong with you?" Melanie backed away, twitching and shaking in disgust.

"Oh God. Straighten it! Quick!" Ricky cried. Panic built within him as his arms and legs rebelled in little spasms.

"How? I don't want to!" Melanie whined.

"Come on you fucktard! Fix it."

"Ricky, don't be an asshole," Melanie said. "I think your neck's broke."

"Okay," he panted. "I'm sorry. I'm just scared. Can you please straighten my head? It's totally freaking me out."

"Me, too, Ricky. You should see it. It's weird. It's fucking creepy."

Melanie returned to the bed, gingerly reached out, and then retracted her hands as if trying to pet a cobra. She repeated the action three times before quickly nudging Ricky's head into a somewhat normal position.

"I'm calling 9-1-1," she said.

"Yeah. Do that," said Ricky. He was wide-eyed and nearly hyperventilating as he watched his wife rush through the bedroom doorway to retrieve her cell phone. She returned in less than a minute with the phone pressed to her ear.

"Yeah. He can't move his head at all. Yeah. Just his arms and legs a tiny bit. Yeah. Just his head. It moved really weird." Melanie quivered at the memory. "Okay, I won't move him any more. No, I don't think he's in pain. Wait. I'll put you on speakerphone. No? Oh, okay. They're on their way. Good."

Melanie ended the call and put the phone on the nightstand. "What happened to you, Ricky?"

"I don't know. I just fucking woke up this way."

"It's probably those ten pounds you gained putting pressure on your spine." Melanie pulled the covers down to expose Ricky's back.

"I weigh a hundred-ninety. That's hardly obese for six feet tall," Ricky rebutted, though in truth he had recently breached two hundred.

"Just sayin', is all. Your back looks okay." She ran her hand down his back and again pulled back uncertainly. "Wait… Ricky. How come you don't have any of those bumpy things going down your back?"

"What bumpy things?"

"You know… like your backbone bumps."

Melanie poked along her husband's spine and felt only sponginess and the blunt ends of his ribs where they should have connected to a spinal column.

"Oh my God! I mean it, Ricky. You ain't got no backbone."

"That doesn't make sense," he spat. "That's not possible!"

"I don't know, Ricky. There ain't no bones there," Melanie insisted. "It's like some kind of miracle or something."

"A *miracle*! How is *this* a miracle?" Ricky barked.

"What would you call it, then?"

Ricky simmered in place until they heard the sound of a diesel engine, followed by a squeak of brakes in the driveway.

"That must be them," said Melanie.

She darted through the doorway, returning after a few moments leading a cop and two heavy-footed EMTs lugging bags, gear, and cases into the bedroom.

"I'm sure his backbone's still there," the cop was saying to Melanie. "Those don't just disappear overnight."

"Yeah. I hear what you're saying," Melanie replied. "But I'm totally serious. I think his is gone!" She pronounced the last word *goo-wan*.

Ricky recognized two of them. The cop's name was Danny

LaCroix—Ricky had worked with him for the last ten or so years... not directly, but on the same squad—and one of the EMTs was a pretty but severe-looking woman named Shelly something-or-other. The second EMT, a young man who didn't look old enough to shave, Ricky had never seen before.

Danny LaCroix squatted beside the bed with the customary palliative cop smile pasted to his face. Ricky recognized the smile because he had used it many times himself. It scared the shit out of him.

"Hey, Ricky. What's going on?" asked Danny LaCroix.

"I can't move most of my body—just my extremities."

"Let's have a look," Shelly what's-her-name said. She pulled on a pair of gloves, grasped one of Ricky's hands, and told him to squeeze. He did.

"That seems fine," she said. "So, you can't move your head at all?"

"No. Well, minimally. Not enough to turn my head."

Shelly probed Ricky's back and muttered something under her breath. He didn't hear what she said, but he did manage to catch the shocked look she and Danny LaCroix exchanged in his periphery, and her faint shake of the head.

"What?" Ricky demanded. "I have a backbone, right?"

"Hey. Whatever's going on, I'm sure it's minor," Danny said, trying to reassure him. "We'll have you right in no time."

The EMT cautiously lifted and then lowered Ricky's head. Twenty minutes later, Ricky was securely bound to a backboard and heading for Lawrence General Hospital.

Ricky was admitted immediately, only to wait an eternity for X-rays, and then another before being transferred to a private room. Doctors, specialists, technicians, nurses, and, for all Ricky knew, ice cream vendors, filed through the doorway to see the peculiar new patient. An endless progression of pinching, probing, and limb manipulation was followed by even more of the same. Ricky wanted to scream, and he would have run away if he could. After another infinite wait, an MRI, and a CAT scan, they returned him to his room and instructed him to wait for a consult... as if he had a choice.

Melanie sat on a pleather chair to the left of his bed, staring blankly out the window toward the Lawrence Mill district. She was conflicted and avoided looking at Ricky, even when he was addressing her.

"Did you hear anything last night?" Ricky asked.

She didn't respond.

"Melanie!" he said, louder.

"Huh?" she answered, but she still avoided looking at him.

"Did you hear anything last night?"

"Like what?"

"I don't know... like someone in the house?"

"No. You know me, Ricky. I would have said something if I had. I slept right through until I got up."

"It's no wonder, you and your fucking sleeping pills."

"Don't give me no shit, Ricky. You didn't wake up either, and it's your spine that got took." She risked a quick glance and returned her gaze to the window. "Anyway, I wouldn't need sleeping pills if you didn't snore like it was fucking D-Day or something."

They wallowed in their uncomfortable silence for forty minutes until Doctor Leiderman returned carrying two X-ray prints. He was a short but sturdy man in his late fifties, with a graying beard and a receding hairline capped with a dark blue yarmulke. Doctor Leiderman clipped the X-rays to a lightbox mounted on the wall. From his angle, strapped to the hospital bed, Ricky could clearly see the prints and that the unmistakable stack of vertebrae was not present.

"To the point, Mr. Briggs," Doctor Leiderman said. "We are

baffled. It's unprecedented. No one here has ever heard of this kind of thing. We've searched high and low and there is nothing that compares to this in any records… not in any database or even online."

Ricky felt reality tilt and his vision took on a purple hue as he fought to stay conscious. "There has to be an explanation. Spines don't just dissolve."

"Not only that…" said Doctor Leiderman. He pointed to the upper back on the X-ray image and ran his finger down along the spinal valley. "…But if they did, there would be evidence of a dissolved spine—a residue in your bloodstream. You have no history of spinal damage. There are no traumatic markings anywhere on your body. In fact—and even more perplexing—your nervous system is still completely intact and undamaged. It's mystifying. Normally, many of the gluteal, tibial, and posterior nerves thread through dorsal foramina—these are skeletal holes in the lower lumbar and pelvic region. To remove this part of the spinal base you would have to deconstruct the sacrum. This is not easy. It would entail hours of intense and precise surgery."

"So, what are you saying?" Ricky asked. "Aliens took my spine while I was sleeping?"

Doctor Leiderman offered a sympathetic glance and shrugged. "Extraordinary occurrence seems as good an explanation as any we can offer. We've had chiropractors, osteopathic physicians, physiatrists, and surgeons here. No one has answers or even speculations… at least for the time being."

"So what's his prognosis?" Melanie asked, pinning Doctor Leiderman with doleful brown eyes. "Is he gonna stay like… like this?"

The doctor weighed his answer before saying, "Unless another event of a similar inexplicable magnitude occurs, I don't see any chance of correction or improvement. You, Mr. Briggs, will most assuredly need to start therapy on your musculature to keep your extremities functioning and to avoid the atrophy that will assuredly occur without exercise. Your skeletal structure has no central support without your spinal column, and your body becomes like a... well...”

“A gummy worm?” Melanie offered.

“Well... uh... yes,” agreed Doctor Leiderman. “A gummy worm.”

“So, I’m going to live the rest of my life as a fucking vegetable, pissing and shitting myself?” Ricky’s eyes brimmed as he awaited the doctor’s reply. He could feel his wife’s eyes on him as he unsuccessfully willed the tears not to fall.

“Vegetable is a harsh term —and not entirely accurate. I’m sure you will be fitted with some form of support system that will secure your back and your head and will allow you to sit and perform minor and moderate arm and leg movements. As for your bodily functions... you are not quadriplegic or even paraplegic, Mr. Briggs. Your nervous system is still functional and so are your abdominal muscles, therefore soiling yourself is optional. Not soiling yourself is optional, as well... with assistance.”

“It all sounds hopeless,” Ricky moaned.

“Never say hopeless, Mister Briggs,” said Doctor Leiderman. “Who knows what technology will bring us? As for now, we will be sending you to Mass General, where they are better equipped to deal with spinal situations. Some of the world’s best doctors and specialists are there to help you, so do not give up hope. Not yet.”

Thursday

Ricky had arrived at Mass General late the previous evening and checked into the orthopedics ward angry and defiant, insulting the attendants and making undeliverable threats. Dr. Chan, the head of the ward, quickly tired of Ricky's tirade, gave him a shot that knocked him out until the next morning.

He awoke early Thursday to the sound of the 6 a.m. shift change and an incessant itching along his spine. He was flat on his back, fastened to the bed by cloth straps to prevent him from toppling. His upper torso was slightly raised and a cervical collar held his head to reduce the possibility of damage to the unprotected nerves of his spinal cord. He was staring at the ceiling, which seemed miles away in the dim glow from the hallway, and at that moment the full brunt of his truth hit him and left him gasping for breath. If things didn't change—which it seemed they wouldn't—everything he would see for the remainder of his life would not be up to him, but to the whim of whoever moved him or positioned him. If they wanted to sit him facing the corner, they could... and there was squat he could do about it.

Goddammit, his back itched!

He tried to maneuver his arm between his back and the mattress, but the resistance was too much. He was absolutely helpless and dependent—an infant. Yet, even infants had backbones.

Ricky was just able to see Melanie sleeping on a rollaway cot the hospital had set up for her on the window side of his room. He felt indignant. He wanted to yell at her—demand of her— *How in the hell can you lie there sleeping while I'm stuck here like a wad of dough and itching like a bad case of poison oak?* He bit his words back, which was uncommon for him.

She slept on her belly, her face turned toward his bed and her arms hugging a balled-up pillow beneath her head. Her pouting lips were slightly parted and a swath of honey-colored hair partly covered her cheek. The diffused lighting softened her, imparting a childlike purity to her features, and Ricky perceived her in a way he hadn't for... well, possibly years.

My god, she's beautiful, he thought. When did I stop noticing?

As if sensing his scrutiny, Melanie opened her eyes and pinned him with soft cocoa irises. She held his gaze, though she was still hazy with sleep's spell and the innocence of the newly awoken.

Those were the eyes that had captured him so many years earlier, when they had met. He would have leapt through flaming hoops to gain approval in those eyes, but once he had gained it, it seemed the reward wasn't so valuable any longer. Of course, there would no longer be hoop jumping... or jumping of any variety.

But they were the same eyes. What had changed?

He thought of how those eyes had regarded him at first: with love, desire, hope, and lust—even in the not-so-distant past. Ricky knew he was moderately handsome, but he wasn't Ryan Gosling and he'd been no Prince Charming in their fourteen years together. He was nice enough in the beginning, but as time wore on, he became increasingly angry, self-righteous, and arrogant. Any love, desire, or lust he had received in, say, the past six years had been gifts from Melanie. He hadn't deserved it, yet he felt it was his entitlement. The understanding that he may never experience it again was an excruciating gash to his soul. He would no longer be looked upon with desire, but instead with sympathy and possibly disgust.

And contempt?

He would never again be able to run his hands over Melanie's body while in the heat of passion or as a soft acknowledgement of her presence. To feel the smoothness of her skin, the rise of her hips, or the heavy swell of her breasts, were all things of the past, and now he felt a powerful yearning he hadn't felt in years. He thought of the times he could have held her and hadn't ... and he mourned.

Awareness of time and circumstance set in, and it was clear

in Melanie's expression. She turned her waking eyes from Ricky and he almost cried out.

Just a while longer... a little more time!

"Are you okay?" she asked. Although her voice had been hardened by the years, the compassion was still there when you listened—if you took the time to listen.

Ricky closed his eyes. A part of him wanted to ignore Melanie and the rest of creation and pretend that nothing was wrong. Another part wanted to beg her to hold him and comfort him like a child. To promise—to lie to him—that everything would get better.

"My back itches," was all he could muster.

Melanie pushed her hand beneath him and scratched as well as the position would allow.

"I don't want to move you in case I hurt you," she said. "I'll do it better when they come to help you go to the bathroom."

"It don't matter," Ricky mumbled, defeated.

"Don't be going all pity-party, Ricky. You're gonna beat this. You just watch."

Ricky turned his head away.

The remainder of Thursday passed with a continual procession of specialists, much in the same way as Wednesday had. There was a priest, a psychiatrist, a physical therapist, a phlebotomist, and a slew of others digging for answers and offering false assurances. By nine o'clock that night, Ricky was so exhausted he didn't fall asleep... he plummeted.

Friday

Sleep eluded Ricky, just as it had the previous night. He lay in the darkness, his mind whirling without direction, when something triggered his senses. There hadn't been a noise or a movement, but a feeling, like knowing that it was raining outside without seeing or hearing the rain. Something had changed.

His bed was slightly elevated, and when he focused his eyes into the shadows, he could just make out a figure sitting in the visitor's chair near the foot of his bed. How had they gotten there without his noticing?

Melanie had left for home earlier that evening. The lure of a shower, a change of clothing, and her own bed was just too appealing after spending a night on the visitor's cot. *Had she changed her mind?*

"Melanie?" Ricky asked, hesitantly.

"Not by a long shot," the figure replied.

The familiar voice was deep and eloquent with a mild rasp, but he couldn't quite put his finger on it. How did he know that voice? Did it remind him of an actor or a singer? The memory of it taunted him.

"Who are you?"

"Who am I?" asked the shadow-man. "Come on, Briggsy. Are you going to lie there and tell me you don't know who I am?"

Briggsy had been his nickname in high school. After that, only one person called him by that name, but he was—

"Mac?" Ricky asked.

"See that? I knew you remembered me," said the man.

His tone was amiable, but Ricky felt an underlying sense of threat, which only increased since the man didn't move, continuing to sit silently in the shadows.

Faulkner "Mac" McFall had been Ricky's partner on the force for nearly four years, until Mac was shot during a drug bust about six months earlier. The bullet had ripped through his larynx and shattered two vertebrae in his neck. The EMTs had responded in top-notch fashion and had managed to save Mac's life against dire odds, but nothing could be done about his blown-out vertebrae and splintered voice box. The last thing

Ricky knew, Mac had been laid up at Whittier Rehab, unable to move or even talk. What made it even more traumatic was that Mac's mental functions were still one hundred percent, yet he couldn't communicate beyond blinking his eyes. The fact that he was here in Ricky's room was nothing short of astounding.

"You're better?" Ricky asked. "I thought you were in rehab."

"Four months," said Mac. "You know, a funny thing about rehabs is that when you're quadriplegic and have no voice, not a whole lot of *rehab* happens."

As Mac spoke, he nodded in his familiar and unique Faulkner McFall way, where his whole upper body seemed to nod in unison with his head, as if promoting his words.

"I tell you, bro, it sucked bad. All I could do was lie there, with no way to communicate and nothing to do but think and fester."

Mac studied Ricky for a moment and then raised his chin slightly, as if he were about to impart some profound bit of wisdom. "You know," he said, "You didn't visit me even once... partner."

Ricky had no words, as the guilty often don't. Mac rose and stepped to the end of the bed. He leaned forward and rested his hands atop the footboard. It was definitely Mac. His face was partially visible in the weak band of light coming from the hallway and Ricky was surprised by how healthy he looked. He was wearing his navy-blue duty jacket with his badge pinned above his left breast pocket and *Lawrence PD* patches on the shoulders. His collar was raised as usual, but Ricky could see no evidence of a bullet wound on his throat.

"Wow. You've healed well," Ricky said. "I didn't hear anything about you returning to duty."

Mac straightened up. "Don't know why you would have," he said.

The door swung slowly open, spilling light into the room as a nursing assistant entered. She was young—early twentyish—

with dark brown shoulder-length hair, prominent freckles, and a pretty and amiable face. According to her badge, her name was Kayleigh. Mac stepped back to the wall, and both men watched the nurse approach the apparatus near the head of Ricky's bed. She started slightly when she saw that Ricky's eyes were open and looking at her.

"Oh! You're awake!" she said. "You nearly scared the be-poopies out of me."

"Haven't been doing much sleeping lately."

She looked at the monitors and then at Ricky. "In case you were wondering... you're still alive. This thingy says so."

She inspected the urine collection, paying no attention to the man standing near her.

She looked at Ricky and repositioned his pillow behind his head.

"Aren't you going to say hi to Mac?" Ricky asked.

Mac offered a friendly wave and bowed theatrically, but the nurse didn't even look his way.

"Mac who?" She asked.

"My partner," Ricky said, pointing at Mac. "We were on the force together for years."

Kayleigh looked around. Mac shrugged.

"Are you telling me you don't see him?"

"Sorry. Don't see anyone. I think your dosage may be too high," she teased.

"I'm not taking any meds."

Kayleigh chuckled. "Then maybe you should. You seem pretty awake. Do you want me to see about getting you a sleeping pill?"

Ricky said nothing.

"Okay. I'll come by in about an hour in case you change your mind." She walked out the door, passing within inches of Mac.

"Have a nice night," Mac said, but she seemed not to hear. He turned to Ricky. "What a sweetheart... and very pleasant.

She might appreciate a thank you one of these days."

Ricky closed his eyes, hoping that it was all a hallucination. Maybe Mac would be gone when he opened them again.

"I'm not leaving yet, partner."

"Go away," said Ricky. "You can't be real."

"Oh, I'm for real, brother."

Ricky opened his eyes and saw that Mac still stood at the foot of his bed.

"Why are you here?"

"First let me tell you *how* I am here," Mac said. "I think you know the answer to *why*. As to *how*... pneumonia. The curse of the bedridden. When you're flat on your back and can't move—pretty much how you are now—that shit will set up camp in your lungs. And you know what? It ain't leaving. You're screwed. It festers inside of you, and even though your body is essentially dead from the neck down, you can still feel it absorbing your life."

Mac walked over to the monitors and studied them as if he were profoundly interested. "You know what the biggest bitch of pneumonia is?"

Ricky didn't respond.

"It hides the truth," said Mac. "You have cancer and the big P sets in... guess what? You've died from the complications of pneumonia. AIDS...pneumonia. Remember Christopher Reeve? Busted his neck falling off a horse? Yup. Pneumonia got him. It's diminishing; it makes molehills out of mountains. And do you know what else it does?"

Mac moved his face within inches of Ricky's. Again, he said nothing.

"Yeah. You do," Mac said with a nod. "It turns murder into simple misfortune." Mac righted himself, moved to the pleather chair near the window, and sat down. "Six months ago, a bullet stole my arms, legs, voice, and in the end, my life. Thanks to four months in rehab and a dance with pneumonia, that bullet was found innocent."

"It wasn't me who shot you," Ricky said defensively.

"You didn't hold the gun, but you pulled the trigger," Mac replied.

…and in the end, my life.

As he absorbed Mac's earlier words, Ricky's expression changed from defiance to disbelief. Mac's slow smile showed that he noticed, too.

"Are you telling me you're a ghost?"

"I didn't tell you that. You figured that out yourself."

"When did you—?"

"—Come on, bro," Mac said, as if trying to reason with a stubborn child. "You might be spineless, but don't try to pass it off as being stupid."

"Wednesday night?" Ricky asked. "Are you the reason I woke up like this?"

"Nope. You're the reason. I did the work," Mac said, crossing his legs. "Other than that, your deduction skills are working well."

"Why would you do this to me?"

"Did you really just ask that question?" Mac said, staring Ricky down.

"What? I'm not the asshole that shot you!"

"You clearly need some time to think about who you are and what you are. Do a little soul searching." Mac stood and started for the door. "Lucky for you, there's little else you can do."

"Wait!" Ricky said, but Mac had vanished, leaving him alone.

Melanie returned a little before noon carrying a plastic food storage container and a purse that could hold an Alpine camp. She set both items on the windowsill and kissed her husband on the forehead.

"How you feeling today?" She asked. "Did you sleep okay?"

"Tired. I slept like shit," Ricky grumbled.

It was clear that Melanie had slept well. The shadows beneath her eyes had faded and she looked refreshed, vivacious, and… well, she looked lovely. Ricky felt as if it was intentional, as if she had purposefully made herself more attractive in defiance of his condition. He knew it was illogical, but so was waking up without a backbone, and it only soured his mood more.

"I made you some hermit cookies… your favorites," Melanie said cheerfully. She retrieved the container from the windowsill, lifted the lid, and showed the contents to Ricky. "Do you want some?"

"Not hungry."

"You sure?" Melanie asked. "They're good. I made them this morning."

"I said I don't want any fucking hermit cookies."

"No. You said you weren't hungry," Melanie snapped back. She sighed and put the box of pastries back on the windowsill. "I was just trying to help you feel a little better."

Ricky looked away when he saw the tears forming in Melanie's eyes. He was disgusted with himself. She had treated him with kindness and he had responded with anger and contempt. He knew he was being unpleasant and unfair, but he couldn't seem to help it with Melanie, she just seemed to bring out the worst in him.

"I'm going to the gift shop to get a book to read," Melanie said.

She paused on her way to the door and then walked out of the room. Ricky knew she was going to ask him if he wanted anything, but had decided against it. He was both relieved and angered that she hadn't asked, but he didn't blame her either.

Melanie was still at the gift shop when Doctor Chan entered

the room followed by two men and a woman, all wearing lab coats. Doctor Chan approached Ricky in a near stutter step as if expecting to be bitten.

"How you feeling today, Mister Briggs?" greeted the doctor.

Ricky said nothing.

Undeterred, Doctor Chan continued. "I am so happy to introduce to you Doctor Shauna Keating from Harvard. I informed her of your situation yesterday, and she immediately called Doctor Kostman. He is Chief of Neurology at Johns Hopkins University, and this is his associate, Doctor Shota Higuchi."

Doctor Higuchi gave a quick bow as Doctor Keating stepped forward to the bedrail. She was a tall and lean woman with a stern face and short, no-nonsense ginger-blond hair that only strengthened her severity. Looking up into that face, Ricky felt even more diminished.

"Pleased to meet you, Mister Briggs," she said. "When Doctor Chan called me yesterday, I must say, I was quite captivated by what I heard."

"Glad I could provide you with some entertainment," Ricky said.

"I can imagine your anger and distress at such a traumatic event," said Doctor Keating.

"Then how about you all stop bending, poking, and jabbing me and fix whatever the hell is wrong with me?"

"Which is precisely why I called Doctors Kostman and Higuchi," said Doctor Keating, unperturbed by Ricky's acerbic manner. "They have seen your X-rays and scans and they are especially interested in your case. So much so, that they flew here overnight to see you."

"So, what do you want to do to me?" Ricky asked. In his peripheral, he saw Melanie enter the room.

"At this point, we're not certain if we can do anything," said Doctor Kostman, stepping closer to the bed. "It depends on a number of conditions being met. At the moment it is speculative, but from what we have seen and heard about you, you may be the perfect subject."

"Are you going to tell me what for, for Christ's sake?" said Ricky, his frustration mounting.

"Are you talking about some kind of procedure or something?" Melanie asked. She placed a calming hand on Ricky's arm. "It sounds to me like you're asking him to be part of an experiment."

"Not an experiment, per se," said Kostman. He motioned to his colleague standing behind him. "My associate, Doctor Higuchi, has been working with a merited team of researchers and scientists in both Sweden and Japan on a neurorobotic prototype. We believe it is a design that may work for you."

"What are you talking about, some kind of bionic spine?" Melanie asked.

"Pretty close," Kostman said.

"We are working on a titanium skeletal model, researching the prospect of using neurorobotics in severe cases of spinal trauma," Doctor Higuchi explained in clear but choppy English. His silence up to this point had had Ricky wondering if he spoke only his mother tongue. "We were focusing on cases where the spinal cord is compromised, replacing the spinal cord, not the vertebrae. When Doctor Keating described that your spinal cord was fine, but your backbone had gone... well, we hadn't considered spinal trauma without neural damage."

"So, you're saying you want to install a titanium backbone in me?" Ricky nearly hollered, but the fear in his eyes downplayed the anger in his voice.

"We'd like to explore the possibility," Kostman said. Doctor Higuchi nodded. "As I mentioned, there are numerous bridges to cross, starting with procurement of financial backing. This would be an undertaking of monumental proportions and we would need support in the form of investors or grants. Success would also depend on you on two levels… physical and emotional. Your body may not be able to support this in strength—or structurally. Both remain to be determined. Last and most important is your compliance. If there is any hope of having your condition rectified, I'm afraid there will have to be an extensive amount of, as you put it, bending, poking, and jabbing. The less resistance we have to contend with, the more effectively we can perform."

"More to the point," said Doctor Keating. "Depression and a level of anger can be expected from anyone in your state, but you are a markedly negative, angry, and aggressive person. If we are to move forward, this will have to change."

"Who says I want to move forward?" Ricky said, bitterly.

"Only you can, Mister Briggs," said Doctor Keating. "Do you really want to live like this? It's your move… so to speak."

Saturday

Ricky lay in his darkened room staring at the distant lights from the neighboring building he assumed was also a part of Mass General. He knew the place was huge and comprised numerous buildings, but where he lay in this city-within-a-city, he had no clue. What he did know was that the view sucked, and hours of lying on his back and staring at four walls and a sliver of the neighboring building was getting old fast. He was in the habit of sleeping days instead of nights, and despite the Ambien, he doubted he'd be sleeping at all. His muscles thrummed with pent-up energy and he could physically feel them atrophying from disuse. He had tried exercising, but it was fruitless without his central support system.

Melanie had returned to Lawrence for the night at his insistence. He could take only so much of her pampering. He was miserable toward her, and hours of reflection had presented him with the truth that he usually was, and had been for quite a few years. Even when he tried to be civil toward her, his sense of his own inabilities loomed hugely and only managed to piss him off more. Christ! He couldn't even give her a hearty slap on the ass. Instead, he became nasty and lashed out at her verbally. He clucked with self-disgust.

"Yeah… life loses its prettiness from that perspective, don't it?" said Mac.

"What the fuck?" Ricky barked. His heart lurched against his ribs as he tried to focus on the figure sitting in the corner of the room. "Jesus H. Christ, man!"

"I see we're chipper as usual," said Ricky's former workmate.

"What are you doing back here? Why must you come at night?"

"Isn't that when hauntings are supposed to happen?" Mac asked. "I told you that you needed time to think… so I gave you some. Have you been thinking?"

"I've been doing little else," Ricky shot back.

"No. You've been doing a lot of sniveling and bitching." Mac rose from the chair. "Let me make something perfectly clear here, brother. The reason you are here, lying like a wad of dough on this bed, is completely your own doing. You are now exactly what you were before—a spineless, self-absorbed, useless bag of bones. And only you can change that."

Ricky glared at him, but Mac laughed it off.

"Are you mad at me? Does your truth piss you off? You can't even swing at me. All you can do is lie there and stew in your anger and hatred and cowardice. When that beautiful woman you've been neglecting for years is finally fed up with your shit and decides to leave—and she will—you won't even be able to run after her to beg her forgiveness."

Ricky hid his face from Mac. "I don't mean to treat her like that. Something about her brings out the worst in me."

"No. Only you can bring out the worst in you. She's your target. Isn't it time you stop blaming everything and everyone but yourself for the asshole you are?"

"Why are you doing this to me?" Ricky asked, barely audible.

Mac jumped forward, leaning over the bedrails until their noses were barely an inch apart. His eyes bored into Ricky's, clear down to his soul.

"You know the answer to that, you spineless coward!"

As close as they were, Ricky couldn't feel or smell Mac's breath, but he was aware of an energy radiating from the man that felt electric and lethal. He wouldn't have been surprised if his hairs were standing on end.

"When we walked into that ambush... what were the last words you said to me before all that shit went down?"

"I don't know," said Ricky. Fear invigorated his every nerve ending and his limbs twitched with his desire to flee.

"Well, let's try something new," Mac jeered. "Think."

Ricky's expression changed infinitesimally, but it was enough to show Mac that he remembered. Mac stood upright with a satisfied smile. The night nurse entered the room, passing right through Mac as she walked to the monitors.

"Say it," Mac hissed.

Ricky tried to clear his throat to get the nurse's attention, but it felt as if something had lodged inside, pinning his larynx. The nurse didn't even look at him as she turned and left the room.

"Stop being a coward and say it! Repeat what you said to me before our little bust went south."

"I..." Ricky started.

"Come on," Mac urged. "I..."

"I gotcha back."

"I gotcha back," Mac repeated, nodding. "But you didn't. You were too busy covering your own ass."

Ricky was silenced by the truth.

"Ricky," Mac said, his tone conspiratorial. Ricky slowly met his eyes.

"Who's got whose back now?" Mac asked—and then he was gone.

Ricky agreed to let Doctors Kostman and Higuchi perform any tests necessary for fitting him with the titanium spine. For the following two days he was flipped, spun, and measured, and then probed, prodded, and punctured. He spent what had seemed like hours nestled within the donut-hole confines of the MRI machine, its knocking and whirring playing in his memory long after he was back in his room, and then well into his evenings.

Melanie, loyal as ever, stood by Ricky's side and patiently weathered his outbursts. To his credit, they did seem to be tapering off a little. Ricky was becoming more aware of his disposition. Mac's words had shaken him to the core.

When that beautiful woman you've been neglecting for years is finally fed up with your shit and decides to leave—and she will— And she will— And she will— And she will—

It played in his memory on a perpetual spool.

Ricky's parents were both gone. His mother had passed away seven years earlier, his father... three. His only sibling, an older sister named Gwen, lived on the West Coast. They hadn't spoken since their father died, and before that... when their mother died. He and Melanie had no children, although she had always wanted them. Ricky would always string her along, promising that they would in time, but always *not yet*. Ricky felt children stole all of your time and energy, and he hadn't been willing to make that kind of forfeit. The math was easy. If Melanie left...

And she will—

…it left only him. He would be utterly alone. Who wanted that? He wouldn't even have the ability to kill himself and escape this prison. That was the truth that made it unbearable. Even with all his faculties intact, if Melanie left, the loneliness would be intolerable. His only choice and hope was to undergo the operation—if not for a second chance, then at least as a way out.

Wednesday

"When would the surgery take place?" Ricky asked Doctor Higuchi.

Standing near the foot of the bed, the doctor perused his notebook and then looked at Ricky as if only just realizing he was there.

"Many surgeries," said the doctor.

"Huh?" asked Ricky. He couldn't remember if Doctor Higuchi was Chinese or Japanese, but whichever it was, his accent was thicker than mud.

"Oh… it'll take many surgeries."

Ricky didn't like the sound of that. Surgery meant pain, and he had always gone to great measures to avoid that. One surgery scared the shit out of him, and the thought of *many surgeries* put his mind on the verge of shutting down.

"How many?" he asked.

The doctor pinched Ricky's big toe, which made his left leg spasm. Higuchi gave a brisk, satisfied nod, and quickly jotted something in his notebook.

"We would need to do it over time. It is a very complex and delicate series of procedures that would involve many hours… too many for one surgery. Surgery of that proportion would be too traumatic for the body to endure. The prototype spine would be installed in single-disc segments. Maybe five discs for each procedure. Each disc has an intricate cluster of nerves that weave between it and the next disc. Each disc connection would be performed with extreme care to avoid damaging the spinal cord and nerve bundles. Nerve weaving for the sacrum alone would take sixteen hours."

Ricky felt as if an eel had coiled in his stomach and was sending jolts of panic from his core outward. When Doctor Keating told him that he had checked out okay to perform the surgery—all systems go—he had felt a level of elation he had not felt since this whole mess started. The funding hadn't come through yet, but they weren't too concerned. A procedure as unique and revolutionary as this one would garner a lot of attention. The funding would come, they had assured him.

Now he wasn't feeling quite so enthusiastic.

The doctor pulled down the blanket and then raised the hem of Ricky's Johnny to expose most of his leg. He withdrew an instrument from his pocket that looked like a metal toothpick with a screwdriver handle and proceeded to poke around Ricky's knees.

"You still haven't told me how many surgeries," Ricky said.

Higuchi gave his left knee a painful jab that made the muscle react such that—spine be damned—Ricky's leg kicked outward and pulled him about two inches lower on the bed.

"Ow! What the hell?"

"Sorry," Doctor Higuchi said, and smiled his *life is good* smile. "Maybe five or six surgeries. One every two months. Twelve to sixteen hours each."

"Will the surgeries be painful?"

"Oh… very painful. Very painful times six," Doctor Higuchi said, and nodded emphatically, that damned smile still pasted to his face. "But you'll be very happy afterward."

The eel flipped and Ricky vomited across the front of his Johnny.

Monday

Ricky's insecurity had been increasingly eating at him. He hadn't seen Faulkner McFall since that night, but Mac's words bounced around in his head non-stop and his inability to act on his anxiety only managed to acerbate it.

—and she will.

"I have to work, Ricky," Melanie said. "I'm sorry, but if I'm here all the time, the bills ain't getting paid."

She stopped coming right after work. The previous week, she'd showed up at five on all but one day. He wondered if she was having an affair… not that he could do anything about it. She gathered a few stray magazines she had brought in and set them on the windowsill.

"You get out of work at three-thirty," he said. "It's nearly seven."

"I had to go register the car. You know how long that takes. And I had to do some food shopping 'cause there was nothing in the house. Life goes on, Ricky." She took a sip from her Starbucks iced coffee and set it down.

"So, is that it? Are you moving on? Did you find someone to screw around with already since I can't anymore?"

He knew he had gone too far, but the words spilled out and it was too late to retract them. Melanie stared at him with cold, empty eyes, and it dawned on him that he had never seen her look at him this way before.

"You know what, Ricky? Fuck you! I've had it. I'm going home."

Dread washed over him. He knew her anger was justified as much as he knew his words were poison, but he had no governor. When shit popped into his head, there was nothing to keep it from sliding out through his mouth.

"Hey. I didn't mean it."

"You wouldn't have said it if you didn't mean it." Large tears pooled in her eyes and dropped heavily to the floor. "I stand by you. I come visit you every day, and you keep hitting me with this shit. I don't deserve this, Ricky. No one does."

"I'm sorry."

"Sorry don't cut it, Ricky. You say those words a lot, but I don't think you even know what they mean. I'm going." Melanie picked up her purse and walked to the door.

"Don't leave, Melanie," he begged. "My first surgery is in two days. I need you."

She looked back at him and the disappointment he saw in her damp eyes rattled him.

"You shoulda thought of that before," she said, and walked out of the room.

"Sure!" he yelled after her. "Leave me now that I'm fucking crippled!"

Why can't I just shut the fuck up? he silently scolded himself.

Her footsteps paused for a moment—and then resumed down the corridor.

Tuesday

"Well," said Mac from the chair at the foot of the bed. "It appears you've mastered the art of the fuck-up. Hell, you've probably earned a PhD by now."

"Leave me alone," Ricky said. He'd had a feeling Mac would be showing up to rub his face in it.

"Not on your life, brother." Mac rose and walked to Ricky's side. "Not on your death, either. I'm going to ride your ass for eternity."

"Why..."

"Don't even go there," Mac warned.

"How could you do this to me?"

Mac leaned on the bedrails. "*How* was easy. I made a little deal with someone. He's not such a bad guy. Certainly not what everyone makes him out to be." Mac leaned forward and whispered into Ricky's ear. "He punishes the sinners."

He nodded and righted himself. He raised as if he just remembered something important. "Oh! By the way, this revolutionary surgery they're going to give you? It's going to be a colossal failure. It will demolish your spinal cord."

"How would you know?"

"Because I won't let it succeed," Mac assured him. "How would that benefit you? What lessons would you have learned? You'd still be the same, self-centered, spineless piece of shit."

Ricky gawked at Mac, an incredulous look in his eyes.

"Do you doubt that I can do this... floppy boy?"

"No! I don't want this!"

"Me either, man. But when I left this little monkey show, my wife was still by my side and still very much in love with me. How're you doing with that? Not so good... you screwed it up even after being forewarned."

"The other night you said something," Ricky said. "You told me that I was a useless bag of bones and that it was my own fault."

"Truth."

"But you also said that only I can change that." Ricky finally looked Mac in the eyes.

"I see you've been thinking things over. I'm impressed and a little surprised."

"Are you saying I can get myself out of this?" Ricky asked.

"Don't know. I supposed that's up to you. Maybe you can say a prayer."

"I tried. He's not taking requests."

Mac chuckled. "It worked for me."

"How? You're dead."

"Which is exactly what I prayed for," Mac said.

"Why didn't you pray to get better?"

"You can bet your ass I did," Mac assured him. "But what put me in that particular place wasn't my doing—it was yours, so it wasn't mine to undo. Maybe if you had visited and said a little prayer of your own, things would have been different."

Ricky tried to think of something repentant to say, but there was nothing to be said.

Mac waved it away dismissively. "Water under the bridge, now."

"What do I do?" Ricky asked, nearly whining.

"Like I said… don't know. That's up to you. But you can start by not being pathetic. Stop the sniveling. Self-pity ain't attractive to anyone." He quickly clapped his hands as if preparing to leave. "I'm going to do you a huge favor, but it isn't because I want you to succeed. In fact, I hope you figure it out. That way you'll have to live on, knowing what you are, and what has happened because of it."

"Will it help me get better?"

"Don't know. What's *better?*" Mac said. "*Better* is debatable. *Better* is relative. Your better and my better are most likely very different."

Ricky sighed and seemed to shrink into himself.

"Alright… enough small talk," Mac said. "The first thing I have to say to you is that shit smells. You fall into a pile of shit, you'll smell like shit. If you don't want to smell like shit, you have to get clean. If you clean a little off, you'll still smell like shit. If you clean most of it off, you'll still smell like shit. You get it?"

"Yes," said Ricky.

"Okay. Now, there once was this really smart guy named Albert Einstein. You heard of him?"

Ricky nodded.

"Good," said Mac. "Well, Mister Einstein said *we can't solve problems by using the same kind of thinking we used when we created them.* That's your problem, Briggsy. You don't change your way of thinking. So think about it... in a different way."

Mac was gone before Ricky could protest.

It seemed that he had no good direction to go in. Mac had said that the surgery would be a disaster, and there was more than enough reason to believe him. Deciding not to go for the surgery was an easy choice for a coward, especially if it meant avoiding *Very painful times six.* He realized that admitting he was a coward was a huge step for him. He had always known he was, but he'd avoided the confession. It was easier to keep it hidden.

Not going for the surgery may sidestep a lot of pain, but the outlook wasn't much brighter, and as Mac had said, the *big P* would probably get him anyway. As far as he could tell, there was only one direction left, though there seemed little to no promise in it.

But in the end, it was all he had. It was time for Ricky to come clean.

Saturday

Melanie walked briskly into the hospital room followed by a short and pretty woman with guarded, tired eyes. Ricky could see the resolve in Melanie's stance and expression. Her guard was up a mile high and she wasn't going to take any shit.

"I don't like being manipulated, Ricky," She said. "You're driving me crazy."

Ricky had barraged her with an onslaught of telephone calls, convincing each staff nurse to ring her multiple times and stressing the importance of his need to speak to her. As he had expected, Melanie was too softhearted, and her resolve to ignore him broke.

"What's such an emergency? Bothering this poor woman, especially at a time like this in her life?"

"Please, pull up a chair," Ricky said. "Both of you. I promise this won't take long, Mrs. McFall, or for you, Melanie, but I need to tell you something of dire importance. You can choose to leave afterward, Melanie. For how long is your prerogative, and if you do leave, I promise I will not bother you again."

Melanie sat in the pleather chair. Her expression was a conflict of emotions. Distrust and annoyance were prevalent, but there was a layer of curiosity she couldn't hide. Dannelle McFall sat opposite Melanie. It didn't escape Ricky that she chose the seat in which Mac always appeared. Ricky didn't know how to start, so after a couple of shaky breaths, he leapt in headfirst.

"I have a confession to make."

Both women stared at him expectantly, their expressions unreadable.

"I'm a coward," he continued. "It's not irony that I have no spine. It's fate... a message."

"I know you put off the surgery," Melanie said. "It's only natural to be afraid..."

"Wait!" Ricky interrupted. He closed his eyes and gathered his thoughts with uncommon patience. "Melanie. You've always been too kind-hearted to see the truth. I seldom had to make excuses for my actions because you always did it for me. What you are seeing, my cancelling the surgery, is just another level of my spinelessness. It runs so deep it has cost lives."

Ricky took another deep breath and released it.

"Dannelle. Mrs. McFall. There are things you need to know about Mac." Ricky saw a defiant light ignite in Dannelle's eyes and he realized that his words had been conveyed wrongly.

"Please, don't misinterpret me. Mac is totally honorable. I'm the one who was and is inexcusable. My actions were selfish and, as I said, cowardly."

"Mr. Briggs," Dannelle McFall said. "I have no idea what you're trying to say."

Ricky held her gaze and had to coerce himself into continuing. "The ambush, Mrs. McFall. It didn't go down the way you heard... the way anyone heard. The real truth—and I'm the only person who knew it until now—is that Mac is the reason I came out of there alive, and I'm the reason Mac was carried out of there."

"Go on," Dannelle said, stiff-jawed.

Ricky felt Melanie's stare, but he refrained from looking at her, knowing that whatever he saw there would prevent him from finishing.

"We got a tip that someone was dealing meth in front of a small market on Broadway. We watched him for a few days and learned his pattern, which always brought him back to an apartment on Buswell. I don't think we did very well, because he was just as aware of us as we were of him. When we finally made our move, they were waiting for us. We were fortunate at first. We busted down the door and charged in to see three guns aimed at us from down a hallway... our perp, another man, and a woman who turned out to be the perp's wife. One of them fired. Maybe it was a warning shot, because it somehow missed us. One of the rules in our training is to look for an out as soon as you're in. There was a door on either side of us... a bathroom to the right and a bedroom to the left. I got off one shot before diving into the bedroom. Mac ducked into the bathroom. Turns out it was a lucky shot. I killed the perp. Could you give me some water, please?"

Melanie lifted a glass from the over-bed table and directed the straw into Ricky's mouth.

"Thank you." He paused and closed his eyes for a moment.

"In the bedroom, I found a young woman in the corner, hiding between a dresser and the wall. She was the fifteen-year-old student from Lawrence High School."

"I know who you're talking about, Mr. Briggs," said Dannelle McFall, her words as sharp and hard as a carbon blade. "Her name was Keira Pierce."

Ricky paused. He had never known the young woman's name and had never stopped to consider that she had one at all. It added a personal element to it, and for the first time he thought of her as flesh and blood. He closed his eyes briefly.

"To avoid getting shot, I decided to use her as a decoy."

Melanie's gasp made him pause. *Onward*, he thought.

"Mac was standing in the bathroom on the ready. When he saw me pushing her—Keira—toward the door, he knew what I had in mind. He shook his head and motioned me to stay back, but I ignored him. I pushed Keira into the hallway. I heard Mac yelling at me to stop, and then he did something incredible. He dove in front of her as the girl's mother and the other man opened fire. I ran out of the bedroom shooting blindly, but it was easy to take them down because they had both stopped shooting and were staring at Keira on the floor. This is why they had a hard time putting it together. They finally figured out that the same bullet that got Mac in the throat also passed through Keira Pierce's eye and lodged into her brain. In the end, there were five people dead. As you know, only I walked out of that apartment on Buswell Street."

Ricky chanced meeting Dannelle's eyes, but they were studying the floor with troubled deliberation. Melanie was staring at him with a similar intensity.

"If I hadn't acted in that way—using Keira to protect myself—chances are everyone except Eddie Pierce might have gotten out of there unharmed. Mac and Keira would most likely be alive today."

After a minute of total silence, Dannelle McFall raised her

tear-streaked face to Ricky.

"Why are you telling me this now?" she asked.

Ricky wanted to look away, but he knew he could not. He said, "The truth needed to be told."

"For whose benefit?" asked Dannelle. "Do you feel absolved?"

Ricky contemplated this for a moment, wishing that it could be true, but he said, "Less now than ever."

"Good," said Dannelle. "And I speak more for that little girl than for my husband. Mac knew the risks of his job. Keira Pierce's life is your penance, Mr. Briggs. Hopefully there's enough decency in you to carry that pain, but I question that. You took from her what was not yours to take. You've gotten away with murder... twice."

Dannelle rose from her chair and gave Ricky one last hard glare. She set a compassionate hand on Melanie's shoulder and then left the room. Ricky watched her departure and then stared at the open doorway until he felt Melanie's stare. Ricky looked at her but said nothing. Finally, Melanie spoke.

"I don't know, Ricky. I can forgive you for pretty much anything... and I have. But this..." her words tapered off into nothingness.

With her silence, her disappointment roared in Ricky's ears. She was miles away from him now, which was a sensation he was not used to. It was clear that he had become content with a nearness that was Melanie's creation and upkeep... he had done little to maintain it, but its undoing was all on his shoulders.

"Anyway, my forgiveness isn't what matters here. Unfortunately, the two people whose forgiveness you need aren't alive anymore. And now look at you."

She lifted her purse from the floor and searched through it until she found her keys. She stood and looked at him with profound sadness.

"God damn you, Ricky," she said, and then left.

Ricky watched her go, saying nothing, as he had promised.

Sunday

The itching along his spine was at an all-time high. For the most part he had become accustomed to it, but this bout was extreme enough to wake him from a deep sleep. He jammed his hand beneath his back and wriggled on the bed until the burning began to subside. The full appreciation of what had just occurred didn't hit him until he started dozing off. Ricky sat up quickly, the movement at once foreign, painful, numb, but glorious.

"Well, look who finally grew a backbone," said Mac from within the darkness.

Ricky rotated his arms. They felt weak, but he kept at it. He gingerly moved to the edge of the bed and let his legs drop over the side. The weight of them felt like it might pull the rest of him along for the ride. A sharp pain lit the top of his ass crack, but he reveled in it.

"Did you do this? Gave me my spine back?" Ricky asked.

"May have had something to do with it, but don't sing praises to my generosity before you look at the gift," Mac said. He stood and took a few steps in Ricky's direction and into the light. "There's going to be a lot of raised eyebrows about this one."

Ricky lowered his feet to the floor and started to transfer his body weight to them. He pushed himself upright, precariously balancing on his unstable legs. Another jolt of pain traveled from his ass, up his spine, and into his neck.

"Hell," Ricky said. "If they can handle a spine disappearing, they can surely handle it coming back."

Mac said nothing, but a shrewd smile spread across his face.

Ricky didn't like it at all. He took a hesitant step forward and pain jolted the base of his spine again. He stumbled, but managed to maintain his balance, and as his weight shifted, he felt a pulling sensation where he kept experiencing the jolts of pain. He reached behind himself and rubbed from the base of his spine and down to the crack of his ass, and he felt what wasn't right.

"What the fuck?" Ricky said in disbelief. Mac only smiled.

Ricky felt the odd appendage, running his hand to the end of it before its shape took meaning. "A tail? You gave me a fucking tail?"

"And a very sensitive one, at that," said Mac. "Let's say it's there as a reminder. Although your confession the other night was mostly sincere, there was a part of you seeking sympathy."

"No... I was..."

"Are you going to deny it?" Mac asked. His voice was heavy under the weight of his challenge. "That tail is there to remind you of what you were, what you still are, and what you could become again... a cowering, spineless dog."

As if in affirmation, Ricky's thick, fleshy tail whipped around his side and struck the over-bed table. He grimaced as a searing flash of pain shot up his spine.

"This tail will always be, if you'll excuse the pun, a pain in your ass... a reminder of how it is to be truly spineless, and of how easily you can go back if you forget. And brother? You don't want to forget. It's time to become a new man... a man of honor... a man of your word."

Mac watched Ricky take a couple more steps and then try to see his tail behind him.

"If you're thinking surgery, it won't work," Mac said. "That tail is special. It's different from most dogs. Its design is unique for you. Besides being jam-packed with nerve endings, your spinal cord runs to the tip and then doubles back... kind of like a hairpin. Any attempt at surgery will cripple you... again. It's yours for the long run, Briggsy."

"Come on, Mac. Is there any way I can… try again?"

"Let's not get greedy. You fared a lot better than a few others who were involved. You blew your chance… which reminds me. How's it going with that pretty woman of yours?"

"As if you didn't know," Ricky said without animosity. "She hasn't called."

"Well, Melanie doesn't seem the type who can hold a grudge for long. If you ask me, she's way too good for the likes of you." Mac looked at Ricky and smiled. "Maybe if you crawl back with your tail between your legs?"

Ricky said nothing.

"But maybe not," Mac said. He backed into the shadows and paused. "Hey, Ricky?"

"What?"

"Remember," Mac said. "I gotcha back."

EYE OF THE BEHOLDER

*"There are more things in heaven and earth, Horatio,
than are dreamt of in your philosophy."*

-- William Shakespeare - *Hamlet*

Senator Brandon O'Rourke stopped outside the door to his son's bedroom and listened to the barely decipherable conversation coming from within. It sounded like a one-sided phone conversation, but Cooper didn't have a phone, and Brandon had heard his son's odd, solitary ramblings so many times they had become familiar. There was no denying it: his son was odd and a social outsider in school and at church, but he was a sweet kid and undeserving of the loneliness he suffered. Being small for his age and the son of a pastor certainly didn't help. Brandon would probably be more surprised if he didn't have imaginary friends, or whoever it was Cooper had his chats with.

Brandon nudged the door open and regarded his son's little pajama-clad form sitting cross-legged on the bed, staring blankly ahead.

"Hey, Bub," Brandon said, getting no response, which wasn't unusual. *He has no clue that I'm here,* Brandon thought.

He set a hand on his son's shoulder. He found it disconcerting that Cooper never started, but seemed only to return to himself as the empty look gradually faded from his eyes.

"Hi, Dad!" Cooper said brightly.

"Hi. Chatting with your friends?" Brandon asked, trying to keep it light.

"Nah, I was just…someplace," Cooper said.

"Apparently," Brandon agreed. "Anyhow, it's bedtime."

As always, Cooper obliged without a fuss and slipped between the sheets. Brandon tucked him in, kissed him on the forehead, and pushed an obstinate wing of the boy's blond hair out of his face.

"The light," Cooper reminded him.

"You sure about this?"

"Yeah. I've thought about it a long time," Cooper said earnestly. "I can't be afraid of the dark forever."

"True enough," Brandon said, hiding a smile while trying to match his son's gravity. "But sleeping without a nightlight is a big step in a man's life."

Cooper nodded his agreement. His normally light blue eyes looked huge and dark in the dim bedroom.

"Six years old today. You're growing up so fast," Brandon said, shaking his head. He looked at his son, and then widened his eyes in a comical show of surprise. "Wait a minute! What was that?"

"What?" asked Cooper, a hint of concern in his voice.

Brandon leaned closer. "You just sprouted a chest hair…right here." He poked his finger against Cooper's ribs. "Whoa! Another one here…and here…and here!" he said, prodding playfully.

Cooper giggled and twisted deeper into the blankets, trying to avoid his father's barrage of jabs, yet wanting it to continue.

"My God, you're practically a sasquatch."

"What's a sashcrotch?" Cooper asked, catching his breath.

"Bigfoot."

"But I don't have big feet!"

"Okay, Bub, you win," Brandon said. He straightened the

sheets and kissed Cooper again.

"Why does mommy always have to go away?" he asked dolefully.

"It's her job, Bub. You should be proud of her. There aren't a lot of female pilots, especially ones who fly the big jets."

"I know, but I wish she could have been here for my birthday."

"I know what you mean. I miss her, too. But she did call and promise we'd do something extra special when she got back on Saturday. In six days," Brandon said brightly, but Cooper didn't look very encouraged. He was such a solemn child.

"Tony Hammond says mommy has humongous boobs."

What to say…what to say…

"Well, you can tell Tony Hammond it's because mom's heart is so big. You're a lucky young man," Brandon said, thinking of Sylvia. *And so am I.*

"Tony's mom never has to go away."

"I know," was all Brandon could say. He, as usual, had run out of encouraging words. He reached for the SpongeBob nightlight on the bedside table and paused. "You're sure?" he asked again.

Cooper nodded and turned to his side, clutching his pillow. In his recent battle for independence over fear, he had retired his favorite toy—a plush Minion doll—to a seat of honor atop his bookshelf. Brandon spun the light toggle.

"Goodnight, my man. I love you."

"I love you, too, Daddy."

"Door opened or closed?"

"Open a bit."

Brandon pulled at the doorknob, leaving a five-inch gap.

"Daddy?"

"Yeah, sweetie?" Brandon asked, opening the door a little wider.

"Can you leave the hallway light on?"

Brandon smiled. "You got it."

Brandon walked down the hallway to the top of the stairs, and then looked back toward his son's bedroom. The house was a late eighteenth-century Victorian with enough gothic aesthetic and dark vertical lines to be intimidating to him, let alone his six-year-old child. It was by no means a mansion, but it was larger than average, pushing five thousand square feet, and probably seemed immense to Cooper, especially when it was just the two of them. Sylvia was a mere five-three, as sweet as honey-dipped sugar cookies, and perpetually soft-spoken, but she presented a sense of stability and security for the two men in her life that was beyond palpable in her absence. Brandon felt a hollowness about the place when she was away, as if the house regarded her temporary absence as more of an abandonment... or maybe it was Brandon who did.

At first, her flights had been mostly short jaunts, the overnights limited to an infrequent two, maybe three, days every two months, but as she built experience and seniority, it turned into five, ten, and then fifteen days a month. It made for a handsome income, but it also had its negative aspects. Through all his encouragements to Cooper, Brandon kept a noble façade, but he wasn't without his concerns, too. Foremost was the fear that with all of Sylvia's travels, her heart might do the same. She must get lonely, too, he figured, but what else could a pastor do other than leave it in God's hands?

In the kitchen, he poured a glass of Sauvignon Blanc, carried it into his office, and set it on his desk beside his laptop. He needed to write sermons for the next two Sundays and update his notes for Wednesday evening's Bible study. He tried to stay a month ahead, but it was approaching campaign time, a time when he needed to shift the weight of his focus from his piety to his party. *A time Cooper would spend more time with a nanny than with his parents,* Brandon guiltily amended.

He had been an ordained minister long before his first stint in government, and he liked to think it was his charitable actions and his contributions to the humanities that had secured his position in both The Senate House and God's House. In a world where corruption and greed presided over ethics, he prided himself for making it as far as he had without bending under the weight of corporate persuasion or the insistence of party leaders. In politics, it was difficult to maintain a clean image, especially if you were a member of the clergy, because someone, somewhere, for whatever reason, was aiming to take you down. Smile at a pretty supporter, some opportunistic photographer would turn it into something more. Tip a valet, you're buying votes. So far, no one had been able to soil Brandon O'Rourke, and there was a good reason: he was clean, moral, and honorable—attributes that were becoming rarer in both his professions. Several certificates and awards hung on his office wall for his humanitarian work. Sylvia had insisted he hang them, arguing that he needed to differentiate honor from pride.

Being a Christian, his leaning was naturally toward the conservative. He was registered as a Republican, although he'd have been happier if there were no party associations. He had a similar attitude with religion. Brandon saw many similarities in the modern ethics of both religion and politics, and as far as he was concerned, both were wrought with corruption. Both expected their associates to adhere exclusively to their philosophies, many with which he didn't agree, and others that he could appreciate viewing from either side of the fence. And then there was money, which had so much influence in both— in everything, it seemed.

He pulled out his chair, sat, and sidled back to the desk. He switched on his desk lamp, an antique banker's lamp that did little to illuminate the room with its dark mahogany walls and volume-laden bookshelves, but which did create a comfortable subdued sphere in which he could work. It also made the reflection of the window behind him visible in his wine glass, which would have gone unnoticed if not for the movement of something outside.

Brandon turned in his chair and peered into the night, where, beyond the porch railing, soft lighting exposed a fine cobblestone path that led to a driveway of the same construct. He wheeled forward to get a closer look out at his property just in time to catch the shaking of the shrubs to the left of his window.

Likely a cat or a skunk, he figured, yet he rose and secured the door locks throughout the house to lessen the unease he was feeling. He returned to his office and sat back down, his attention returning to the window's reflection on his wine glass. Thankfully, nothing moved outside the window. He tapped the touchpad to wake the computer and then typed his password, bringing up the Word file with the sermon on which he was currently working. He read his words and was pleased to fall quickly back into the rhythm of his teaching, adding a few paragraphs he hoped were eloquent enough to inspire, and that held truths profound enough to spark epiphanies.

A little more than an hour later, feeling content with his work, he took the final swallow from the wine glass. Recalling the earlier movement, he casually glanced through the window. What he saw there was inexplicable, yet ignited a surge of fear so intense he could only sit and stare at first.

A thick, yellowish substance coated most of the double-paned window. It appeared gelatinous and wet and the word that first came to Brandon's mind was *snot*. Its edges quivered and appeared to fold into the central thickness of the matter, undulating with slurping sounds as it slowly moved upward on the window. As a whole, its movements were hypnotic. Standing slowly, Brandon moved a little closer and watched as wet pustules erupted where the gummy mass touched the glass, forming into gaping cavities that quivered and suctioned onto the surface as it climbed, causing the window to creak with stress. Moist popping noises accompanied the release of each orifice like the snap of quick kisses, moving with a liquid flux to wherever it was heading.

Brandon leaned forward, peering into the curious depths of one of the grotesque maws when what looked like a black, metallic honeycomb emerged from the crater and pressed against the glass. About three inches in diameter, he had never witnessed anything even remotely like it before. He swore it was an eye of some sort, and felt it looking at him. Panic and revulsion drove an all-encompassing shudder throughout his body as he acknowledged the truth that the horrific object on his window was alive. That it was looking at him spoke of some type of intelligence, which made it all the more ghastly.

There was a depth to its honeycomb eye that was oddly seductive and he felt as if it were trying to draw him in. He backed away slowly, trying to make sense of it. No creature that he knew of was even remotely similar, except maybe a jellyfish, but those didn't bubble and boil—or survive out of salt water.

How big is this one? It hadn't covered the window entirely, but was that just a fraction or an iota of the whole…*thing? Host?*

Are there more? he wondered.

Had the human race finally become so corrupt that God had opened the gates of hell, releasing these hideous obscenities?

Is Cooper safe? The thought came out of the blue and rattled him deeply.

"Sweet Lord, I beg of you, keep Cooper safe," he said aloud, but a voice inside of him replied, *that's your job.*

Brandon forced himself to look away from the revolting mass, rushed into the kitchen, and was relieved to see nothing obstructing those windows. He chanced a look outside to confirm that the yard wasn't swarming with the things or that hordes weren't falling from the inky, moonless skies.

What he could use for a weapon? Could it be stabbed or sliced, or would it simply ooze around the blade, unharmed?

Considering the amorphous consistency of the creature, it seemed knives would be useless. And even if he didn't disagree with his conservative colleagues on the right to bear arms, he imagined a bullet would simply be absorbed into the gluey mass of the creature.

He continued staring out the window and calmed himself. For his entire life he had believed in the supernatural qualities of a Christian God, and for that matter, Satan, but never had he considered anything beyond that. The irony was that despite his beliefs, he'd never witnessed anything miraculous or even slightly extraordinary of a supernatural bent. He'd heard plenty claim such things, but he'd sincerely thought most of them were whacks, quacks, or opportunists. If someone were to have relayed what Brandon had just witnessed, he'd have labelled them as well.

The more he thought about it, the more at ease he became. There had to be a logical explanation, but just in case, he'd check on Cooper.

A walk by his office offered a window with a clear view of the lighted yard; no booger-monster with a honeycomb eye, and although he considered it, he didn't look closer for slime tracks on the glass. *Got to have faith*, he reasoned.

As Brandon had hoped, Cooper was sleeping, but evidently restless. He was now upside-down with his head near to the footboard. The SpongeBob nightlight was aglow with six-watt splendor, and Kevin the Minion had found his way into his arms.

FLUMP!

The sound was muted, not distinct, yet startled Cooper, who sprang into a sitting position, looking frantically around the room. It had come from the first floor, in the direction of the front of the house, sounding as if something had hit the floor, as his father used to say, like a sack of wet shite.

Or a two-hundred-pound jellyfish, thought Brandon.

"It's okay, Bub. It's nothing," he quietly said, the lie sounding feeble to his own ears. The look in Cooper's eyes said he wasn't convinced, either.

He was certain that whatever had created the impact was the same thing that had adhered itself to his office window, but he was torn: should he confront the vile thing, which he knew nothing about, or grab his son and run? Instead, he repositioned Cooper correctly in the bed. "Go back to sleep, son."

The most important thing was to keep Cooper safe at all costs, and at the moment, inside appeared safer than out. He'd have to assess the situation. Maybe the thing was harmless, but maybe…. What was that Sun Tzu quote? *If you know the enemy and know yourself, you need not fear…* something like that.

He gently closed his son's door and headed downstairs to find the source of the sound. Only a short hallway ran from the base of the stairway to the front of the house, so it didn't leave many possibilities. From the entryway into the foyer he looked through the front-door window onto a screen-lined, three-season veranda which opened onto the farmer's porch. To the left of the porch, the gentle glow of the outdoor lighting made it just bright enough to settle everything in obscure shadow. He neither saw nor heard anything out of the ordinary so he switched on the porch lights. Nothing reacted to the sudden flare that, although not considerably bright, seemed dazzling to him until his eyes adjusted.

After a small eternity, Brandon unlocked the front door and stepped into the confines of the screened veranda. He looked onto the front lawn, which had been relinquished into darkness outside the reaches of the porch lights. He reached inside the doorway and flicked the lights off, which returned the yard to its previous ambient glow and made visible the long ropes of viscous slime that trailed along the farmer's porch and disappeared around the corner. His office window was located around that same corner, but what concerned him most was that his son's room was directly above it. Whatever that hellish creature was, it would only have to traverse the underside of the porch roof to get to Cooper's window.

And it can climb! He had witnessed that through his office window.

And what had fallen and made that sound?

Brandon approached the screened wall and tried to peer around the corner without leaving the enclosure of the three-season veranda. He was met by the slurping, squishing sound of the creature's movements, and he became aware of a briny odor with the underlying hint of sulfur that was pushed toward him by a mild breeze. It reminded him of the salt marshes of Cape Cod, where his family had vacationed in his childhood. It was not entirely unpleasant, but a foreign smell for Adelphi, Maryland.

Shaking, he fumbled at the screen door-lock until it hooked into the eyelet, and then he backed away just as a putrescent yellow flap of the gelatinous substance breached the corner of the house like a huge infected tongue and sloshed onto the screened wall. It paused as if in contemplation, and then the black honeycomb emerged from within the ghastly organism and pressed to the screen. Sensing the strange, mesmerizing magnetism he had felt earlier, Brandon feared that if he didn't look away immediately, he never would.

A hissing, not unlike the sound of sizzling meat in a frying pan, started emanating from the entity, which instantly traversed to the inside of the enclosed porch, still latched onto the screen and still intact. It had somehow sieved through the screen's mesh unharmed.

"What the fuck?" Brandon blurted, shocked by his own use of the expletive. One that would have surely raised a few eyebrows in his congregation, yet one that was so appropriate for the situation. He said it again. "What-the-ever-loving-fuck?"

FLUMP!

It fell to the porch floor like a pus-filled balloon, hitting and spreading out, splattering against the walls and oozing between the decking. Brandon's gorge rose, yet he could only watch, morbidly fascinated, as it started to gather itself, pooling together but for the three extended splashes nearest him, which merged to form a smooth proboscis that elongated in his direction, reaching for him. Brandon backed away, but the creature compensated by sending more mass into its stretching tentacle.

Don't let it touch you! Brandon didn't know what would happen if it did, but it seemed intent and he felt it was imperative that it not touch him—not even the slightest brush.

Would it steal his soul, farm his blood, or just melt him into its next meal? He backed into the house, slammed the door, and twisted the deadbolt lock. Wildly contemplating his next move—if he even had one—he back-stepped to the foot of the stairs.

What do I do now?

How would he protect them from this thing...this profanity that could flow unfazed through a screen like water? He looked up the stairway toward Cooper's bedroom and then the cellphone in his pants pocket vibrated and rang simultaneously.

"Fuck!" he yelped, nearly sprinting for the kitchen.

Third F-bomb in less than five minutes. *Appropriate,* he reminded himself, and pulled the phone from his pocket to see his wife's pretty, smiling face on the screen.

"Hello?" he answered in a hushed voice, his heart slamming.

"Hi, baby! How's it going?" Her voice was so normal it nearly brought him to tears.

Should I say anything? Should I have her call the cops...the National Guard? No, I could do that. What could she possibly do, except worry?

"Good, good," he said, forcing a cheerful but tentative voice. *Now I'm lying,* but it's a good lie—a compassionate lie, he reasoned.

He heard movement at the door and then the door lever quivered ever so slightly.

"Are you okay? You sound out of breath," said Sylvia, ever observant.

"I'm fine. Just doing some chores."

"Chores at ten-thirty at night?"

"Yeah. Wide awake and Cooper's asleep, so I figured..." Brandon stopped talking when he saw that a thin, phlegmy strand had started seeping through the keyhole of the old door. The skeleton keys were long gone, but the locks remained, long unused until now. "Uh..." he said.

"How's our little guy?" Sylvia asked. "Was he very upset that I wasn't there for his birthday?"

"He's...good...uh, honey? Listen. Can I call you right back? I left the door, the cellar door open, and I don't want anything getting in."

The pool of slime in front of the door was now a foot across and quickly expanding.

"Oh, okay," she said hesitantly. "Are you sure everything's okay?"

"Scout's honor," Brandon lied again as two thin appendages grew from the mass like antennae. "I just slapped a couple mosquitos and I want to get ahead of it before they get really bad, okay? Love you. Call right back."

He disconnected the call before Sylvia could reply and slipped his phone into his pocket. The feelers extended, twisted, coiled, and extended again, blindly searching for Brandon as he cautiously diverted away from the stairway, hoping to lure it to the kitchen and distance its access to Cooper's room. The feelers rose in unison, like twin cobras preparing to strike, and then those damned black honeycombs formed at the tip of each one, swinging and swaying back and forth while its malignant, popping suckers gripped and released the floor as it advanced on him.

"Daddy?" Cooper called suddenly, from the top of the stairs.

The heinous blob immediately stopped and its soulless honeycomb eyes turned to the sound of the boy's voice. Time stood still, as if all three were at an impasse, waiting for the other to make a move.

Oh shit—oh shit—oh shit! It can hear? How can it hear? It has no fucking ears!

"Daddy? What's that noise?"

"It's nothing, sweetie!" Brandon said, alertly watching the slimy creature's movements. "Go back to bed. I'll be up there in a few minutes."

The black-tipped probes appeared intently locked in the direction of Cooper's voice.

Now! Brandon thought, forcing his fear aside, and with two long strides he leapt over the abomination, clearing its reaching probes by mere inches. With a celebratory *whoop,* Brandon landed in the hallway just outside the kitchen threshold, both feet landing squarely on the floor in a patch of slime. His feet cherry-pitted from beneath him, sending him hurtling across the floor in an involuntary backflip. He hit the bottom of the stairway with bone-jarring impact, sending a lightning bolt of pain through him by way of his elbow.

With a succession of sopping slurps and pops, the gurgling form immediately reversed direction, its probing appendages seeming to slide front-to-back like the barrels on a tank turret. Without stopping to assess his injuries, Brandon scrambled to his feet and mounted the stairs, taking two at a time.

Cooper stood at the head of the stairway, watching wide-eyed and uncomprehending. "What *is* that, Daddy?"

"Get in your room, quick!" Brandon ordered.

The boy stood frozen as the undulating form seemed to contemplate the stairs.

"Go! Quick!"

"But..."

"Go!" Brandon yelled, giving his son a push.

Shocked by the unfamiliar urgency of his father's voice, Cooper darted for his room, wailing in fear. Brandon quickly glanced over his shoulder and then followed his son down the hallway, thinking that never before in his life had he seen something pour *up* the stairs.

Inside Cooper's room, he slammed the door, tore the sheets from the bed, and started jamming them against the base of the door, trying to seal the opening. Cooper stood in the center of the room, mouth agape, hands clasping and unclasping as he silently wept. Anger and self-disgust swept through Brandon at his failure to keep his son safe from such trauma and ugliness.

As he worked the fabric into the gap, Cooper started a terrified, high-pitched keening. Brandon looked at him and saw movement in his peripheral, feeling the slightest shifting in the air near his head as a tentacle swayed from the keyhole like a long, infected worm, hovering frighteningly close to his son's face. Brandon sprang away from the door, landing on his back at Cooper's feet, pulling the boy down on top of him.

Rising, Brandon tucked Cooper behind him and backed away from the searching probe. Again, a honeycomb eye formed and locked first onto Brandon, who was busy opening the bedroom window, and then refocused on the little boy.

"Get on the porch roof and go to my bedroom window," Brandon said, lifting his son to the lip of the window.

"Noooo!" Cooper cried, seeming more scared by the thought of climbing onto the roof than the atrocity behind them.

"Cooper, listen to me! Go! I'll meet you there."

Brandon pushed his unwilling son through the window opening and onto the roof. He closed the window and twisted the latch, hoping the hellish beast couldn't sprout fingers, although it wouldn't have surprised him. He stood at the foot of the bed and watched until the last of the slime secreted from the keyhole, and waited for the slime bag to round the bed with eye-tipped appendages flailing, but it didn't show.

Brandon leaned forward to see over the bed when it occurred to him that it could easily move beneath it. He leapt onto the bed just as an infected-looking arm-like extension shot out, swiping where his feet had just been. Sparing no time, Brandon bounced to the floor and raced to the doorway, halting just outside. Inside the room, the oozing obscenity ignored him and began climbing the wall toward the window.

It doesn't give a shit about me, Brandon realized. It only wants Cooper!

"Hey!" he yelled at it. "Hey, pus-bag!"

Still it ignored him and continued to climb, spreading its semi-fluid malignance over the window. To his horror, Brandon could see his son's distorted image through the creature, inches away on the outside of the glass. Fortunately, it appeared that the abomination couldn't manipulate the window hardware or penetrate the seams.

"Cooper! Get away from there!" he yelled, and started for the stairs.

He stopped halfway down when he heard the familiar *Flump!*

Had it given up trying to breach the window? He started back up the stairs when he heard the approaching sound of its movement and watched it ooze through the doorway and past his and Sylvia's bedroom, intent on him. Brandon descended the remaining stairs, grateful that the creature was as slow as it was abhorrent, and wondering if he had unconsciously said something offensive to God during a service, and that The Almighty was exacting vengeance.

As repugnant as it was, couldn't God have come up with something more menacing than a slow-moving bag of pus? Maybe God only wanted to scare him, or maybe it wasn't God's doing at all. He liked that thought better. He had always been so careful not to offend his maker. It seemed more befitting—or at least he hoped it was—that Satan was attacking him, and that God was protecting him by making Satan's underling a bumbling blob of booger. Wouldn't Beelzebub likely be responsible for creating something so repulsive?

"Come on, you snot sausage," Brandon coaxed, while opening the front door.

He stepped out onto the veranda just as the glugging and slewing mess tumbled down the stairway leaving an explosion of viscous debris in its wake. It quivered at the foot of the stairs as its gungy remnants amalgamated, and then followed him across the porch and onto the lawn.

Brandon jogged across the lawn toward the garage as the oversized globule rippled over the edge of the walkway and across the grass, rolling toward the garage like a malignant water-baby.

Brandon looked up to see his son sitting on the roof, his forehead on his knees and his back against the wall near his parents' bedroom window. "Stay right there," Brandon ordered, and then ducked inside the doorway on the side of the garage.

Somehow comprehending that Brandon was talking to his son, the hideous being reversed direction in one fluid shift, again intent on Cooper. When it was halfway across the lawn, Brandon leapt out from behind the doorway of the garage with a plastic three-gallon gas container raised high in his arms and started splashing the pungent liquid all over the creature. It recoiled when the gasoline hit it, all its extremities folding within its central mass.

Cooper had scooted closer to the edge of the roof and was shaking his head and yelling. Encouraged by his son's reaction, Brandon released a shout that sounded as if it was treading the fine line between victory and insanity. He poured the remaining contents of the gas can over the huddled mass and ran a small gasoline trail to the edge of driveway.

Let's put an end to this, he thought, drawing a long butane grill striker from his rear pocket. He flicked the wheel and touched the tip to the small track of fuel, which instantly ignited, engulfing the recoiling mass with a *whoomp!*

The piercing shriek that emanated from the undulating ball of slime was unlike anything Brandon had heard before, and one he hoped never to hear again. It was the sound of a million souls wailing and it carried on as the creature twisted and writhed, its bulk sizzling and splattering. Its cry was so loud and long that Brandon felt a growing sense of sadness, and when it finally stopped moving, he felt an inexplicable sorrow for the remains of the being before him.

Brandon stared at what looked like a large pile of blackened Vaseline for a long time, unaware of the cries of his son. Its demise seemed anticlimactic. He had been expecting more of a fight, or for it to spill a million deadly insectile offspring to the ground. The monstrous thing's cries had been so mournful that it confused him. He looked at his son sitting on the lip of the roof; the little boy's tear-streaked face was drawn in profound grief.

Brandon hurried back to his son's bedroom and brought Cooper inside.

"I'm sorry you had to see something like that," Brandon told his son, sitting on the bed with him. "But it's okay, now. It's dead."

"You killed her, Dad," the little boy stammered. "Why'd you kill her?" He brushed his forearm against his eyes, spreading tears and mucus across his face.

Cooper's tone surprised Brandon. His words were thick with accusation, and although he'd seen his son angry before, he had never seen him enraged. It seemed out of place for a child his age, and especially for one as…mild as Cooper. It was unsettling. Brandon looked at his son curiously.

"Why are you calling it *her*?"

"I know her. She likes me. She cares, like mom is s'posed to."

"Cooper, what are you talking about?" Brandon asked. Maybe it was too much for the kid. He was clearly distressed and surely traumatized.

"She looks different here, but she told me it was her when she touched me tonight," he said, raising a hand to his cheek. "She said she changed when she came here, but she's pretty. Prettier than mommy. They all are."

It sounded like babble to Brandon. It didn't make sense, but then again, that thing smoldering in the front yard didn't make sense, either.

FLUMP!

Brandon wanted to ignore the sound—or pretend he had imagined it. Was it—*she*—still alive? Was it possible?

"Where's she from, Cooper?" Brandon asked. Was it true? Did Cooper actually know what this thing was?

FLUMP!

"She's from…the place."

"What place?"

"Where I go when I'm sad or mad or alone," he said irately, and then shrugged. "I don't know."

"And where is this place? How do you get there?" Brandon asked.

FLUMP!

FLUMP!

"I don't know. I just sit here and go there," Cooper said, his chin quivering. "But this time I wanted her to come here."

His rambling was madness, some kind of dissociation, Brandon thought, but then…there was that thing outside.

FLUMP! FLUMP!

FLUMP!

FLUMP! FLUMP! FLUMP!

"Are there more of these, Cooper?" Brandon asked, looking up at the ceiling, where the last sound seemed to have originated.

"Yes. When I was on the roof, I told them you were hurting her. They are really mad you killed her."

FLUMP! FLUMP! FLUMP! FLUMP! FLUMP!

FLUMP! FLUMP!

FLUMP!

FLUMP! FLUMP! FLUMP!

FLUMP!

"How many are there, Cooper?" Brandon asked

"As many as I want."

A TRUNK STORY

As proprietor of Huddy's Quality Used Autos and father to thirteen offspring of varying intellect and repugnance (who local folk referred to as *the Brood* for want of a more appropriate designation), Fergus Huddy was a busy man. His dedication to the former was fueled more by his aversion to the latter than by necessity, so his car lot generated plenty of revenue.

Overburdened by neither instinct nor morals, Fergus Huddy was not a man to turn his back on opportunity, and a pristine Mercury Grand Marquis—regardless of its age, and especially considering it was offered to him for free—spelled opportunity in bright, Day-Glo splendor. That the trunk of said vehicle had once served as a makeshift casket for a number of weeks was not a deterrent to our less-than-upright car salesman, and it seemed too good an opportunity to risk losing by asking too many questions—so he asked none.

So, the car has a bit of history and the trunk has a lot of stink... big deal, Fergus figured. He could remedy that! Wash the offending trunk lining, give it a good citrus douche, and voila! Or so he thought. That had been his belief when he'd first agreed to take the four-wheeled atrocity in 2013, four years prior.

It had been sitting for five years by that point, awaiting a beneficiary who never turned up. The attending lawyer, of whom Fergus had never heard, despite being local, seemed oddly anxious to put the abandoned car in Fergus Huddy's hands.

In hindsight, Fergus should have seen these as omens, but the old weasel had never believed in omens. He did now, because he had no doubt the 1994 Mercury Grand Marquis was haunted. He believed the lawyer knew it, too—sure as the sun sets.

Fergus was seated inside his office the day the tow truck dropped off the car. He watched the driver back the car into a spot near the overhead doors and was surprised to see someone sitting in the front passenger seat of the towed vehicle. This was highly frowned upon from a safety aspect, but when he got outside to accept the delivery, the car was empty and the truck attendant swore no one had been inside.

Deal done, Fergus returned to his office, settled behind his desk, but soon became aware of a hollow, rhythmic hammering that seemed omnidirectional.

After nearly an hour of the incessant banging he was ready to pop a vessel. He followed the sound outside where it surrounded him, filling the air, the ground, and his head, but seemed to originate from the trunk of that wretched 1994 Mercury Grand Marquis. It sounded as if someone were inside, hammering for escape, but it stopped as soon as Fergus opened the trunk.

Nothing was inside—ever—except for an astounding stench that never dissipated, even after half-a-dozen cleanings by his son, Henson. Fergus personally stripped the trunk interior down to the metal and pressure-washed it with an industrial-strength detergent.

It intensified.

His next endeavor was to isolate the trunk from the cabin of the car, closing the access behind the rear seat with six-mil poly sheeting and silicone sealant. This stopped the permeation of stench from the trunk to the car's interior, though a hint of the abhorrent scent was always present. All he or Henson had to do was to keep prospective buyers from opening the trunk. Once the car was off the lot, it would no longer be his concern.

The hellish drumming became his daily companion, a personal solo that assaulted only his ears during the workdays, and resided in his memory's ears during the nights; Fergus hadn't enjoyed a decent night's sleep since the car was towed onto his lot.

A sensible man would have surrendered the car to the depths of Lake Winnipesaukee long before, but Fergus Huddy had never been a sensible man, just greedy, hopeful... and now scared. Not afraid of the car so much, but of the headaches.

Dear God, what headaches!

The few times he had come close to selling the car—if the smell didn't discourage the buyers, which it usually did—he suffered nauseating, crippling migraines that throbbed in tempo with the pulsing trunk music. If he tried to get rid of the car, have it towed, give it away, or junk it, he would suffer the same ailment, and would have to terminate the transaction for fear his head would explode.

But, this particular day, it wasn't happening. When Henson informed him that a couple was interested in the Mercury Grand Obscenity, he realized there hadn't been any drumming that day.

"It's hideous. I hate it."

Todd Ingram didn't disagree with Rachel's assessment, she could read it in his expression, but at nine hundred dollars— three hundred less than the *Kelley Blue Book* suggested price— the 1994 Mercury Grand Marquis was difficult to resist... and the dealer was currently presenting Todd's six-hundred-dollar offer to his boss.

"Aw, it ain't *that* bad," he countered.

"My father drove one just like this. Same color, same fake convertible roof and everything." Rachel squinted at him, trying to shield her eyes from the brilliant late-morning sun that haloed Todd's head. "It's a gas-guzzling beast with a hundred-eighty thousand miles on it. It'll probably keel over as soon as it makes the street."

"One-eighty's great for a twenty-three-year-old car, and it's in solid physical shape!" He pointed at the data sticker on the rear driver-side window. "CARFAX says it ain't never been in an accident."

"And you believe that?"

"Why wouldn't I?"

"Of course, Mr. Gullible," she said, walking to the opposite side of the car. "You believed I was still cherry when we met," she muttered under her breath.

"What?"

"I said it ain't exactly a cherry-red Corvette!"

Todd nodded and settled his non-existent rump against the front fender. He barely broke one hundred and forty pounds and was rail-thin at five-eleven, despite a perpetually ravenous appetite. Rachel was five-two and—as Todd put it—a *salacious* one-forty-five. She often bemoaned the unfairness of their dissimilar metabolisms, though much of the blame lay in her penchant for Ben & Jerry's Cookie Dough ice cream and most any form of chocolate, the latter of which she surreptitiously stashed throughout their apartment: tucked under couch cushions, wrapped in her winter socks, and even secreted in tampon boxes.

Rachel had a natural beauty and the good fortune that her extra weight migrated mostly to the areas enhancing her hourglass contours, making her more enticing to the male eye—and a fair share of female eyes, too.

"Well, we can't exactly afford a cherry-red Corvette...or any other color, for that matter. This here car's about all we can manage. Plus it has an engine that actually works." Todd slapped the dulled black hood. "And barely any rust."

"Plenty of Bondo, I'm sure," Rachel said.

"Well, Bondo ain't rust!" Todd responded, the words leaving his lips like a bullet. "Christ in a rickety rowboat, Rachel! I can't exactly yank ten thousand dollars out of my pucker-hole, now, can I? We either get this here car, or we just keep on walking ever-where!" Todd seldom became angry; he was so even-keeled that it startled her when he did.

Her feet still throbbed from the three-plus-mile walk from their apartment, and they still needed to fetch groceries at The Bargain Basket. The thought of lugging a dozen bags all that way nearly brought her to tears.

"You're right," she agreed, averting her pretty blue eyes.

As if on cue, Henson Huddy exited the office and headed their way. A mile-wide charlatan's smile beamed on his pasty face and Rachel wondered if he'd been listening in on them.

A thought occurred to her. "Did you look in the trunk?"

"What for?" Todd asked.

"Remember the Camaro?"

Todd had owned a 1988 Camaro when they'd met in 2002. It had been his pride and joy; a pretty car—navy-blue with white pin-striping—but as the adage went, beauty is only skin deep, or where Todd's Camaro was concerned, paint deep. While the surface shined, the car festered with a rusty cancer that had scabbed over the unseen parts and nearly devoured the undercarriage. The only thing between the trunk lid and the ground was a gas tank, also well on its way to demise. The floorboards were riddled with so many holes, those inside the car ended up knee-deep in water whenever he hit a sizeable puddle. Nonetheless, to a starry-eyed sixteen-year-old lass from upstate New Hampshire, it may as well have been a Bugatti.

"Yeah, I remember," Todd said sadly, then brightened. "But this here has back doors! We can put stuff on the seat if we have to."

Rachel rolled her eyes. "Can we *please* look inside the trunk?" she asked.

"No need," said Henson Huddy. "Daddy…I mean, my boss agreed to your offer of six hundred."

"I still want to see in the trunk," Rachel insisted.

Henson Huddy's smile faltered. "Why you want to do that?" he asked. He pushed back a lock of his stringy black comb-over as greasy as his reputation.

Rachel jabbed her finger against the trunk lid. "We ain't agreeing to nothing 'til I see inside that there trunk!"

Henson Huddy changed tack. "You let your lady make all your choices?" he asked Todd, boring into him with his black pencil-point eyes.

A larva, Rachel realized. That's what Henson Huddy resembled. She set her blazing eyes on the maggot of a salesman and Todd took a preemptive step away lest he catch some shrapnel.

"If you don't open that trunk right now, I'll jam my foot so far up your ass you'll taste your colon," Rachel warned, her words metered and menacing. "How's them for choices?"

The black, pinpoint eyes shifted to Todd, who simply stated, "That's my girl."

Seeing no alternative, Henson drew a single key bearing a small white tag from his pocket and tossed it to Todd. "Be my guest," he said, and furtively moved away from the car.

Todd slid the key into the lock and turned. The trunk popped open with ease, revealing a cavernous compartment. Rachel stepped closer to inspect its integrity. Her nose crinkled in disgust and she fought back a rising nausea. She glared at Todd.

"Did you fart?"

"Weren't me," said her husband, cupping a hand over his nose.

"You?" Rachel set her eyes on Henson, who shook a rapid

denial.

"Ain't no fart smells like that," said Todd.

"Your Keystone beer farts do," Rachel countered. Her stomach lurched again.

"Yeah, they're pretty thick, but this ain't the same..." Todd noticed Henson Huddy's covert retreat. "Hey, bub!"

"I didn't fart!" Henson insisted.

"Then what ain't you telling us? Someone die in there?" Todd asked.

Henson Huddy shook his head again. And he wasn't lying, for Lionel Freemont had been quite dead for nearly a week before his wife had wrestled his bloated corpse into the Grand Marquis' vault-sized trunk on that August morning of 2008. Mildred Freemont then pulled Lionel's beloved car behind their abandoned barn and parked it. For three weeks, Lionel simmered in the relentless summer sun by day, and cooled by night. By the time his body was discovered, he'd been reduced to a festering stew so wretched that the coroner—once he'd vomited himself dry—decided to forgo the body bag and opted for a large fishing cooler.

With the exception of her discarded muumuu and a trail of heavy footprints into the adjoining forest, no further traces of Mildred had ever been found. It was believed she'd become a hearty bear feast, though a number of locals claimed to have seen her pale, naked form dashing through the trees on moonlit nights, cackling wildly at her lunar guide.

"Nobody died in there," Henson assured them.

"Holy shit, close it before I hurl!" cried Rachel. "We don't want it!"

"But..." Todd and Henson started in unison, but their spoken thoughts were cut off by the impact of the dealership's door against the building's tin walls.

A short, rotund man hastily wobbled through the doorway, waddling in their direction. He was unmistakably related to

Henson Huddy, and simple logic tagged him as Fergus Huddy, but to Rachel's eyes there was more than sufficient evidence that somewhere in Huddy history, a Morlock and a penguin had fucked.

"Hold on a moment there, folks!" said the repugnant troll. "Let's not be hasty and miss out on this golden opportunity." He extended his hand to Todd, who shook quickly. "Fergus Huddy," he said.

"Were you listening in on us?" Rachel asked.

Fergus Huddy's eyes went directly to Rachel Ingram's breasts as if no other part of her existed. "Well, my dear," he said to her chest, slowly advancing. "Any businessman worth his own weight puts his customer's concerns before all else. I make sure my staff treats my customers fairly."

"That so?" asked Rachel.

"Yes, ma'am."

"In that case, I'm concerned," said Rachel.

"About what, my dear?" said the squat man.

He was sweating profusely and Rachel was afraid he'd try to hug her, or something worse. "Well, I'm concerned I may have to poke your eyes out if you don't stop staring at my tits," she said. "And I ain't your fucking 'dear.'"

Stunned, Fergus Huddy quickly composed himself. His little piggy eyes seem to regain focus, but avoided looking at Rachel. Todd hid a satisfied smile.

"In that case, I apologize for offending you, young lady, and I wish to make amends," said the porcine proprietor. "I'm determined not to let the two of you leave this property without this car, at a price you can't refuse."

"I said we don't want it," Rachel insisted.

"The trunk reeks like Satan's asshole," said Todd.

"Simple water stagnation," Fergus explained. "The trunk was accidentally left open before a downpour. One of our staff closed the lid without looking inside and it sat that way for nearly a month. You may have noticed, we replaced the old lining with new one-hundred-percent polyester. The smell will fade in no time."

Rachel stared at him in disbelief. "I said no! We ain't paying a fucking thing for that car."

"Deal!" said Fergus Huddy. He grabbed both of their hands and shook.

"What?" asked Todd.

"Huh?" said Rachel.

"It's a deal. You said you ain't paying a fucking thing for that car and I agreed. It's yours."

Fergus Huddy presented them the car the way Vanna White presented a new puzzle, with a big, fake flash of teeth, though his were far from pearly whites. Rachel thought she saw a nucleus of terror in his eyes, and she had no idea how right she was.

When Henson had returned with the offer, Fergus hesitantly accepted, swallowed three anticipatory Percocet, and braced for another skull-splitter, but it never came. Encouraged, Fergus decided to monitor the interaction on the surveillance system. All seemed to be going well until they opened that goddamned trunk. When the woman said, "We don't want it," the hammering started and the resultant headache almost leveled him where he stood.

Fergus had had to act quickly and salvage the sale— anything to relieve the pain. He'd barreled his way through the door, approaching them as fast as his little pistoning legs could carry him. They stared at him as if he were an alien, and he guessed, in some manner, he was.

Things quickly went downhill. It wasn't intentional, but when he noticed the young woman's bountiful breasts and the relief they promised, all he could think about was settling his pounding head against them and going to sleep.

He slogged through his agony as the annoyed woman reprimanded him, and forcefully returned to the situation at hand. He offered a two-hundred-percent bullshit explanation for the infernal reek emanating from the trunk as the slamming in his head intensified, and he understood his chances to be rid of the car were slipping away… but then everything changed.

"We ain't paying a fucking thing for that car," she had said. Fergus latched onto those words like a lifeline. He knew the woman wasn't interested in the car, but the man was.

"Deal!" he'd said, and like magic, the metallic hammering and the headache were gone. He knew he had succeeded.

Speeding northbound on Route 3 toward Holderness, Todd pushed the car to fifty, sixty, and then seventy, pleased with the power of the old V8. Rachel wasn't moved. She didn't like or want the car, but she couldn't dispute Todd's argument that it ran great and the price was certainly right. *At least the trunk stench was staying in the trunk,* she reasoned.

Todd ran an appreciative hand over a section of faux wood trim running the length of the dash. "Why you think he just gave the car to us like that?"

That also concerned Rachel. The previous owner had kept it in great shape, the upholstery was clean and whole, and the tires seemed deep-threaded to her untrained eye. Surely the car had *some* value, so why give it away?

Rachel jabbed the power button for the radio. The display illuminated with little green digits, but no sound came from the speakers. She pressed the volume "+" button to continued silence.

"Maybe because it smells like swamp-rotted assholes and

the radio's a piece of shit?" Rachel exclaimed, driving her closed fist into the radio.

"Still… can't complain," said Todd.

"I can."

"I can't argue that," Todd agreed. It took Rachel a few moments to recognize the jab.

A sound of rustling plastic came from behind them.

"What was that?" Rachel asked.

Both chanced a look in the back seat but saw nothing.

"Car's old, could be anythin'," Todd said, shrugging a dismissive shoulder.

Rachel poked a button on the radio and a cassette ejected from the tape player to swing suspended by its oxide ribbon. The speakers roared to life and both she and Todd jabbed blindly in search of the volume. Todd hit the power button and the car fell into silence… almost.

"Jesus H. fucking Christ!" a voice behind them complained.

"Was that the radio?" Todd asked. His eyes remained fixed forward, but they looked confused and worried.

"Radio's off," Rachel said. She turned in her seat and shrieked.

"What? What?" Todd scanned every direction, expecting to see a vehicle barreling toward them.

Rachel didn't answer, only stared in terror into the back of the car.

Todd pulled to the side of the road so he could see what had Rachel so troubled. At first, he thought the mottled green fingers poking out from between the rear seat sections was a prank, until they wriggled as if offering a dainty greeting.

"Well, that's just fucked up," he said, eyes glued to the deteriorated digits, but Rachel was already out of the car, standing ten feet away.

"What are they?" she asked.

Todd rolled his eyes. "Ain't you ever seen fingers before?"

She took a few timid steps toward the car and looked in the rear passenger window. "Not like those."

They watched with fascination as the fingers clutched the leather seat and then shot forward until the putrefied limb was exposed to the elbow. Rachel jumped back with a shriek.

"That there's an arm," said Todd.

"Whose arm?" asked Rachel, wide-eyed, her fisted hands to her mouth.

"Ain't sure, but I imagine there's a body attached to it."

Todd leaned into the glove box and hit the trunk release. He then climbed from the car and walked to the rear. Rachel stood behind him as he lifted the lid, both turning their heads to avoid the assailing stench.

"Hey, Rach! There ain't nothing in here. Even the stink is gone," he said, hoping she'd be pleased by this revelation.

"No way! A stink like that? Where would it go?"

"Beats me. Just up an' left, I guess," he said. "Ain't no body in there for that arm to connect to, neither. I'm starting to suspect something ain't quite right with this here car."

"Ya think? I told you I didn't want this... Oh, Todd! Oh, shit... oh, shit!" She pointed in the window and Todd stepped beside her to look inside.

"Holy freaking basket of batshit! Now, that there just ain't proper!" Todd said, backing from the car.

A full arm had extended from between the upper and lower seat section, which was bad enough, but a head was also pushing its way through—with difficulty, judging by the expression on its gangrenous face.

"Son-of-a-bitch!" it said, grimacing. Another hand appeared and extended.

Terrified but intrigued, Todd moved back to the window. "Reminds me of when Gertie was calving."

"Fuck Gertie!" snarled the thing in the car, both its hands latching onto the front seat. It pulled itself up, and within seconds a tall, lean man in a bedraggled flannel shirt and jeans was sitting in the back of the car. He was—or had been—handsome, despite his surly countenance and before his festering flesh.

Rachel found herself unable to look away from the cold, soulless eyes or the thin, tight lips.

"What in the hell are you two idjits looking at?"

Idjits? She only knew one person who pronounced 'idiots' that way. "Father?" she said.

"Well, it ain't the goddamned pope!" Said the ghost of Lionel Freemont, with a dry rasp.

Yup, that's him, Rachel thought. "You're dead?"

The man looked at his blotchy, frog-belly arms, then back at Rachel. "Still sharp as a sponge, I see. Stupid shit."

"And you're still a mean old man!" Rachel shot back, sour memories eradicating her fear.

"You and your mother made me mean!" he said.

"Because you were never satisfied with anything we did!"

"Because neither of you could do anything right!"

"I hate you! You're an asshole!"

"You're a little bitch!" he said.

Freemont glared at Rachel as she glowered back, and she realized they were exactly where they had left off fifteen years earlier. Todd stood beside her, looking too baffled to be scared.

"And who the fuck are *you*?" asked the cantankerous old bastard.

"Todd Ingram." Todd offered his hand through the open window. The ghastly man only scowled. Todd retracted his hand.

"You the son of that hack carpenter, Frank Ingram?"

"Yeah, that was my dad. He used to say you were the cheapest bastard east of the Pacific," Todd said, responding to the insult in kind.

"Hah! That son-of-a-whore couldn't make a straight wall

with a steel I-beam."

"Yeah? Well, speaking of whores, Daddy said there wasn't a one that wasn't on your payroll."

"No wonder Mama hated you!" spat Rachel.

"I wouldn't have needed them if she knew how to please a man!"

"Maybe if she had a man worth pleasing!"

"Daddy said your mama had quite a few men," said Todd.

"Shut up!" both Lionel and Rachel yelled.

Rachel noticed a shadow cross Todd's eyes. She had seldom seen this in their relationship, but she'd always remember the great displays of rage that followed.

"I think it's time you got out of our car," Todd said, his voice curt and unyielding. He opened the door and stood back.

"It's my car," said Lionel.

"No, we just bought it," Rachel told him.

"They *gave* it to you."

"Correct, which adds up to the same," said Todd. "Our name is on the title, so get out."

"Make me," challenged Lionel, his chin proffered like a stubborn child's.

Todd grabbed for his arm but his hand passed through as if he were smoke. "Well, don't that just figure," Todd sighed. "How do we get rid of a ghost?"

"I don't know," said Rachel.

"C'mon, you watch all those shows about ghosts and the periodontal stuff."

"Paranormal," Rachel corrected. In her mind, she reviewed past episodes of the dozen or so reality shows she used to watch that had the words *ghost* or *paranormal* in the title, while Lionel would smirk at them, looking smug and rather like the asshole he was.

"They often say ghosts have to be anchored to someone or something in this realm for them to stay."

"Is it you, seeing as he's your daddy?"

"He might be my father, but he ain't my daddy," Rachel said. "A daddy has to earn that title. It don't make sense, anyhow. I've been his daughter all my life, and even after he died, but he shows up now?"

"Ever since we got the car."

"Ayup," said Lionel, patting the car seat in front of him.

Rachel snapped her fingers at a memory. "That makes sense! I think the thing… the… *host*, that's it! The host has to be present when they die. It can attach to anything, like a doll, a dress, or a car. We have to get rid of the car."

"Well, I ain't giving up this car!" Todd said. He climbed into the driver's seat and motioned for Rachel to follow.

Rachel regarded the two men. How different they were. She congratulated herself for rebelling against her father by finding a compassionate man. The decision to support her husband was an easy one and she slipped into her seat, ignoring the dead man behind her. Todd shifted and pulled onto the road.

Freemont started a loud, tuneless humming, intent on irritating his car mates, but Todd had nerves of steel and the patience of the virtuous, and his wife carried a lifelong grudge that was close to impenetrable. Undeterred, the ghost increased his volume. Retaliating, Rachel jabbed the radio's power button and cranked up the volume, introducing her father to the heavy riffs of AC/DC's "For Those About to Rock."

Lionel Freemont slapped his hands over his ears, a pained expression crossing his face. "Christ in a cradle! What is this clatter?"

A small, satisfied smile on her lips, Rachel bumped the volume higher yet and she and Todd nodded in rhythm while her father uselessly prattled on. AC/DC faded out and Lionel's hands lowered.

"Thank all that is fucking sacred and sane," he said, then pointed at the cassette suspended from the player. "What in the holy jumping Jesus did you do to my Hank Snow tape?”

“Oh God. Is that who that was? I remember you playing that stupid tape every waking hour.” Rachel grabbed the tape and yanked. It unwound with a high whine but did not release. She wrapped the ribbon around her hand and yanked again until it freed with a satisfying snap that severed it in two.

“Hey!” Lionel complained as the liberated cassette passed through him and hit the seat. “Hank is not stupid!” he pouted.

“He sounded like a neutered goat,” Rachel said.

“You know… he does,” agreed Todd.

“And what do you know, smart ass?” Lionel challenged.

“Well, I know I ain’t no genius, but I know I’m probably a lot smarter than I really am,” Todd said.

Lionel held his gaze for an extended spell. Rachel looked confused.

“Did he just say…” he started to say, but froze. “Ho-lee shit, did I hear that right? Did the radio announcer just say *President Trump?*”

“Yeah, you heard right,” Rachel said, unable to contain her disgust.

“The orange angst monkey? That one?”

“Yes.”

“Well, you fuck-ups sure let this place go to shit since I’ve been gone, didn’t you?”

Though Rachel agreed, she wouldn’t admit it. “Trump always reminded me of you. You’re both deplorable.”

“Ha! He doesn’t hold a candle to me!”

“Told you,” Rachel said to Todd, who shook his head sadly.

“So schmuck, she give you the *marry me I’m pregnant* pitch like all the others?” Lionel asked.

Rachel’s face reddened until it felt ready to blister. Todd looked at her inquiringly and she became quite interested in the stitching of her Levi’s.

“You did tell me you were pregnant a couple months after

we met," Todd said, doubt coloring his words. "That's why we got married."

Lionel barked a laugh. "What a sucker!"

"I was!" Rachel said, trying to sound hurt by the allegation. "I miscarried, remember?"

"A stewed tomato and some puree in the toilet bowl. I'd put money on it," said Lionel with a nasty laugh. Rachel looked out her window, staring into the distance and rubbing a tear from her eye.

"That true, Rach?" Todd asked.

"It was tomato sauce, not puree," she admitted. "But you were the nicest guy around and I knew you'd love me and treat me right... and you have," she added hopefully.

"Then what did he mean by 'all the others'?"

Rachel remained silent. In the back seat, Lionel chortled.

"Well, were there others?" Todd pressed.

"Yes, but not a lot," Rachel said.

Lionel barked again. "The Berman boy, the Simmons kid, the Jones kid, both McCready boys, the Harrington boy, the Keen..."

"*Shut up!*" Rachel roared.

Todd looked stunned. "But you were hardly sixteen when we met."

"Whoopsie!" Lionel said, and then giggled impishly.

She turned to him, rage burning in her eyes. "You ain't nothing but a heartless, ugly, *green* old man! I'm glad you're dead!"

He stuck his bleached, swollen tongue out at her. It looked like a slug squirming from his lips.

She knew Todd must be feeling betrayed, because she would if she were him. "Todd," she implored. "We've been married almost fifteen years... happily married. We love each other a lot, and I've always tried my best to make you a happy hubby, haven't I?"

She watched his eyes for a sign. He glanced at her teary face and softened. Rachel saw the opening, dove in, and hit him where he lived.

"Like you always say, our sex life is crazy good from all the good crazy sex. And I love it, too."

"I bet you do," said Lionel, but they both ignored him.

"Why'd you lie to me 'bout all that stuff?"

"I was afraid you wouldn't want me."

"Couldn't blame him. Tramp," said Lionel.

"I was with women before you and you still wanted me. Why do you think it'd be different for me?" asked Todd.

"I don't know. I was young and insecure and dumb…"

"Bingo!" said Lionel.

"And I wanted… *needed* to get away from that fucking son-of-a-bitch, the way he treated me and my mother!"

"Young lady! Is that any way to speak of your father?"

"Fuck you, you ain't my father! You're dead!"

"I guess I can see why you'd want to get away from him," said Todd.

"Did she tell you she used to sell herself on the corner of Bartlett and Prospect?" asked Lionel, waving the question at Todd like a lure.

Rachel spun in her seat and glared. "That is not true at all! Why are you doing this? Why are you such a shit?"

"I just want my family back," Lionel said, choking on the false solemnity of the words.

"Oh, bullshit! You never wanted me around, and all you wanted from mom was a live-in slave."

"Yeah, you're right." Lionel laughed scornfully, then glowered at his daughter. "I just want to get back at the bitch. *You* are the only thing that mattered to her. She lost her nut when you ran away."

"Get back at her for what?" Rachel asked. "All she ever did was cater to your whims."

"She did this shit to me." He gestured to his deteriorated body.

"Momma killed you?" Rachel asked, a satisfied sparkle in her eyes.

"Nasty old shrew poisoned my whiskey. In my own living room while I watched NASCAR, no less!" He said this as if there were no greater indignity. "Never figured she had it in her."

"She poisoned you?" Rachel felt a burgeoning pride for her mother. She found it difficult not to smile, so she did.

"Sure, you think it's funny now, but wait until I'm done with you, you spoiled rotten shit!"

Rachel sneered at the ranting presence in the back seat.

"Let's go food shopping," Todd said, nodding to the passing buildings through the car's window.

"Really? What about him?" Rachel asked.

"He can't leave the car. It's his anchor, right?"

"I think so," she said.

They both felt the brutal assault of an instant migraine as the car filled with the ungodly stench that had occupied the trunk earlier.

"Ha! I figured!" Todd barked, speeding the car into the plaza to an open space near the market. "Out of the car!"

"What? Why?" Rachel asked, confused and clutching her head.

"I think it might be like with a Wi-Fi signal, and weaken if you're far enough away." Todd squinted at the pain.

"Don't you dare dismiss me!" Lionel growled.

Rachel paused, but Todd insisted. "Go!"

Rachel quickly walked away, her head low under the weight of the headache.

"You get back here! Listen to your father!"

As Todd suggested, the farther she got from the car, the more the pounding eased. Rachel stopped about two hundred feet from the car, a point where the pain became tolerable. She was startled that Todd was not beside her, but still at the car, kneeling in the opened trunk, ass pointed skyward as he shifted around inside. It appeared he was grappling with something, but then he leapt out of the trunk and opened the rear door on the driver side. He had a hand pressed to the top of his head as if he were trying to keep it from splitting open.

"Get away from me!" yelled the wretched old spirit.

"Screw you!" yelled Todd.

"Todd!" Rachel cried.

"Arrhhhh!" Todd bent low to ease the pain.

Rachel started forward, wondering if the old man was somehow holding her husband there. She approached, but the pain increased, as did the putrescence. Fifty feet from the Grand Marquis, she was gagging and woozy from the slamming in her head.

"Stay back!" Todd hollered. He dragged the rear seat from the car.

"No! Get away from her, you recalcitrant fuck!" Lionel howled.

"Shut up! I don't even know what recalcitrant means, you asshole!" Todd screamed in reply.

"Leave!" The older man swatted at Todd ineffectually, hands passing through him.

"Fuck off!" Todd hopped from the car, clutching something in his hand. He staggered to Rachel and displayed a small object.

"Was this his?" he asked. Rachel squinted at him, not comprehending. "Was this your father's?" Todd's breathing was hard and ragged, matching the pulsing warfare in Rachel's head. He was close enough for her to recognize the object: a man's ring with a large black onyx.

"Yeah, that's his," Rachel said, remembering how her father would turn the jewel side of the ring downward to get optimal impact when slapping her on top of the head.

Todd took three long steps, reeled back, and let the ring fly with every bit of his strength. It was an impressive throw, the ring disappearing into the distance. The only evidence it still existed was a distant, barely audible *ping*.

Rachel looked at Todd, his eyes red and watering, as were hers, she suspected, but *her* head no longer hurt. "Your headache gone?" she asked.

"Yeah," he said, turning to the car. "And so is that nasty old bastard, by the looks of it."

They approached the car with timid steps until they stood beside the detached seat cushion. Rachel carefully leaned in the opened door.

No smell, no cantankerous apparitions.

"You in there, Mr. Dickhead?" Todd called. There was no answer. He looked at Rachel. "Help me put the seat back in."

Rachel climbed in and sat on the rear seat. "You here, Daddy-o? Daddy asshole?" she sang as she bounced girlishly on the cushion. "How'd you know about the ring?" she asked Todd.

"I didn't, but you said a ghost has to be attached to something he died with, but he said your momma killed him when he was watching NASCAR. It ain't likely he was watching NASCAR in his living room and in his car at the same time."

Rachel grabbed him by the shirt, yanked him onto the rear seat, and planted him a warm, wet kiss that set his mind on something else warm and wet.

"You are a fucking genius," Rachel said.

"Well, I have my moments, and I'm smart enough to know I ain't fucking."

"Then you best take me home so I can give you something so crazy freaky you'll think you're being pulled inside out," Rachel said.

"I have no clue what you mean by that, but I like it."

Todd slammed the trunk shut, climbed into the driver's seat, and closed the door as Rachel clambered between the front seats and settled into hers. Todd started the car, pulled forward, then stopped.

"What's the matter?" asked Rachel.

"Okay… so, no more fibbing, all right?"

"All right," she agreed.

"Good. So, just how many were there before me?" Todd asked, his cheeks flushing.

"Never mind that," said Rachel, matching his hue.

"More than five?"

"No! Well, okay… maybe."

"A dozen?" Todd pulled the car forward to the parking lot exit.

"Umm… maybe."

"At the same time?"

"*No!*" Rachel nearly yelled, her face now a furious red. She sighed and admitted, "Uh… maybe."

"You film it?"

Rachel turned and glared at him.

Todd shrugged and pulled onto the main drag.

"Maybe," said Rachel.

Henson Huddy was lifting the third case of Black Label he'd purchased from The Inebriation Station into his car when he heard a metallic *clink*. Something bounced off a vehicle behind him and ricocheted past his ear into the trunk. He scanned the parking lot for stone-throwing pranksters—which wouldn't be the first time—but saw nothing. He searched the confines of the trunk, moving a large collection of debris around, looking for the projectile that sounded as if it had landed inside, but came up short.

It aggravated him. Whatever it was—maybe the way it had rung out when it impacted the car—left him with a hell of a headache.

Thinking about a healthy dose of Black Label to quash the headache, Henson slammed the lid, climbed into the car—and nearly gagged. Someone must have pulled a fast one on him and dumped a bag of ripe dog shit—or worse—in the car. It wouldn't be the first time, either. He turned to check the back seat.

The mottled green-skinned man laughed.

John McIlveen

NOBODY'S DAUGHTER

Foster Square, despite its name, is triangular in shape. The plot of grass acts as a median in our small city of Riverside, Massachusetts, separating a variety of buildings—the post office, the town hall, and a five-story, nondescript business center. A tribute to a forgotten historical figure, the square is adorned only by two Revolutionary-period cannons, two benches, four large, neglected flower urns, and a statue. It is well tended and attended by humans and pigeons alike. All in all, Foster Square is nothing special...except for the statue. The statue makes it special.

It is a life-size rendering of a young woman seated on the ground, arms held out before her, palms up as if in meditation, her legs folded beneath her to her right. Her dress, modestly draped over her knees, speaks of spring. Her fine features, full lips, hair flowing mid-back in a slight wave, offer softness to the exquisitely carved black granite. Her beauty is not that of goddesses or princesses, but of suppleness and youth: the all-American girl.

A small commemorative plaque on the base reads *"Nobody's Daughter."*

She arrived four years ago, on a Saturday, with no celebration but for a brief article in the weekly paper. The town accepted the anonymous gift, for she was tasteful and added beauty to the otherwise ordinary square.

I often have lunch on Foster Square, save for inclement days. I am a loner. I overhear conversations about the origin of the statue, or as to who the young lady is. They amuse me. Most are off the mark, others painfully close, none of them fully accurate.

For the true story, we must backtrack fourteen years to a young man named Ammar Sardell. At sixteen, Ammar was bright, adventurous, and mildly rambunctious. He walked the line, though the opportunity to veer to either side reared often for him and his friends, Chris Tremblay and Jimmy Ruiz. All three lived in the same mid-town tenements converted from abandoned mill buildings two decades earlier.

Always open to adventure, they often searched old structures or tried to impress one another at parkour, an activity that the more daring took to an extreme, often falling—sometimes from great heights—with painful or fatal results. Fortunately, Ammar and his friends were not so foolish.

One bitterly cold evening in November of 2003, Ammar, Chris, and Jimmy, tired of watching Comedy Central, moved to the basement of the tenement to waste time and smoke a couple joints. The boiler room door was secluded in a darkened alleyway at the rear of the building. Though locked, Jimmy could quickly manipulate the door using a switchblade. Jimmy was not only his name but also his talent; a sad portent into a future of repeat stays at Massachusetts Correctional Institute at Concord for forced entry.

The three boys darted inside, intent on the storage room where management stored furniture, decorations, and office surplus—a comfortable place to do little. They bustled through the boiler room, weaving around pipes and rumbling machinery, but Ammar caught sight of something that made him pause and backpedal.

Seated on a piece of cardboard beside a large water heater was a young woman, legs splayed and back to the wall. Her hands palms-up on her legs, her eyes closed as if afloat in a state of enlightenment. She wore an oversized, thick winter coat and a tattered woolen hat pulled low over her ears. Ammar stepped closer. He recognized her from somewhere or sometime.

"Hi?" he said.

Nothing.

"What the hell, Sardell? Come on!" came a distant voice.

Hesitant, Ammar watched her.

"Just go," she said, emotionless, no room for a response.

Ammar went.

Ammar returned shortly after midnight; images of the girl had hijacked his thoughts and claimed his sleep. He breached the door in reasonable time, but with less dexterity than Jimmy, and entered the heat and clamor of the boiler room. Safety lights nestled high amidst pipes and conduit dispersed conical shafts reminding him of UFO retractor beams.

He returned to the water heater to find her still there, eyes closed, a depleted backpack as a pillow. Her stillness ignited a spark of fear within him until she hitched, shaking her body, and freeing his breath. Her thin, dirt-streaked face was pretty, freckled across the cheeks and nose, and again begged recollection.

A discarded Taco Bell wrapper lay near her leg. He had the impression it was retrieved, not purchased, and a profound sadness swept over him. Ammar left and soon returned with two bottles of water, four slices of American cheese, an orange, and two apples. He left the offering beside her and returned home.

She preoccupied his thoughts throughout the night and during the following day, making school and communication difficult. At work he stocked shelves and front-faced cans, garnering accolades from his boss for not socializing. He begged off hanging with Chris and Jimmy.

"I feel like shit, man," he lied, and hurried home.

She was not there that day, nor for the next six days, but late the following Saturday evening as Ammar walked home from work, he noticed her moving purposefully down the dim alleyway. She paused at the boiler room door and then entered the building.

Ammar followed. He triggered the door latch, and with light steps, made his way to the water heater.

"Shit!" she said when Ammar appeared. She hastily pushed something between the wall and the water heater.

"Hi," Ammar said, maintaining a buffer between them so not to intimidate her, but also for escape if perchance she turned feral.

She stared warily, her eyes seeming to cycle in and out of

focus ... and then a flicker.

"Hey Amma-what-cha-face," she said, offering a lackadaisical wave.

"You know me?"

"Fuck, yeah. Saint A's. You were a skinny little shit. Taller now but still skinny. From Arabia or something."

Saint Augustine's school. It seemed so long ago, another lifetime, though it had only been three years. A better place and time before the planes hit the towers and his father took off to parts unknown, foreclosing on their American dream.

His mother had lost her job when the semiconductor industry crashed. She was never able to match her previous esteemed position and was forced to mop floors and swab toilets in office complexes, burying her self-respect deep inside to fester like a tumor. They moved to *The Mills* and he transferred to public schooling.

"Afghanistan," Ammar corrected.

"Whatever."

She was drunk or high and Ammar experienced a blend of sympathy and revulsion. She freed a half-smoked cigarette and a lighter from her coat pocket and lit up. He studied her brown eyes, her freckles, and a memory of a younger, fresher, and much rounder cheeks arose. Her beautiful face, once plump with adolescence, now reduced to this drawn visage, was utterly heartbreaking.

"Wait, you're Selene Carras!" Ammar barked, unable to govern his surprise.

"Shocking, huh?" Selene looked away. "Smack ... it seduces you and makes you ugly."

"You're not ugly, just...thinner."

Selene shrugged. "You bring me food the other night?"

Ammar nodded.

"You expect a blowjob or something?"

Ammar had often fantasized about it, but not in this

situation. "No, I just figured you were hungry."

"Really?" She pinned him with curious eyes and he wondered if she was insulted or grateful.

"I'm not like that," Ammar said.

"You gay?"

"No."

She studied him at length. "Thanks," she said sincerely. "Now get the fuck out of here so I can ride."

"Do you have to?"

"Try and stop me," Selene said.

Ammar returned the next day. Although Selene was gone she tormented his thoughts. At Saint A's, she had been a year ahead of him, but very much in his field of vision. She had seemed an infectiously happy child of wealthy parents, the personification of youth and spirit with her mile-wide smile and effervescent personality. Boys liked her and girls envied her.

Near the water heater, under the edge of the cardboard, he found a discarded orange syringe. He crushed it under his sneaker.

What had happened to her? Where were her parents?

Selene took the rotisserie chicken and bottled iced tea Ammar offered her. It was nearly a week later. He had sensed she'd be there, and if not, the meal would have tasted fine to him.

"Why are you doing this? I'm not looking for sympathy."

Ammar shrugged and pointed to the cardboard on which she sat. "Can I?"

"Suit yourself, hero."

Ammar sat.

Selene pulled a section of skin from the chicken, put it in her mouth and chewed. She wiped her nose, looked around the room as if confused, and then started crying.

Ammar felt useless. He wanted to hold her and comfort her but was afraid she'd think he wanted more. "What can I do for you?" he asked.

"Stay a while. I don't want to be alone."

Ammar obliged, a silent sentry while Selene drifted off, still there when she jerked awake, panicking, short of breath.

"Can you lend me twenty bucks?"

Twenty was all Ammar had left before payday and he knew what it would be spent on. He looked at the barely touched chicken, making sure she noticed.

"What for?"

"Woman stuff."

"CVS is down the street. Walk with me and I'll buy it, or I'll go get it for you."

Selene stared at him with sleepy eyes and then lay down, spouting out a melodramatic *Fuck you.*

"Can I ask a personal question?" asked Ammar.

"Do I have a choice?" Selene muttered into her cardboard bed.

"Yes."

She was silent long enough that Ammar thought she'd fallen to sleep. "What?" she finally asked.

"Have you tried getting help?"

"For what? My life is perfect." She huffed with derision, then conceded, "No one wants to help me."

"I do," said Ammar.

"There's always a price."

He wiggled his fingers. "No strings."

Selene huffed again. "Right."

"What about your parents?

Selene snorted. "What about them?"

"Where are they? If I remember, they were wealthy."

"They're alive and well, living out their plastic fantasy in Castle Carras." Selene sat up and slumped against the wall, her arm draped over a metal junction box at the base of the water heater.

"You don't get along with them?"

Selene's expression emphasized how foolish his question was.

"What went wrong? You seemed so happy at Saint A's."

"Nothing *went* wrong that wasn't always wrong," she sneered. "Tricked you all, didn't I?"

"What happened?"

"Long story, talking about it won't help. Go away now, I'm tired and need my beauty sleep." She lay down again. "Gonna change the world tomorrow."

"When will you be back?" Ammar asked.

"I don't know."

"Come back tomorrow night."

"Why?"

"I want you to."

She opened one eye. "Why?"

"Promise you will."

"Go away."

Ammar waited until Selene was snoring lightly, her arms and legs twitching from inner energy or demons. He retrieved a throw pillow from the storage room, gently lifted Selene's head, and slid it beneath.

She watched him as he left the room.

Selene returned the following night looking worse for wear, simultaneously sweating and shivering. Ammar feared she'd drop the hot soup he'd brought her and burn herself.

"Why do you care?" Selene asked.

"I lived in Afghanistan until I was eleven. When war and death surround you, you do anything to stay alive. I don't understand why you do this...*to yourself!*" He gestured to her arm. "Life is valuable. You are valuable. You don't deserve to live this way...or die this way."

"Maybe I do." She sipped, clutched her stomach, and setting the soup down, grimaced.

"You okay?"

"Hardly," she said, teeth clenched. The pain subsided and she smiled for the first time in the two weeks since he'd found her. It was sweet, heartwarming, and Ammar was relieved her addiction hadn't progressed to where her teeth had started falling out. A glimmer of hope.

"Have you tried going home?"

She raised a shaking hand and pulled her hat off to reveal greasy, stringy hair.

"Tried once, can't now. His majesty changed the locks."

"Because of you?"

"I stole money... almost a thousand."

"What for?"

Selene gave him a look that asked *really?* "Before that, he said I'd left the family in shambles, ruined the good Carras name, and then he slammed the door in my face."

"Why?"

"Because I did. Got picked up for prostitution. Got to make a living, you know." She shrugged it away but Ammar knew she was watching his reaction. It was a gut punch, not because he hadn't expected it, but because the mental imagery was so painful. "I was seventeen. They caught me with a high-profile lawyer. He was an acquaintance of my father's, but he didn't know me...at least at the time. They never mentioned his name in the paper. I was released to the street."

That she talked about it so easily that it showed the depths to which her self-respect had fallen. She wiped her nose and clenched her stomach again.

"Still care?" she challenged.

"Yes." He knew there was more to it. "How'd you end up on the street the first time?"

"I ran."

"Why?"

"My father slapped me across the face … hard. I thought he snapped my neck."

"What'd your mother do?"

"Like always, cowered and sniveled like a dog."

"She didn't protect you? What about your brother … Mark?"

Selene's laughed loud and sharp, a gunshot. "Ha! He's why my father slapped me." She tucked her chin to her chest and mimicked in a deep voice, *"How dare you accuse your brother of such … rubbish?"*

Another gut punch.

"What did he do?" Ammar asked, knowing the hideous truth.

"Raped me," Serene said, blasé—as if she had said *he crossed the street.*

Mark Carras, everybody's buddy. Solid-bodied with chiseled handsome features … beautiful on the surface, repugnant beneath.

"Your fucking brother?" Disbelief and outrage contorted Ammar's face.

"Precisely, but he preferred blowjobs."

Ammar stared at her, aghast. "He did it more than once?"

"A hundred, two hundred, a thousand times … as long as I can remember. It's not something you keep track of. He's seven years older than me. He had plenty of time."

No fucking wonder she shoots up, Ammar thought. He wanted to hurt Mark Carras and the hateful people who had parented them. How did they not know what was happening under their roof, or was denying it easier than dealing with it? It seemed *too* bizarre and Ammar felt a fragment of doubt, but the broken soul slumped against the wall made it believable.

"I'm sorry they did this to you." He hoped she recognized his sincerity.

She pulled a battered pack of Winstons from her pocket, jiggled a torn cigarette from it, threw it to the floor, freed another, and lit up. She blew smoke toward the ceiling. "Shit happens."

"It's not right."

"Which matters, how?" She dug at a hangnail.

"You be here tomorrow?" he asked.

"I don't know, hero," she said, drowsy.

"Maintenance doesn't usually work weekends," Ammar said.

Her eyes cycled between agitation and exhaustion until they closed.

The horrors Selene had suffered tormented Ammar through the night and he fought the urge to check on her. Despite her being eighteen, he had embraced a sense of responsibility for her and feared she would go in search of another fix. He tossed and turned enough to awaken his mother in her bedroom across the apartment; not easy since she would collapse into bed each night under the weight of total fatigue. He felt guilty. She was scheduled to work seven to three on Sunday and was gone when he arose at eight.

Ammar dressed, brushed his teeth and hair. He scanned the refrigerator, grabbed a leftover burrito, took two bites and tossed it, noting never to eat burritos again after brushing.

Multiple scenarios played out as he headed for the basement: Selene gone, Selene blitzed on smack, Selene with a man, Selene lifeless. He pushed the thoughts away.

What he did find was Selene lying on the floor, her body shaking, and her face drenched in enough sweat to dampen the cardboard beneath her. A puddle of vomit near her head also clung to her hat and matted her hair. Ammar was no authority on addiction, but he knew what he was seeing. It had been two to four days since she had last shot up.

Ammar knelt and gently rested a hand on her.

"Ffffuuuccckkk! My fucking head. Don't touch me," Selene croaked.

"You're having DTs," Ammar said.

"No fucking shit," she said between rapid breaths. "I need some candy, just a taste. Get me some, please. Just this once."

"I don't have money," Ammar said. Not entirely true, but he had no intention of feeding her craving, not that he'd know where to find any.

"You said you care. You don't fucking care or you'd get me some."

"Sorry, can't do it."

"Then just kill me, pleeese!"

"Can't do that either."

"You're an asshole. I hate you."

Ammar rose and headed for a paper towel dispenser near a utility sink.

"Don't fucking leave me!" Selene demanded.

Ammar smiled despite himself, returned and gently wiped vomit from her face. She pulled away but then let him press the cool paper towel to her forehead. He remained with her for two hours, fearing maintenance workers would show up and formulating an explanation in case they did.

Selene drifted in and out of a troubled sleep. Ammar wanted to do something for her, but being sixteen and financially limited didn't present a lot of opportunities. He couldn't take her to a movie or a meal looking the way she did, not that she'd eat anything.

"Hey," she croaked.

"Hi," said Ammar.

"This sucks."

"I can't even guess. You impress me."

She rolled her eyes. "I puked?"

"A little."

"Oh, God, I'm fucking disgusting. How can you stand looking at me?"

"I've seen you looking better," he admitted. "Hey, I work four to eight today, my mother works until four. Come up to the apartment and hang for a while."

"I don't think your momma would like catching you with a whore." Selene laughed, dry and raspy, as if her laughter had sat idle too long and had rusted. She rocked in place, lightly kneading her arm.

"Don't call yourself that," Ammar said, but she was right. His mother was devout. If she found a woman in their apartment who'd been arrested for prostitution, she'd have him doing Salat at the mosque in minutes. "Nothing personal, but I figured you'd like to shower, maybe sit after and watch TV."

"Do I smell bad?"

She reeked of sweat, vomit, and addiction, but he had acclimated to it. "You don't smell good, but I've smelled worse."

"What the fuck. Help me up … slowly." She extended her hand.

Ammar led her to the fourth-floor apartment, getting curious glances but passing no one he recognized.

Selene entered the bathroom and closed the door behind her. "Can I take a bath instead?"

"Of course."

"You have a washer and dryer?" she called from the bathroom.

"Yeah."

Ammar retrieved his robe from his bedroom, returned to the bathroom and timidly knocked. Selene opened the door and stood before him, naked and unabashed. Ammar reflexively averted his gaze from her as she dropped her soiled clothes into a pile at his feet.

"There's more in my backpack," she said. "Can I?"

"Yeah." He held the robe out to her, which she grabbed.

He stole a glance as she closed the door. She was painfully thin, childlike. Anger seared in him, toward her father, her mother, her brother, at the bastard lawyer and anyone else who had ever hurt her. He loaded her clothes into a washing machine set behind bi-fold doors near his bedroom. Her small collection of possessions was as heartbreaking as everything else about her.

He sprawled on the couch and watched *Lizzy McGuire*, *The Proud Family*, swapped the wash to the dryer and watched half an episode of *Kim Possible* before Selene emerged from the bathroom. She dropped onto the couch beside him, looking smaller than ever draped in Ammar's oversized robe, a towel wrapped around her head like a turban. He smiled.

"Welcome back. I was ready to send a search team."

"I had to scrub the tub. Had a ring like Saturn."

Again, her bluntness knocked him off center. "Feeling better?" he asked.

"I feel like shit, but I feel like clean shit, so that's better. The bath helped a lot," she said, holding his gaze for the first time since he'd brought her the soup.

"Your clothes should be done soon."

"Sending me packing already?"

"No! Just saying. My mother doesn't come home until four."

She smiled and removed the towel from her head, her arm visibly trembling. She shook her head, fanning her hair out, increasing her appearance from twelve to fifteen years old. Two small lesions near her lips and a mild darkness beneath her eyes confirmed her addiction, yet were evidence of a relatively new dependency… as addictions go.

"In the bathroom cabinet, there's—" Ammar struggled.

"What?" Selene pressed.

"You know … woman things. You said—"

"I lied," she admitted, shrugged. "I haven't had a period in months. Benefits of smack. You have a brush?"

He retrieved one of his mother's brushes, thoughts of lice crossing his mind. He'd boil it once Selene left. She ran the brush through her hair with a quivering hand as they shared small talk, the *Power Rangers* flickering on screen.

"In another life, I would do this five hundred times every morning," she said.

Ammar looked at her familiar spray of freckles. She was still pretty, but the wholesome beauty had dampened. She set the brush on the couch and turned to him.

"We can fuck if you want," she said.

A flicker of panic and a stream of thoughts sped through Ammar. What do I do? What if mom comes home early? How do I explain a woman wearing nothing but my robe? She spilled a drink? She puked? At least that was somewhat true.

He had often deliberated when and how his first sexual encounter would transpire, and while the prospect was certainly appealing, Selene's condition, childlike appearance, and his mother's many warnings about STDs were huge deterrents.

Seeing his hesitance, Selene said, "Yeah, I don't blame you."

"No! I want to. You're very pretty, but if it happens, I want to be sure it's what we want and that you don't feel obligated."

She searched his eyes. "Are you for fucking real?" she asked.

"I think so."

"Will you hold me for a while at least?" she asked, almost plaintive.

Selene curled against Ammar and he held her,

reverberations of her dependency humming through her and into him.

"You know," Selene said, breaking a long silence, "right now, at this moment, I feel like I could kick this thing and someday maybe have a normal life."

"I'd like that for you. I think you can," Ammar said. "How'd you get started?"

"Mother's Vicodin. Heavy-duty stuff, ten milligrams of hydrocodone per tablet. Life was warm and fuzzy on *vikes*, not so much once the bottles were empty." She rubbed her forehead and then took Ammar's hand. "Vicodin's hard to find on the streets. Heroin and meth are easy. You don't need a prescription. Someone told me it gave the same high."

"Does it?"

"Yes and no. It's the best-worst feeling ever. I love it, I hate it. I don't recommend it."

When the sweats and shakes again took hold of Selene, she lay down, restless, agitated, often crying out. "I want to rip off my skin," she groaned, fingers clawed.

Slightly after noon, she leveled out. Ammar made peanut butter and jelly sandwiches, and Selene ate a quarter of hers with mouse-like nibbles before her stomach knotted. It was the most Ammar had seen her eat since he'd found her and it encouraged him.

At two-thirty, Selene carefully dressed and stuffed her few extra items in her backpack. "I need to go—before I can't," she explained.

Ammar followed her to the parking lot where she kissed him sweetly.

"See you soon, hero?" she said.

"Hey, I need a favor!" Ammar said.

"What?"

"If you get the urge to use, don't. Okay? I promised to hang with Chris and Jimmy after work, but I'll be home later.

Promise you'll come back here. I'll help you through it."

"I know you will." She kissed him again and walked away.

Ammar waited in the boiler room until midnight but Selene never showed. He wandered downtown with little hope of finding her; if she were anywhere, it wouldn't be the city's main drag, Washington Street. He checked the boiler room again. He was frightened for her, desperate to know she was okay. He imagined her passed out or walking the streets, oblivious, or doing tricks to buy a high. He closed his eyes to the images but understood he had no power over her choices, and regardless how hard he tried, he couldn't drive them from his head. He stared into the darkness for a long time before sleep finally claimed him.

Ammar's mother had already left for work when his alarm woke him. His first thought was of Selene. He had an hour to dress and get to school. He hurried through his morning routine, grabbed his book bag, and sped out the door. Exiting the apartment complex, he turned for the alleyway between the buildings and froze, panic congealing his legs.

Outside the boiler room door, a police cruiser and ambulance idled, red and blue lights flashing and strobing defiantly. A crowd of onlookers had gathered, crowding yellow cordon tape that read *"POLICE LINE"* and *"DO NOT CROSS."*

Coaxing his legs, he walked and then ran toward the scene. As he neared, he saw a stretcher near the ambulance, covered by a sheet ... completely covered.

"No...no, no...no no!" He tried to duck beneath the tape. A police officer stepped in front of him and corralled him backward.

"Please stay behind the line, son," he said, but Ammar surged forward again and the officer grasped his arm.

"No, no!" He said, trying to string his words together. He bounced on the balls of his feet, staring at the small shape outlined beneath the sheet, child-small.

Who else could it be?

The officer spoke to him but Ammar was beyond hearing. Near the doorway, a maintenance man stood looking troubled and pale.

"Roger!" Ammar yelled.

Roger glanced his way and sullenly turned back to the officer, without acknowledging Ammar.

"Wait! Is she dead?" Ammar asked, but he knew. His words got the officer's attention.

"How do you know it's a she?"

"I know her. She's homeless!"

"Wait here. Don't move."

The cop walked to the other officer, spoke, and then both policemen returned. They gently led Ammar away from the crowd and the stretcher, though his eyes couldn't leave it.

"Is it her?" Ammar asked.

"I don't know, son. Can you tell us who you think it might be?"

"Her name is Selene Carras. She's homeless but it's not her fault."

The officers shared a glance. "Please wait near the cruiser. We may need to ask you a couple questions."

The questions were quick and perfunctory. *How long have you known her? When was the last time you saw her? What? How? Who?* They answered none of Ammar's questions, acting deaf to them. The paramedics loaded the stretcher into the ambulance and drove away, not confirming who lay beneath the sheet. He knew.

Ammar suffered through school and work in a daze, thinking only of the girl he had met a month earlier ... now gone forever.

His mother was asleep when he arrived home, but sleep evaded him, not from wondering when he'd see Selene again, but knowing he never would.

He dozed sporadically until his mother's activity dragged him from his stupor. He joined her at the table where she, already in her janitorial garb and kerchief, drank coffee and read the paper.

"You're up early. Can't sleep?"

"No," He leaned to kiss her cheek.

"You okay?" she asked, ever intuitive.

"Yeah."

"Coffee on the stove."

"You know I don't drink the stuff, Mom."

"Forgot you're an alien. You hear about the homeless girl they found dead in the basement?" she asked, seeming slightly animated.

"Yeah, it's freaking sad," Ammar said, hoping she'd mention it no more.

"Poor thing, just looking for a place to stay warm and she gets electrocuted."

"What? What do you mean electrocuted?"

"Says it here." She pushed the paper forward, looking at him oddly. "Daughter of some local bigwig. We clean his offices on Thursdays."

Ammar grabbed the paper. The article buried on page four read:

Riverside Woman Electrocuted In Tenement Basement

The body of a homeless teen was discovered in the basement of a Riverside apartment complex early

Monday morning by the complex maintenance head, Roger Demeister. The deceased, identified as Selene Marie Carras, estranged daughter of local financier Alexei Carras, appeared to have inadvertently come in contact with exposed electrical conductors after forcing her way into the building's boiler room. Police Captain Greg Foley said there will be an investigation, but believes no foul play is involved.

Reportedly, Selena Carras had run away from home in 2001 after a family dispute resulting from an arrest. Alexei Carras believed his daughter had fled to the West Coast.

Selena Carras is survived by her parents, Alexei and Dorinda Carras, of Riverside, a brother, Mark Carras, also of Riverside, and a number of aunts, uncles, and cousins residing in Greece. Holland Funeral Home will be handling Services.

Ammar read the article three times, saddened and confused. It was the last line *'Holland Funeral Home will be handling Services,'* that that troubled him. Would they be pretentious and insincere enough to put on airs after the way they had abused, neglected, and denied Selene? Would they shower their deceased daughter with traitorous love and provide a beautiful funeral only to impress observers?

Ammar intended to be present at Selene's funeral.

Ammar knocked on the boiler room door. A plate had been installed, restricting access to the latch. He knocked again with no answer, searched the property for twenty minutes before finding Roger Demeister seated on a stairway, smoking a cigar.

"Hi, Roger."

The maintenance man looked at him and nodded. He still appeared pale.

"Ammar, right?"

"Good memory," Ammar said. The only time he recalled talking to the man was the day he and his mother had moved in.

"I remember the names of the people I like … and the people I don't like. You I like. You don't cause trouble."

It was difficult telling Roger's age. He was short with ropey arms, his hair graying at the temple and mostly gone, wrapped around the back of his head like a laurel wreath. He released a stream of cigar smoke from beneath a walrus mustache.

"Thanks," said Ammar. "Roger, can you tell me what happened to Selene Carras yesterday morning?"

"Electrocuted. Fucking shame, poor kid dying like that. Excuse my French."

"I know, but what happened?"

"You know her? You were pretty upset."

So he did notice me, Ammar thought. "She was a friend."

"She was troubled," Roger said.

"She was still a good person."

Roger shrugged. "Fair enough. Stupid shit luck, as far as I can tell. She knocked the junction box cover off the water heater when she tried to sit or something—bumped into the element. She was still holding onto a copper water line when I found her. Two hundred and seventy-seven volts makes every part of you contract. No letting go of that pipe until it tripped the breaker. Pretty much cooked her from the inside out, poor kid."

"Oh God!" Ammar said, choking out a sob. He turned and fled without another word.

Ammar entered the Greek Orthodox Church unnoticed, sat

in the last row, and counted seventeen heads in attendance including himself. Selene's casket, a beautiful exhibition of craftsmanship, was a light-colored hardwood, maybe hickory, and polished to splendor. A spray of pink and white roses covered most of the lid. Its opulence was obscene to Ammar and he hoped Selene couldn't see such an insult. Mark Carras was seated in the front row, as broad-shouldered and handsome as Ammar remembered. Alexei and Dorinda Carras sat to Mark's right. The man was solid, a fireplug with granite hair and an emotionless face that appeared to be carved of the same. Dorinda Carras, also emotionless, looked dead inside, a petite husk of a human devoid of life. To Mark's left sat a woman with lustrous hair and an enviable figure, even in black dress. *His wife?* Ammar wondered.

At the conclusion of the service came the next insult, when Mark lined up as a pallbearer.

Ammar followed the procession along a side road on the outskirts of Riverside, to a cemetery he never knew existed. He stood back during the ceremony, standing last in the short line of people offering condolences to Selene's remaining family. Ammar stepped before Alexei Carras who met his eyes and offered his hand. Ammar didn't shake.

"Hello," Alexei greeted in his businessman's voice. "Did you know Selene?"

"Better than you did, it seems," Ammar said.

The man's brow furrowed and his hand fell to his side, all professional composure. "Excuse me?"

"She was your daughter," Ammar said.

"Yes."

"No, she was your *daughter!*" Ammar repeated, louder, tears forming at the unfairness of it all.

Dorinda and Mark Carras looked at Ammar. Alexei stood straighter, pulling his shoulders back, but Ammar wasn't intimidated.

"How does this concern you?" asked Alexei, civility gone.

"Why didn't it concern you?" asked Ammar, his voice rising. He pointed at Dorinda Carras. "You knew! You both knew what your son was doing to her, but you hid it and let it continue! All to protect your image!"

"You'd best leave!" said Mark Carras.

"Why? So no one finds out? She was your sister!" Ammar sputtered. "Your *SISTER!*"

The beautiful woman in black looked at Mark and then at Ammar. Ammar saw Mark Carras' punch coming, and ducked from most of it, though he'd probably have a sizable bruise on his cheek.

Dorinda Carras burst into tears. She moved from her husband, striking at his hands as he tried to hold her at his side. Ammar wondered if maybe she didn't know.

"Who the hell are you?" Alexei Carras roared.

"Who the hell are *you*?" Ammar responded. "*Nobody*. You are *nobody!*"

Ammar turned and left the cemetery.

There is a statue downtown on Foster Square, a tribute to a young woman who deserved better. It faces southwest, toward the offices of Carras Financial. I saved a long time to buy it; it wasn't cheap. It's made of polished black granite, meticulously sculptured. Its resemblance to a young Selene Carras is striking. The artist used a photo in my freshman yearbook from when Selene was a sophomore.

I often wait on the park bench until *Nobody* leaves work. He could leave by the back door, but he never does. Sometimes he pauses to look at the statue, other times he walks by, averting his gaze. I've never seen him walk past without looking at *some* point. Some days he looks at me…some days not.

I heard that *Nobody*'s wife left him. Now *he's* an empty, lifeless shell.

Selene's autopsy showed signs of previous use but no opioids were found in her system.

She was clean. How's that for a kick in the ass?

There is a statue on Foster Square
A tribute to Nobody's Daughter...
Who deserved so much better.

THE MAKING OF MONSTERS

PART I

"Beauty and folly are old companions"

-- Benjamin Franklin
Poor Richard 1734

What were the chances? Chet wondered.

Not by the standards of the day, but by what he called "The Chet Farner Barometer." Chet felt the majority of world's population had lost its self-respect and honor. All one had to do was search the internet to see that anything was possible. Name your perversion and you'll likely find it, from college orgies to farm animals…and so much worse. Chet was fine with these, and even browsed them once in a while, but in no way would he want to be associated with them. He kept his kinks well below the radar. He had always thrived to *appear* the benchmark for thoughtfulness and respect; he had always prided himself as being seen as one of the "Good ol' Boys." Chet felt he was the epitome of self-respect and honor. Unfortunately, they had no connection to moral decency.

By modern norms, Chet felt his crime was trivial. Married to a beautiful, elegant, and socially accessible woman for years, few would have expected it, but it had happened. Chet Farner had fallen for another woman.

Sure he had several clandestine trysts with anonymous women, but those were simply for relieving tension. His job was stressful. They meant nothing.

But Anna was different. More than just *another woman*; she was sensuality in a Venus wrap ... a hedonistic vision of pleasure. He was smitten. *Another woman* could never make such an impression on him.

For Chet, modern perceptions of beauty seemed characterized by physical and facial anonymity, portrayed so well in the magazines and tabloids that congested most checkout counters. He found the sameness of the silicone, scalpel, and digitally honed cover girls discouraging at best, and could not understand why women would endure such extremes to be a replica of nearly every other tight-skinned fashion model or starlet, sporting gravity-defying breasts and pouty, knockwurst-thick lips. His assessment of beauty lay principally on individuality, in which Anna flourished. He had never seen desirability and uniqueness presented so well.

Anna dressed in trendy styles—aesthetic skirts and blouses that, even when loose fitting, appeared to be a part of her, emphasizing and delicately conforming to her alluring curves. Hers was not a hard body like those common to beaches and health clubs, but the feminine softness of her figure demanded attention and promised nirvana. She had more curves than a box of macaroni.

Karla, Chet's previous personal assistant, in her eighth month of pregnancy chose to pursue the domestic arts. Despite his loyalty for the ever-affable Karla, hiring Anna was akin to trading a pencil for a computer. She modernized Karla's old-school system, making most aspects of it paper-free and accessible with a few finger-taps on her keyboard.

Another significant change since Anna had enhanced the lobby outside of Chet's office was the increase in male traffic.

Through the sidelight window to his door, he would see men strut comically by with arms flexed and chests extended. Anna would ignore them or dismiss them with a roll of the eyes.

The kicker was, she appeared to be interested in Chet...only Chet, though she kept it low-key. At first, he had dismissed it, figuring she was little more than a gold-digger...wishful thinking on her part. Why else would a twenty-eight-year-old Aphrodite who could get practically any younger, more athletic, and single man be interested in a forty-two-year-old married man? But as Anna's attentiveness increased, so did his interest; he cycled from humored, to flattered, and ultimately to infatuated.

He knew he could not act on it since she worked for him; it would jeopardize his position and his marriage. Both were seen as idyllic by many.

The simple remedy would be to have Anna transferred to another department or site altogether, but she excelled at her job to where his reasoning might be, *"I fantasize about my personal assistant?"*

Plus, he didn't want her to go and...

And what?

...and he liked the flattery, the fantasy, and he was...

Admit it, Chet.

...Hopeful.

Ironically, his wife, Marilyn, had encouraged him to interview Anna Paxton. She had met Anna at her hairdresser and, as she explained it, idle chatter segued into Anna's gut-spilling account of a corrupt and abusive relationship with "Mr. Perfect" that had rendered her jobless and alone. Anna had decided the best way to rise above it was to pack her possessions and resentments and return to her native roots in New Hampshire with an understanding that life was unpredictable and time was irreversible regardless of setting.

Aware Karla was leaving, Marilyn suggested Anna apply at

Essential Analytics, since she appeared more than qualified to fill Karla's shoes. Chet wasn't thrilled by the prospect of interviewing or ultimately hiring a friend or acquaintance of his wife, but there were many things that Marilyn excelled at, including persistence and persuasion. He agreed, but made no promises.

Chet nearly flipped in his chair when Anna flowed confidently into his office, meeting his stare with bold and intelligent ice-blue eyes.

"Anna Paxton?" Chet asked, and motioned to a chair.

"For now," she said with a mild accent. She poured into her seat and brushed back chestnut hair that churned halfway down her back. "Anna Buccheri, soon."

"Ah, getting married?"

"No. The other direction."

"Oh, I'm sorry."

"I'm not," she assured him.

"Is Buccheri Italian?"

"Sicilian," Anna said with a slow smile that seemed to mask a million secrets.

Chet wasn't sure if "Sicilian" was a confirmation or a correction. *Sicilians are Italian, right?* he wondered and then thought, *Please God, let her know how to type.*

She could type ... and possessed a bounty of additional skills. Chet had explained to her that more applicants were scheduled to be interviewed, but promised to review her references and reply to her regardless of the outcome. Despite his words, he had already decided. He hired Anna three days later, so as not to appear anxious.

Later that same evening, Chet humoredly asked Marilyn if she were testing him by sending him someone as young and beautiful as Anna.

"Don't flatter yourself, old man," she replied. "Don't kid yourself, either."

He figured this as true… at least at first. Then Anna started in with flirtations that were furtive, yet too direct to ignore. *Is she being playful, or is she really coming on to me?* he wondered.

Karla and Chet would occasionally go to lunch together. There were no rumors and nobody appeared to think much about it. In her fifth week at EA, Chet invited Anna to lunch and she quickly accepted. The rumors were instant and widespread. Chet was hesitant about taking Anna to lunch again, fearful that Marilyn might somehow catch wind of the envious yarns.

The novelty of Anna eased with the company men as the ensuing weeks passed, but her subtle flirtations toward Chet increased, escalating from stares and smiles to physical contact. Whenever proximity allowed, but always clear of the public eye, she would nonchalantly stroke a hand over his back, or brush a hip against him. During dictation, she would sit cross-legged, her skirt raised enough to divulge a liberal amount of flesh, yet concealing enough to make Chet yearn to dive over his desk. He managed to keep himself under control … barely.

On the Wednesday of Anna's eighth week, Chet saw that her desk was still unoccupied at 7:30 a.m. Anna's day started at eight, but she was consistently first in the office. When she arrived just minutes before eight, he was surprised by the relief he felt.

"Sorry I'm late." Anna placed her purse under her desk.

"You're not late. Is everything all right?"

"Just my car. It wouldn't start. Had to call the garage and arrange a pick-up."

"How'd you get here?" he asked, absorbed by Anna's shapely bottom as she bent over to insert a K-cup. The urge to run his hand over the rising landscape of her hip was intense, but held back. She started the coffee maker.

"Cab," she answered. The machine dispensed a stream of brew, saturating the office with its aroma.

"Why didn't you call me? I could have given you a ride."

"You would have?"

She passed Chet his coffee, her fingers lingering on his hand.

Was that intentional? Should I react? He had never wavered when coming on to women who attracted him but there was something different about Anna.

"I would have liked a ride from you."

For the first time in recent memory, Chet wished there wasn't a Marilyn Farner.

Shortly before 4 p.m. there was a gentle knock on Chet's office door.

"Do you need anything before I go for the day?" Anna asked.

"How about a backrub?" Chet stretched, stifling a yawn. With a seductive smile, Anna started closing the door.

"Kidding," Chet said.

Anna pouted, twirled, and gave a provocative peek over her shoulder before leaving his office. The gesture radiated innocence, but her sparkling eyes and mischievous grin set Chet's nerves abuzz.

Is she looking for a father figure? Chet smiled at the irony, if that were the case. He and Marilyn had never had children. Early in their relationship Marilyn had explained that she suffered infertility due to endometriosis, hoping it would never become a problem. It never had, and at forty-two, it never would. Chet had no particular desire for children…his own, or those of others. If Marilyn regretted not being able to have children, she never brought it up. Besides, her schedule was always full, practically day and night; she never had time for him, never mind children.

What if he had consented to the backrub, or if **he** had

advanced **her?** Would she have consented? Would she sexually devour him if given the opportunity?

Then the sobering thoughts worked their way into his fantasy. Anna had been very cautious with her flirting. If he reciprocated and she screamed sexual harassment, he would have no defense. It would create anarchy. His could become the next job opening at EA. Marilyn wouldn't take well to the humiliation it would cause her. It would smear her shining veneer amongst her trendsetting peers. The divorce would be quick and brutal; tear down the damaged marital structure and rebuild, new and improved—and single—in the blink of an eye. Marilyn could and would take everything he owned to assure she could maintain her socialite ways; she was that driven. Chet would naturally sit and watch it all transpire; he was that passive.

But Anna resided inside his head. *I must be crazy,* he thought. He had so much at stake: a top-level job, a marriage others envied, and a home he had busted his hump to get and keep. Besides, Marilyn hadn't exactly slithered out from beneath a rock. She was only thirty-six and reliably turned heads. After sixteen years together—eleven married—she could still arouse him, not that she often made any effort. Would he throw it all away for another woman? For Anna? For a stab at some hot little honey who might end up being merely lukewarm...or even cold?

For all Chet knew, Anna could have peculiar quirks or hang-ups...or maybe hang upside-down to sleep. She could be into BDSM or pain, neither of which appealed to him. She could be horrendous in the sack and maybe think an orgasm is something cultured in a petri dish.

He shut down his computer, rose, put on his blazer, and drifted out of his office. Anna was picking up her purse, on way out.

"Going my way?" she inquired.

"If that's out the front door, I guess so."

They walked to the front lobby together, past Beth—the company's receptionist and premier scandalmonger—and out the front entrance. A taxicab was idling near the curb.

"Does she remind you of Miss Piggy?" Chet asked.

"Beth? Now that you mention it," Anna chuckled.

"You need a ride?" Chet asked, and instantly thought, *don't do it, you fool.*

"Already called," she said, motioning to the cab.

"Forget the cab. You'll need the money for your repair bill," he persisted, his words continuing to defy him.

"You sure?"

"Come on."

As they ambled past the battered cab, Chet nodded a greeting to the driver who returned a feeble salute. They rounded the corner of the building and stopped beside Chet's car. Anna eyed the blue Lexus LC 500 with open appreciation.

Chet opened the passenger-side door for her. As Anna slid into her seat, he tried to recall the last time he had done the same for Marilyn.

"So posh," Anna said.

"Why does everyone say that? There are nicer cars here," Chet said, knowing it wasn't true.

"Where?" she asked. "Must be nice to have a car you can rely on."

Chet disregarded her remark as he saw Mark Houseman from engineering exit a side door. Mark grinned knowingly and offered a thumbs-up. He was one of those people who talked too loudly, laughed too loudly—especially at their own jokes—and seemed to thrive on making people uncomfortable. One morning he covertly whispered to Chet, "You plank her yet?" This was not good.

"Shit," muttered Chet.

"Fuck him," Anna said.

Mark Houseman climbed into his Hummer, started it with a roar, and rumbled past them with a piercing blast of tractor-trailer air-horns.

"Big SUV, giant tires, loud horns…I wonder what he's compensating for?" said Anna.

"Fuck him," Chet said, latching his seatbelt and shifting into reverse.

A few minutes and about four miles later, Chet maneuvered his car into Ken's Service Station, stopping in front of a bay door. Anna's neglected blue Subaru waited alongside a brilliant, candy-apple red '57 T-Bird.

"Nice," Anna said.

"Very."

"Ken has a jaded sense of humor, parking *my* car near *that*," Anna said. "How about a drink?"

"They serve them here?" Chet asked, trying to screen his anxiety.

"I live there." She pointed to a sizable red colonial across the street and three buildings away.

He tightened his grip on the steering wheel to steady his quivering hands. "I probably shouldn't. Marilyn will be expecting me."

"Wednesday night…yoga night until seven," Anna said.

Chet had nothing to counter with. Anna kept his calendar and took his calls; she knew his schedule.

She patted him on the leg and squeezed gently.

"Don't worry, I don't bite… unless you *want* me to," she said, her words so packed with intent and promise their seams were splitting.

Oh God! Chet couldn't ignore the stirring itch below. "I guess one drink won't kill me."

"That's better." Anna exited from the car and closed the door. She spent a moment inside the garage, sauntered out, and climbed into her car.

Chet followed her, fighting the uneasy feelings with illogical reasoning. *I can turn around if this starts going too far. I've done nothing wrong, yet. Marilyn can't read my thoughts.*

He recalled the word Mark Houseman often used to describe him when he would refuse Friday night drinks with the staff.

Henpecked.

Was it true?

No, Chet concluded. It was simply that he didn't like most people on his workforce.

He parked in the spacious driveway, wishing his car wasn't quite so unique or so visible, or that he had a nice *Kenworth* to park behind. Every vehicle that motored past looked like Marilyn's white Audi, but then it would morph into a green Toyota, a black Mustang, or otherwise.

I've only given her a ride, for Christ's sake!

With renewed confidence and purpose, Chet climbed from his Lexus.

Anna slid from her car and stood beside him as her car gasped and shuddered, finally expiring with a resounding backfire and an impenetrable swirl of inky smoke.

"It's an improvement," said Anna. "This morning it wouldn't start, now it won't die."

Anna's apartment was on the second floor. A distinct blend of potpourri and coffee wafted over them when she opened the door. She showed Chet her apartment, room by room. He couldn't determine if it was what he had expected or not. Several well-tended plants hung before windows, rested on shelves, or grew in large floor urns...many, but not *too* many. A diverse balance of handcrafted décor added character with an argument of styles.

"What's your desire? I have vodka, gin, rum, tequila..."

You? he thought, then asked, "Beer?"

"Sam Adams?"

"Perfect."

Chet waited in the den, his favorite of the apartment's five rooms, he'd decided. A telephone rang in the kitchen and Anna entered the room covering the mouthpiece. "It's your wife," she whispered.

Dread lit Chet's spine and the soles of his feet with what seemed like a thousand volts. He stared at Anna in disbelief, wanting to run.

Anna tried to refrain from laughing but failed miserably. "Oh my god, your face!" she said.

"Oh my god, my heart!"

"I'm thinking a little lower." She handed him the beer, coquettishly slipped past him to sit on the couch and patted the cushion nearest her.

"Come and sit down. I promise I'll be a good girl."

"Then what's the sense in sitting?"

"We could lie down." Anna winked.

Chet sat beside her, wondering how this came to be, that Anna, so stunning, so brazen, so…young, could be interested in him. He felt adolescent, that the shy and introverted schoolboy he had been, had returned. He sipped his beer, looking around the room, expecting her to pull the rug out from beneath his horny and eager feet.

After a few minutes of uneasy silence, Anna said, "I guess I'll get a drink, too."

"Of what?"

"Rum and Coke."

"Make it two," he said, hoping it would settle his nerves.

Anna returned with the drinks, handed him one over his shoulder from behind the couch, and set hers atop a coaster on the end table. Her hands settled on his shoulders and she started massaging and kneading with practiced skill.

Anna's breath caressed his face as her lips brushed his ear and against his cheek. "You're so tense. Relax," she whispered.

Good hands, Chet thought, *good strong hands*. The tautness in his shoulders started to recede and he leaned his head back and closed his eyes. Anna's lips tenderly touched the corner of his mouth and her tongue gently traced his lips.

This is it, he thought. *Time to go.* But he didn't leave. He surrendered to her gently searching mouth as she slid her body over the back of the couch and settled in his lap, never taking her mouth from his. She kissed a burning trail along his jaw and gently nipped his earlobe.

"Want me to stop?" she purred. Chet said nothing, his breathing heavy and becoming rapid.

Unbuttoning his shirt, Anna worked her way to his neck and shoulder, descended to a nipple, delicately biting and sucking, and effectively driving all thought from Chet's mind except for the intoxicating woman before him.

Anna lowered herself to the floor between his legs and worked her hungry mouth lower, to his navel, and placed a hand on his erection, repositioning it to twelve o'clock, so the tip was just visible above his belt. Anna ran her tongue ever so gently over his glans, met Chet's eyes, and it was all he could do to keep from exploding right then and there. She gifted him with a telling smile, making it clear that she now possessed him.

Chet moaned his frustration as Anna slowly rose to her feet. She took his hand and led him into the bedroom. Directing him to stay in place, she unbuttoned her blouse and let it drift to the carpet. Her skirt followed, leaving only her bra, nylons, and a confirmation that she wore no panties.

"Help me," she mouthed inaudibly, motioning to her legs with a nod.

Chet knelt down and put his lips against her belly, marveling at the softness and relishing the heat of her skin. Rolling her nylons down with shaking hands, he unveiled her center of desire. Rising, he nimbly unfastened the clasps of her bra.

"No tan lines," Chet said, drawing a sweet and rigid nipple

into his mouth.

"Shhhh," Anna hushed him. She steered him to the bed, instructed him to lie on his back, and then deftly removed the rest of his clothing.

Anna rose up, knelt on the bed, and straddled Chet. Leaning forward, she grabbed onto the headboard and maneuvered upward until her passion and sweet musk saturated his lips. So bold, but for Chet, no single act was more arousing. Anna slowly rocked her hips as he tenderly kissed and teased her most tender spot. After what seemed too little time, Anna's gentle rocking stopped, she tightened a hand in Chet's hair and her limbs started quivering ever so slightly. Setting his hands on her hips, Chet centralized his attention, softly flicking his tongue as Anna's tremors sharpened. Her breathing becoming vocal and ragged and she rewarded him with vibrant bucking as she vaulted into a lingering climax.

Taking little time to regain her breath, Anna moved lower on the bed, curled like a kitten with her head on Chet's leg and took him into her mouth. She caressed him with her silky lips, her tongue tantalizing every nerve. He felt the white light of pleasure mounting, summoning him until he felt he would dissolve...and then Anna would stop, denying him release. Remaining completely still, she would ease her hold on him while the sensual clutches ebbed, and then she would resume.

Again, denying him release, Anna stopped, making him nearly scream in need. She straddled his legs, and slid forward until her core touched the warm firmness of him and she slowly guided him inside, pulling him deeper and deeper. Leaning forward, pressing the heavy warmth of her breasts to his chest, she dug her nails into his shoulders and ground against him.

She whispered in his ear, "Cum inside me, it's okay."

Those words—the offer, even with its devastating potential—combined with urgent need for release, were beyond resistance...there was no turning back.

Chet's climax hit him with the fury of a runaway train, embracing him with paralyzing paroxysms as Anna rode him, coercing him to a level so intense, he feared for another breath.

"I got you," Anna breathed into Chet's ear. She collapsed atop him, and again she said, "I got you."

Chet thought of those words as Anna lay with her head on his chest, and understood their truth. Within minutes, they both surrendered to a welcomed sleep.

When Chet awoke, Anna was lying beside him, tracing her fingers over his chest.

"Welcome back," she said.

"I may never walk again," he mumbled. "I need a wheelchair."

"Let's hope it's turbo-powered, it's 6:54."

"What?" He vaulted upright to look at the clock. "Shit!"

"I just woke up, too."

Chet scrambled out of bed, gathered his clothes, and started dressing. He tried three times to put both feet into the same leg hole.

"Slow down, you'll get there faster," Anna said, laughing. "Don't worry, your administrator can attest that you stayed late, working *very* hard."

Finally dressed, Chet gave Anna a quick but impassioned kiss, and then raced out the door. He saw her watching him through the window as he hopped into the car and drove away with a squeal of rubber.

The drive home was sheer misery. He had cheated on his Marilyn, and while cheating was nothing new, he had never put so much at risk before. He had never given someone so much power as he had just given Anna. The act was irreversible; it couldn't be undone, you can't unfuck someone. Discovery and the ramifications that would follow could be devastating. His would no longer be honorable.

Innumerable thoughts paraded through his mind, landing like marching soldiers with spiked boots. *Will Marilyn know? Will she smell Anna on me? Maybe I should have showered! Did Anna leave evidence, like hickeys, nail marks…herpes? Oh God, what if she has something?*

Holy fuck, I came inside her! What an idiot I am! "It's okay," she had said. What in the hell did **that** mean?

What would Marilyn do if she found out he slept with the woman she recommended to him for a job? Would she leave him, take everything but the shirt on his back? Or broadcast the insult far and wide, costing him his job and his reputation?

Chet veered to the edge of the road and waited for his hands to stop shaking. Gazing in the mirror, he raked his fingers through his hair, confirming that it bore no evidence of the night's endeavors.

Collecting himself, he drove the rest of the way home, but his heart plummeted when he saw Marilyn's Audi in the driveway.

"Damn it!" he muttered, urgently searching for a convincing alibi. He scanned the glove compartment and found what he needed: a new 12-pack box of *Callaway SR1* golf balls.

Yeah, you have balls, all right! he thought wryly. *Something you may end up lacking if Marilyn finds out.* He broke the seal on the box, making sure to tear the flap a little for validity's sake. *Will she check them for scuffing?* He wondered, his paranoia swelling.

"Honey, I'm home!" he announced from the front door, instantly despising how he sounded … hollow and counterfeit like an inferior actor trying to impersonate Dick Van Dyke.

"Hello, baby, be right there," Marilyn called from the kitchen. He heard the rattle of the landline phone being returned to its cradle. "Did we take the scenic route home?"

And what a scene at that! Nothing compared to the scene you'd make if you knew, he reflected. "I went to Gormans' to fantasize over some golf clubs. You'll be happy to know I controlled my urges, though I couldn't resist playing nine holes. Time got away."

He was surprised at how easily the lies slipped out and his confidence rose a notch. *I might be able to have my cake and eat her, too.*

"Shocked and proud." Marilyn shuffled across the living room on slippered feet and gave him a quick hug. "I still regret that I have to compete with a bunch of woods and irons. Someday you'll realize that I have an admirable set, too," she pouted playfully and kissed him.

"Do I taste chocolate chip cookie?"

"I might even bake *you* some, if I don't eat all the batter."

Chet set the box of balls onto the counter, hung up his blazer, and then sprawled on the couch.

"How's Anna working out?" Marilyn asked, catching him off guard.

Is she testing me, or toying with me? Stay calm, he warned himself.

Maintaining composure, he said, "She's working out perfectly." *The truth would make you shit.*

"That's good," Marilyn said from the kitchen. "How about we take a stroll along the mine trail after the cookies are done?"

Chet knew what *that* meant—Marilyn was feeling playful. Whenever they went for a stroll along "The Mine Trail", Marilyn returned flushed, whimsical, and erotically charged. The jaunts had started as a Saturday night standard for them, but with the passing of years had tapered off to once about every six months. Sex had become rare and perfunctory, at best. What were the chances, the one night in half-a-year Marilyn felt frisky is the night that he is fucked nearly inside out by a woman he's cheated on her with?

"It's Wednesday," Chet said.

"I'll make it worth the trip," Marilyn promised.

Trying to demonstrate his usual eagerness at such an offer, Chet rolled off of the couch and stood up, aware of the tingling numbness that still suffused his groin. "Well, if you're going to put it *that* way."

"It works for Dunkin' Donuts. We still have to wait for the cookies, though."

Chet stretched out on the couch and pondered how the walk would evolve. Would he be too preoccupied to perform in bed? What if he mistakenly called her Anna?

I could close my eyes and think of Anna? Chet wondered, remembering the feel of her. There was an awakening below his belt and he thought everything would be all right.

After their walk, Marilyn and Chet reveled in a fervent lovemaking session. His apprehension about not 'rising' to the occasion departed minutes after returning to the house. Marilyn was upon him with a ferocity he hadn't seen from her in years, and he responded with an intensity generously fueled by the novelty of getting away with having amazing sex with two highly desirable women on the same day.

He wondered if Marilyn sensed it—smelled her on him, maybe—and, desperate to save the relationship, wanted to prove she still craved him more ardently than anyone else could, or she knew, and in some sordid way it got her juices flowing. Wouldn't it have been revealed sooner if she had that kind of kink, not eleven years into the marriage? Was it that eleven years of wedlock had become mundane for her, and this lit a little spark in her? Whatever it was, it intrigued him.

PART II

Chet had never seen Anna looking so flawless, and seeing her brought everything back in a flourish: the sensations, the heat, her desire, and her wonderful indulgence in *him*. The memory staggered him and he knew he wouldn't give her up. What complicated it more was that he didn't want the stigma of divorce, either.

"Good morning, Mister Farner," Anna greeted, not looking up from her work.

"Um...hello," he said, grateful she kept a professional demeanor in the office, even with his inability to do the same.

"Thank you for *the ride* yesterday," Anna said. Her eyes flashed mischievously and then returned to her work.

"Uh, sure. No problem," said Chet, embarrassed by Anna's ability to fluster him like a schoolboy. He had always been confident, if not downright arrogant around women.

He entered his office and set his workbag on his desk. Anna came in shortly afterward and set a steaming cup of coffee on his desk.

He looked at her and he gasped comically. "Did I do that?"

Anna shielded her neck with her hand. "Is it *that* noticeable?"

"I don't remember doing that."

"Well, I can't exactly suck my own neck."

What felt so fantastic about the previous day was the youthful and enthusiastic recklessness of such an encounter, the exhilaration of discovery, or the rediscovery of passion long forgotten or lost to the automation some suffer with matrimony. It was like venturing into new realms.

Rubbing the blemish on her neck, Anna said, "According to your calendar you're free tomorrow night. Come to my place for dinner?"

It irritated Chet, not that Anna was so tuned to his life schedule, but that his life had become presumably routine and easily forecasted. Marilyn obsessed about schedules: yoga on Tuesday and Thursday, tennis on Wednesday and Friday, grocery shopping on Monday morning. Any deviations made her antsy.

"You'll love dessert." A tantalizing promise.

Chet knew he should end it, but he couldn't. Anna was stunningly beautiful, voluptuous, smart, and witty. She seemed too good to be true. The promise of another libidinous revelry with her was too alluring, and knowing that Marilyn would be none the wiser made rejecting it impossible.

Although he never cared for the game, Chet was suddenly fond of tennis, and then a thought staggered him. *What if Marilyn didn't go to tennis on Wednesdays and Fridays, or Yoga on Tuesday and Thursdays?*

He felt an illogical stab of jealousy with the awareness that Marilyn could also have someone on the side, maybe for years, and it had never crossed his mind until that moment.

"I'd like that," he said, feeling unduly vindicated.

Chet found himself at Anna's apartment Friday night, while he assumed Marilyn was at tennis, and Sunday while Marilyn thought he was playing golf. Nearly every Wednesday night and Sunday afternoon for the next four months, Anna and Chet spent them together.

Marilyn never appeared to suspect anything. *Did she even think about me? Did she care?* he wondered, a little hurt.

Then came the day Anna said what he most dreaded hearing. They sat on the floor, naked, leaning against the sofa. Anna had just proved that a hassock had far better use than as a simple footstool.

Anna stroked her hand softly over his thigh. "Chet?"

"Hmm."

"What's going to become of us?"

"What do you mean?"

"Are we always going to be part-time lovers? Will our relationship always depend on Marilyn's tennis or your golf? Love shouldn't be canceled on Sundays because of rain."

"Are you getting sentimental?" Chet teased.

Anna sat up to face him directly. "No, I'm getting desperate. What kind of life can I have if this continues? I have no future in this situation. Believe it or not, I want a future. Sex isn't all I'm good for."

"It isn't?"

"Oh, *screw you!*" Anna jumped up and stormed into the bedroom.

"I was joking!" Chet called, rising to follow her, a sense of panic rising. *So here is where it ends...and where my nightmare begins.*

Anna returned wearing her robe. "Well *I'm* not joking. I have dreams, too. Someday I want a house and some children ... to be a mother."

Chet sat on the sofa, distressed. Marilyn's inability to bear children had always left a void in her, but not him. He had no desire to play catch with a son or buy stuffed animals or dresses for a daughter, and Anna's desire for the same shouldn't have surprised him. He should have seen that coming. Chet felt vulnerable and disoriented and could only see disaster looming. His career, his reputation, his marriage, all doomed.

"I love you, Chet, but I feel trapped. It scares me *a lot.*"

"I don't know what to do."

"Have you ever heard of divorce?" Anna asked, as if addressing a child. "Why do you continue living with her if you don't love her, or do you love her and I'm just a convenient diversion?"

Love? There was the rub. Chet wasn't sure he'd ever felt love. He looked at Anna and contemplated what he felt. Lust? Definitely. Possessiveness, jealousy? Sure. But love? If Anna or Marilyn both disappeared from his life, would he be heartbroken? He figured he'd feel a void he'd want to refill...

"Tell me so I can resume life with at least an inkling of hope," she appealed.

He nearly reminded her that *she* had been the aggressor. *She* was the one who'd advanced *him* with no reservations about his marital status at that time.

He kept quiet, but pondered. Divorce frightened him; it would be so messy. He would lose at least half of everything he'd ever worked for ... his house and his savings, which at this point were respectably strong.

To lose Marilyn without losing his shirt was improbable. Marilyn was not the 'Win-some-lose-some' type. Though she was not scholarly, she was far from dim. She had a strategic mind that usually recognized an advantage.

"I've contemplated divorce already. I lie awake at night striving to find an easier solution," he admitted. "I could lose virtually everything."

"Everything?" Anna said and turned away from him. "I guess that settles it."

"Wait!" He had to think. If he let Anna go, Marilyn would surely find out and he'd lose Anna, Marilyn, his job, and a huge portion of his life's work. If he stayed with Anna, he'd lose just about everything except Anna.

Was four months with a woman he still didn't really know worth surrendering eleven-plus years of his life?

He stood, naked, feeling vulnerable. "We've been together, what, four months? I think it's still a little early to be making life-long commitments."

"It's not just the commitment. It's knowing that you go home to *her* every night and probably still making *love* to her. I want you to come home to *me*." She clutched his arms and turned him toward her, her eyes pleading with him to understand. "How would you feel if *I* went home to someone every night?"

Jealous, possessive, cheated, he thought. "Okay, okay," he said, "just give me a little time to figure how I'm going to go about it, all right?"

She gave him a little time—very little, in fact.

The following Wednesday Anna approached Chet with an exemplary solution. One Chet didn't favor, nevertheless, one he could not disregard.

"I'm pregnant."

"What?" Chet choked out. The room dipped as he groped for his chair.

"You heard me."

"How?"

"Really?" Anna snapped.

"I mean, I thought you were on the pill."

"I am … I was, but they never professed to be one-hundred percent effective, only ninety-nine." Tears welled and she crossed her arms protectively over her abdomen. "And no, I won't abort."

Christ what a nightmare! How had he let it happen? What a hole he had dug for himself. He was damned either way.

"If I have a child growing in you, I'm going to take responsibility for it," Chet said, surprising himself and not sure if he meant it.

"You're not going to dump me?"

At that moment Chet understood how callow Anna truly was; a woman, yes, but preserving an adolescent edge. "No," he said, deflated and defeated, yet feeling inanely paternal to Anna. "Go back to work and we'll talk about it later, at your place. Okay?"

"I guess so," she said, still wary.

"But we have to keep this quiet," he told her, leading her to the office door.

"I don't like it."

"At least for now," Chet said, and closed the door. Oblivious to Anna's victorious smile, he returned to his desk.

What a mess! If there had been any chance of breaking up with Marilyn quickly and efficiently, it was gone. Not only was he having an affair with his secretary, he had knocked her up, too. He wondered if she was truly pregnant.

He returned to the door and opened it. "How do you know?" he asked Anna.

"E.P.T. *Very* dark lines. Doctor tomorrow."

He closed the door again.

Holy shit, what a mess. Lawyers. Courts. Lose at least half of everything. There were difficult days coming, he knew.

He sat forward in his chair and placed his forehead on his desktop. *Yess'm Mr. Farner, you fucked up big-time. Gonna be some strange times a-commin.* And fathering a child was out of the question.

Knowing Marilyn and her disposition, there would be no way of escaping it, short of murder. Chet laughed in spite of everything. *Murder,* he reflected, *and you call her extreme?*

Chet arrived at Anna's apartment promptly at four-thirty to discuss their predicament. That evening they dined, made love, and schemed the murder of Marilyn Farner.

It evolved quite innocently—actually as a joke.

They retired to the living room, sated with food and liquor, as well as each other. Anna reclined against the ottoman with Chet's head resting on her lap. Chet, on his fifth (maybe sixth or seventh) drink, griped about starting anew after so many years. He emphasized the financial relapse that would evolve.

"One hell of a way for you to start a life," the whiskey-propelled words fell from his mouth. "Wish we could just get rid of her, make her disappear."

"And how would we do that, a blender?" Anna quipped.

"Be too messy…too much blood," Chet chuckled.

"Bad Karma. How about a good garroting?"

"Nope … still a body. Too much evidence." Chet rolled over and knelt, savoring the numbness of his body. "We can't kill her, she'd haunt me. Showing up at night looking for her bingo inky dab thingy."

"Huh?"

"Never mind. Need another?" Chet pointed to Anna's empty glass.

"Sure."

Chet quickly returned with drinks in hand, splashing some as he struggled to sit. "We could push her down a mine shaft."

"Sure, FedEx her to Pennsylvania. Maybe Loretta Lynn will sing her eulogy."

"Nah, copper mines. There's about a dozen of 'em behind my house," Chet slurred.

"Really? Copper mines?"

"Bell Hill. No copper left in any of them now, not enough to matter, at least."

Bell Hill, once a rich source of copper, remained pocked with evidence of its former wealth more than 130 years later. Vegetation-choked mineshafts burrowed into the hill at astounding angles, purging the Earth to even more riveting depths.

"They just left the shafts there? They didn't cover them or fill them?"

"Take a lot of filler," Chet snorted. "There are 'keep out' and 'danger' signs."

They sat quietly for a few minutes, sipping their drinks until Chet broke the silence.

"Talk about the perfect alibi," he noted.

"What?"

"The Mine Trail," he explained. "We take walks through the trail. It's one of the few things we both enjoy. Our friends know we do. Shit, stuff a couple of drinks in her. Take her to the top and flip-bing-boom! Nobody knows any different." Though influenced by the liquor, he would swear it was a near-perfect plot.

"Take me there," Anna blurted, bright-eyed and animated.

"When?"

"Now!"

"But it's right behind my house."

"There must be other ways," Anna persisted. "Anyway, she's at tennis."

Chet thought it through. "I guess we can park on the old mining road."

"I'll get my coat."

While not as dependable as the Lexus, Anna's Subaru had four-wheel drive. Chet maneuvered the protesting car through the dilapidated access road until the furrows and holes became too brutal to permit passage. They exited the vehicle and leaned on it until the vertigo of drunkenness waned.

A delicate breeze whispered through the trees, making the shroud of leafy branches sway lazily overhead. A soft smattering of moonlight dappled the uneven ground, beckoning them onward, guiding them.

Chet held Anna's hand as he led her gingerly through the familiar but unpredictable path that weaved its way up Bell Hill.

"Watch your step," he warned her, the thought of twisted or broken ankles flashing through his mind. He was in no condition to carry an injured woman—let alone himself—back down through the barrage of pits and gullies.

About fifteen minutes into their climb, Chet stopped and stared into the darkness. "Right here," he said.

"What?"

He moved forward, Anna sticking close to his side. "I think this is the deepest shaft."

Anna peered into the shadows of the knoll before them. At the base of the mound, she could barely discern the mouth of the cave, an oblong chasm of utter darkness, hardly seven feet long by five feet high.

"People used to climb down *there*?" she asked with wonder.

"Someone had to." Chet picked up a baseball-sized rock and lobbed it through the opening. "Listen."

The rock vanished down the shaft emitting resounding, hollow cracks. They listened until the sound was no longer distinguishable, but still aware that it had yet to reach bottom.

"This is where you wanted to push her?" Anna asked.

Chet looked at her. She seemed ghost-like in the satiny glow of the moon. "I didn't say that."

He returned his expressionless gaze to the mine.

"Could you?" she asked.

"I don't know," he answered, then turned to her. "Could you?"

She shrugged. "I'm not sure. Now ... yes. It would make everything so much easier for us."

Chet pulled a pint of whiskey from his coat pocket, uncapped it, and took a long pull. He passed it to Anna, who did the same.

"Maybe I could," she said. "If I hid behind that brush." She pointed to a spot not far behind them. "You could throw another rock down and while you're both listening, I could come from behind."

"Maybe, but what if one of us backs out?"

Chet looked at the sky. It was what he and Marilyn had always considered a perfect night for a walk, mild with a soothing breeze. Chet chose another rock and tossed it through the mouth of the cave Marilyn had titled the 'Hell Hole.' They both listened.

"Chet, Anna?" someone said from behind them. They both turned as Marilyn walked up to where they stood, looking confused and uneasy.

"Wow! I was hoping you'd show up," Anna said, girlish and animated. "Please don't mind, but after Chet told me all about the infamous 'Mine Trail,' and how you two walk up here all the time, I made him promise to show me how to get here. I want to surprise my boyfriend and bring him here."

"Oh," Marilyn said, her eyes volleying between the two of them.

"No tennish tonight?" Chet asked Marilyn, thinking Anna was the smoothest character ever.

Marilyn eyed Chet. "Are you drunk?"

Anna lunged and thrusted with all of her strength. The sickening impact as skull hit stone reverberated from the shaft followed by sliding, sounding like a heavy linen bag plummeting down a laundry chute.

They listened until the sound faded.

"Dead?" Anna asked nervously.

"No question about it."

"I didn't think I could do it."

"You were perfect."

Anna stared into the dark maw of the narrow cave, contemplating. "We won't be caught, will we?"

"Not if we keep quiet. We better not stick around. I've got a missing husband to report," Marilyn said.

"You think he was drunk enough to cover your story?"

"They'll never reach him. As far as they'll know, he went for a walk and never returned."

"Still…"

"It's all ledge here. No footprints…nothing. We'll be fine," Marilyn said. She wrapped her arms around Anna and kissed her fervently.

Anna sighed. "I hope so. I don't think I could have done it again."

"What?"

"The sex. His dick in my mouth. Acting as if I enjoyed it. Pretending to be a lush. That was hard enough, but four months waiting for that positive E.P.T. result was torture."

"You did say you came pretty hard."

"That first time, yeah. I admit there was something really arousing about the whole plan. It just took so long. I just pretended it was your tongue."

They started down the path. "I can't believe he bought the bit about me being pregnant," Anna said.

"But you *are* pregnant."

"Yes," Anna rubbed the slight bulge of her belly. "You know, you're weren't entirely right about him being good for nothing."

John McIlveen

A PERSPECTIVE

A knock awakens me. This isn't unusual, since sleep is now what I do most.

"Grandmother, may I come in?" my granddaughter's sweet voice asks from beyond the chamber door.

"Yes, my dear. Come in," I say, and watch as the door swings slowly open.

She slips through the seam of light that shines from the hall and approaches my bed. Her face is beautiful, angelic, framed by a defiant wreath of golden curls that escape from beneath her nightcap. She lifts the hem of her nightgown and moves wraithlike from the cherry wood floor to the thick pile of the carpeting.

"Grandmother?" she asks in her hummingbird voice, her eyes instantly brimming with tears. "Is it true what they say— that you are dying?"

"Yes, sweetie," I answer. "But please don't lament for me, dear, I've had a long and wonderful life with many beautiful children and grandchildren. This part of my journey is nearing its end."

Seven-year-old children may not understand the mechanics of death, but they do know its finality. I rub my hand over her lovely velveteen cheek and brush away her tears, amazed that my wizened, parchment-wrapped shell once had flesh as hearty and vital as her own.

"May I stay here with you for a while?" she asks. Her

demeanor is stoic, yet I can sense distress in her question.

"Of course, my dear…always. Are your father and uncle still fighting?"

"Yes Grandmother," she says. She sits beside me on the thick down mattress. Her honeysuckle eyes grow distant in thought, and again I pray that both of my sons be prudent in their actions and words in her presence.

After a long and profound silence my granddaughter says, "Grandmother?"

"Yes, dear?"

"They are so angry. They throw things and say such hateful and terrible words to each other."

"Sadly, sweetheart, yes," I agree, disheartened that she must witness such dissension.

"Why? I don't understand," she says. "It's just a silly crown."

YANKEE SWAP

"Leaving already?"

Damn it! Kat cursed inwardly, cringing as if pincers had claimed the back of her neck.

Randy Oberlein was the personification of "insufferable." The son of affluent socialites, he was born with a silver spoon inserted so far up his ass he could stir his pancreas. It meant nothing to him that Kat was engaged and very much in love. *And pregnant,* she mentally added, although it didn't show yet.

As assistant division manager, Randy was her superior, which put her in an undesirable position as a subordinate. She was a Purchasing Manager, a station she had been proud of...until she'd actually started the job.

Randy wanted her—had for months—and as far as he was concerned, she was his right...his entitlement. Evidently, "no" was a word he was not accustomed to and which he had difficulty acknowledging. She had considered reporting him, but he was as sly as he was arrogant and the best offense she could present was a *he said/she said* scenario she feared would cost her her job. Her lack of action or reaction only seemed to encourage him.

Randy was the primary reason she had dreaded attending the holiday party, but she'd felt obligated to show up. That it was held in the Doubletree Suites ballroom had made her even more apprehensive. The smug bastard surely had a room reserved and expected her to throw herself upon the mercy of his unhinged whims.

Unfortunately, Kat's fiancé, Vernon, was in Singapore doing whatever it was field engineers did, otherwise he would have been there for her and for their baby. Kat could envision him with his rugged gunslinger's confidence and overprotective daddy-swagger, planting a size-eleven boot against Randy's forehead. She calmed herself but didn't look at the greasy bastard, instead focusing on the memory of Vernon's glowing smile when she'd showed him the two thick pink lines on the pregnancy test. His eyes shone as he joked about trading in the Harley for a mini-van and designer diaper bag. He had posed like a fashion model and asked her if she'd still find him irresistibly sexy with a papoose strapped to his chest.

"Leaving already?" Randy repeated, as if she hadn't heard him the first time.

"Yes. I'm not a fan of crowds or loud parties," she said, knowing it sounded like the bullshit it was, and that he saw right through it. She remained composed. What she truly wanted to do was embed the pointy toe of her Franco Sarto pumps into his grapes.

"I've rented a top-floor suite. We could go there if you'd like to be someplace quieter."

Bingo!

"No. I really have to go…somewhere."

"Are you okay to drive? I can give you a lift."

"I'm fine," Kat said. "I didn't drink anything." She clutched her evening bag tightly between her arm and ribs and headed for the door. As expected, Randy fell into step beside her.

You fucking fatheaded snake, she thought, and realized that was exactly what he reminded her of, with his large forehead that tapered down to sunken cheeks, and those beady black eyes. He was a dangerous, cold-blooded serpent. He was a cobra.

Shaking inside and out with fear and anger, Kat stopped abruptly, her eyes locked on the floor before her. "Stop—

following—me!" she said, assertively enough that a few heads turned toward them.

Randy noticed, too. He held his hands up and took a step away from her in a show of harmless submission, but his hostile eyes promised she would pay for her defiance.

Kat rushed forward, through the ballroom doorway, and away from him. She claimed her coat from the check, walked past a bank of elevators, and shoved open the heavy steel door that opened into the parking facility. She was taken aback by the rigid winds that sliced through the garage, unhindered, it seemed, from the Charles River. With her notoriously poor sense of direction, she was disoriented. By the time she found her car, her face and fingers were in agony, and she cursed herself for not having brought gloves and a hat…mussed hair be damned.

The blow that caught her on the back of the head was sharp and unexpected. She had not heard anyone approaching, and her single thought before she lost consciousness was *Randy*.

A rattling sound brought her around. When she tried to move her head, the pain defined her and owned her, radiating from the back of her neck, over the top of her head and across her shoulders. A woman cried despondently from nearby, her sobs repetitive and shrill, piercing. Kat wanted her to shut the fuck up before the sound split her skull. She thought she might be in the hospital and tried raising her left arm to feel the small but reassuring swell of her belly, but something metal and unforgiving restrained her movement. She yanked and there was a tightening around the front of her legs and her other arm was tugged downward.

She opened her eyes to nearly complete darkness, except for a small red light that blinked every five seconds. Although bright, it seemed distant and offered little help. She couldn't see what was binding her arms, but it rattled like heavy, steel chains. She panicked and yanked, ignoring the nauseating pain that flared up her neck and into her skull, driving her to tears. She was seated, her hands tethered together by a chain strung beneath her chair. Any movement of one arm was countered by a pulling on the other and pressure on the front of her legs.

"Ain't no use," came a man's voice, originating from a few feet to her right. "Just going to fuck your wrists up, is all."

Kat tensed. Her nerves buzzed with anxiety and she expected to be touched—or worse—at any moment and from any direction. *This is bad,* she thought.

"Randy?"

"No, ma'am."

"Who are you? What do you want?" she demanded, with a fear-fueled bravado she wasn't feeling.

"I'm Shep. I'm not the one who did this to you, if that's what you're thinking," he said. "Or I wouldn't be sitting here chained to a fucking chair, either."

"Who did this? What do they want? Why…"

"Whoa there, cupcake. I don't know any more than you do," he said. "I woke up like this a couple hours ago, I guess…hard to tell. Head's splitting. Last thing I remember was closing up my office. Fucker said, 'excuse me,' and when I turned to him, he popped me good on the head. Sounded like Richard Simmons, the twisted little prick who did this."

Shep didn't sound scared, which had Kat suspicious despite his words. She was terrified, her breathing elevated, and she teetered on the edge of hysterics, though not like the woman still blubbering miserably somewhere to her left. She was incoherent, but her deep, hoarse cries made her seem a mature woman of fifty or more.

"Hey," Kat called to her, "can you give it a rest?"

"Yeah, don't bother. She's zoned out," he said. "And if she

doesn't stop carrying on that way, I'll be going over the fucking edge, too. By the way, if he strung you up the same way he did me, you should be able to free a foot or more play for your arms by lifting your legs over the chain. It's work, but it's worth it."

It took Kat a couple minutes, but Shep was right: the small freedom was nearly blissful.

"Christ, I have to go to the bathroom," said a young woman at Kat's near right. *Or maybe it was a teen or a younger boy.*

"That there's Gwen," said Shep. "Name's about all I could get out of her; I think she's in shock."

A man to Kat's right released a contemptuous chuff, startling her. He sounded near enough to touch.

"Who's that...is that him?" Kat sputtered, leaning away from where the sound had come.

"No. He's been fading in and out for a while, but that snort sounded like derision. It's dark as unholy fuck in here, but there are five of us, maybe six," said Shep. "I tried centering in on the breathing."

The man near Kat moaned in agony. "Mierda," he mumbled, a word she was familiar with. Chains rattled softly, and then more determinedly. "What the fuck? What's with the chains, man? This some kind of joke or something?"

"No joke, hombre. Asshole's got a bunch of us penned up here in the dark," said Shep. "Took my phone. Reckon he took all of yours, too."

"What does he want?" asked the man.

"Fuck if I know," said Shep. "You Mexican or something? What's your name?"

"Miguel. I'm Dominican, but why the fuck does that matter?" he answered, and then said, "Come on, lady, shit's bad enough without you squealing like that, you know?"

"Please?" Kat said. It was getting on her nerves, too. The woman kept at it.

"How about you? What's your name," asked Shep, and it

took a while before Kat realized the question was directed at her.

"Kat," she said. "Katrina."

"You got an accent, too," said Shep. "Fucked if I can tell where from, though."

"Philippines," said Kat. "You like that word, don't you?"

"What word?"

"The F word," said Kat.

"Fucking right I do."

She actually smiled, not that anyone benefited from it.

"Seems we got us an ethnic smorgasbord... a Filipino, a Dominican, a Texan, a Gwen, and by the sounds of it, a banshee," Shep said. "Maybe he's putting together some kind of collection. A set. Any of it make sense to y'all?"

"I'm black," said a nervous voice to Kat's right, somewhere between Shep and Gwen. "If he's collecting..."

"That you, Gwen?"

"No. I'm Delanna."

"That's a new one on me. Well, howdy, Delanna. I'd shake your hand, but that ain't in the cards right now. How long you been eavesdropping?" asked Shep.

"Fifteen minutes or so." She said. "Trying to evaluate the situation."

"Any luck?" asked Shep.

"No," she admitted.

"HOLY FUCKING CHRIST, LADY, SHUT UP!"

The room fell into a dead hush; even the keening woman became silent. What was more unexpected than the sudden shriek was that it had come from the one named Gwen.

"Amen," Miguel whispered.

They sat for an immeasurable amount of time, appreciating the quiet, when the room burst into blinding light. They all cowered, lowering their heads and covering their eyes as much as their fastened hands would allow. Although it seemed to Kat as if a bank of stadium lights were turned directly on them, by the time her eyes adjusted, it was difficult to believe that only six standard incandescent light bulbs on a wagon wheel chandelier, and two or three strands of Christmas lighting, could provide that brilliance.

They sat in matching chairs around a large, round, distressed-wood table. Each of them was equally distant from each other and the table, but all beyond reach due to their manacles and chains. The room was rectangular, with double windows on either side. An opaque material covered the glass, making it impossible to determine whether it was day or night. Kitschy Christmas decorations festooned the place, hiding a Southwest décor. Kat wondered how far they were from Boston and if Shep, Southern accent and all, was as innocent as he professed.

At the far end of the room was a door, but no windows. To the left of the door—behind Shep—was a sideboard with a lamp and a nativity scene, complete with baby Jesus and the full cast of characters. Beside the manger was the source of the blinking red light—a small desktop cam, the likes of which you could purchase from Best Buy for fifty bucks.

Kat looked at the five people who sat around the table and saw that they were all just as screwed as she was. Facing her, Shep was easy to recognize with his blue denim shirt and thick moustache on a weathered face that might have been handsome if he hadn't been so gaunt. Wholesome Delanna sat directly to his left, staring back at Kat with frightened, intelligent eyes. She looked barely old enough for college.

Miguel, directly to Kat's left and across from Delanna, leaned forward, only his wavy black hair visible as he searched beneath his chair, trying to decipher the mechanics of his confinement.

"Son of a bitch," he said. "Chains trapped by the support rails. No slipping out of this, man."

He had intense black eyes, a rugged body, and thick arms, both of them sleeved with intricate tattoos. He intimidated Kat. Although she hated to admit it, he was the kind of man she would not meet eyes with in public, and completely avoid in a dark alleyway.

The familiar high keening emanated from the woman to Miguel's left. She lowered her head and managed to fan herself with one hand, a generous hammock of fat swinging loosely from her upper arm. Probably in her late sixties and easily two-fifty, Kat would have wagered a week's pay that the woman had twin teacup poodles named Mitzy and Fitzy that yipped incessantly at nothing in particular. Her eyes were red and swollen above bloated cheeks covered with a patina of tears and snot.

"Oh, don't fucking start that shit again," said the petite woman to Kat's right.

It was intriguing, such aggression coming from such a tiny woman with so adolescent a voice. If Gwen broke ninety pounds, Kat would have been surprised. Alabaster skin, hair dyed coal-black, with matching black fingernail polish and lipstick, she was a teen Goth dream come true. Yet on closer inspection, Kat detected lines near her mouth and eyes that gave evidence of someone years older.

"Agreed," said Shep. "How about telling us your name there, Buttercup?"

The keening woman didn't answer, only carried on sniveling.

Fear dominated the table, but Kat saw something underneath the others' terror that kept her from dissolving into a hopeless, blubbing mess like…well, like "Buttercup."

Shep looked like a doer, constantly scanning the room for answers and a means to escape, as did Miguel, but Miguel also was a mover, pulling at the chair arms, trying to manipulate the chains. If they were to get free, Kat figured she would follow his lead. Delanna looked as confounded as Kat felt, though sentient, and Gwen just looked utterly pissed off.

Kat turned in her chair as far as the restraints would allow and looked behind her. A large Christmas tree, heavily swathed with lights and ornaments as generic and tacky as she had ever seen, stood to the right of another door. Beneath the tree, presents of various sizes lay strewn across the floor in a haphazard offering. Farther to the right, cornered with the windowed wall, was a small side table on which was set a landline phone and another camera that winked ominously.

"We're being watched," Kat said.

The far door slammed open, crashing heavily into the sideboard. A figure leapt into the room and flung its arms skyward. "Correctamundo!" he blurted, and then took a moment to look at each one of them. "Oh, look at you all…so adorable!"

He wore a red mid-length jacket with a white fur collar, green tights, and a wide black belt that cinched his middle. On his head was a pointed red cap that bent to the left a third of the way down. The Santa's helper get-up might have been cute and even disarming, if not for a hideous rubber goblin mask, which made the whole display terrifying. Buttercup crescendoed into a completely new level of wailing.

"What the fuck?" Shep said upon seeing this display.

"Oh, we're going to have so much fun!" The masked oddity skipped closer to them. "I'm Flea…get it? Backwards it's A-E-L-F, a elf." He sounded proud of himself.

His voice was high and did have a Richard Simmons intonation to it, but Kat thought it sounded contrived.

"*An* elf," Gwen corrected, her lip slightly lifted in a sneer.

Flea's grotesque face snapped in Gwen's direction and he scuttled behind her.

"Oh, are we *an* English teacher?" Through unseen eyes, he watched her intently, swaying slightly. "No, honey, you're *a* tattoo artist and I'm still Flea, because I said so…so there."

He touched Gwen lightly on the head with his index finger and hurriedly moved around the table to Buttercup's side. He leaned close to her, their faces inches apart. His circus-clown theatrics gave him unsettling stop-motion intensity.

"What's wrong, my blubbery, blubbering butterball?" he asked, his tone syrupy sweet.

Buttercup stared at the grotesque mask, quivering and sniffling, her fingers fumbling nervously.

"BOO!" Flea screamed in her face and then pranced off, giggling manically.

Buttercup squealed childishly and managed to squeeze her girth deeper into the chair.

"Why are you doing this?" Kat asked.

"Oh, isn't that obvious? 'Tis the season, sweetheart." Flea spun, raised his arms in a less than impressive pirouette, and sang, "It's the most wonderful time of the year."

"Pardon me there, amigo, but what the fuck are you talking about?" asked Shep.

Flea stopped spinning and faced him. "Christmas, silly! It's the season for giving, and I've got gifts for all of you to open!"

He clasped his hands together and dashed to the Christmas tree, squatted, lifted three of the presents, and carried them to the table. He set them neatly at the center and repeated the process.

"There! Isn't this fun! We're going to have a Yankee swap!"

He patted Miguel atop the head. Miguel recoiled, and Flea, unperturbed, skittered around the table. He situated himself behind Gwen, grabbed ahold of her chair, and pushed her closer to the table. He repeated the process with the five remaining chairs and their occupants. To Kat, it seemed he moved Shep's, Miguel's, and Buttercup's chairs just as easily as Gwen's.

Stationing himself behind Delanna, he merrily clapped his hands together. "So...does everyone know the rules for a Yankee swap?" he asked, and waited. "Come *on*, people, somebody answer me!"

"Fuck you," Shep muttered.

"Oh, I don't think so."

Flea quickly maneuvered behind Shep and ran a hand affectionately over his head. The Texan's eyes widened and his entire body began convulsing as a rivulet of drool ran over his bottom lip and fell onto his shirt, forming a dark blue Rorschach pattern.

Buttercup amped up her squealing and Miguel let out a dismayed "fuck," trying to scoot backward in his chair. They all stared at Shep in dismay, and then at Flea, when he proudly displayed a black device to them.

"Nothing inspires cooperation like one of these...they're stunning, if you'll pardon the pun. Whether you want to or not, you're *all* going to cooperate." He put the stun gun in his coat pocket—his left one, Kat noted.

"Okay, sunshine, time to come back. You need to hear the rules," Flea said cheerily, as if speaking to a toddler. He slapped Shep's cheeks lightly. Shep groaned and glared at him. Flea cocked his head disturbingly to one side and then righted himself.

"Good!" he said dismissively. "So the rules *are*...the participants – that means all of you – draw numbers." Flea drew a handful of papers from a pocket on his jacket, removed his cap, and pushed them inside. "I *love* this! Okay! Whoever draws number *one* goes first and opens a gift from the pile. Number two then opens a gift. If he or she prefers the gift number one opened, he or she can *trade* for that one instead." He paused thoughtfully. "You know what? Fuck it, I'll tell you the rules as we go."

His masked face regarded each person seated around the table, moving from one to the next with a jerking motion that reminded Kat of a bird, especially with the black hollows of the mask's eyeholes that betrayed nothing of the man inside. The goblin face abruptly jolted and faced Kat, and with a flourish of the wrist, he pointed at her.

"You first!" he said. He bounced to her side and held the opened cap toward her.

Kat looked at the faces of the others seated around the table. In their eyes, she encountered terror, hatred, anger, and hopelessness, but not the salvation or inspiration she thought she'd seen earlier. That he had chosen her to go first was a terrible omen that seemed to validate her fear of not leaving there alive.

"Ka-at, pick a number," Flea said in a singsong voice, bisecting her name into two syllables.

She was frozen. She couldn't move or speak, but only stared at the collection of gifts centered on the table and Delanna's countenance in the hazy background, slowly shaking her head in fearful denial. Seeing no alternative, Kat slowly reached a shaky hand into the hat and pulled out a square of paper. The rest of them followed suit as Flea moved clockwise around the table.

"Okay, kiddies, unfold your papers and tell me who has number one." He rubbed his hands and shuffled around the table. "Who is it? Who is it? Oh, who is it, already, or do I have to get zap-happy?"

"I do," Delanna whispered.

"Ooooh, hurray!" Flea said with delight. He capered over to her and plucked the paper from her fingers. "Okay…pick a gift!"

Delanna stared at the colorful packages, saying nothing.

"Come on!" Flea cajoled.

Silence.

"PICK A FUCKING GIFT!" Flea erupted. It started as a shriek and ended as a throaty growl. Everyone around the table started and Buttercup recommenced her soggy sniveling. Kat heard insanity in his words, but they resonated in the back of her mind, as if they had awakened something familiar, yet out of reach.

"The blue one," Delanna said, her voice no more than a whisper.

"Snowflakes or *Frozen*?" asked Flea.

"Snowflakes."

Flea grabbed the chosen package and tossed it to Delanna, who mechanically caught it, her chains rattling with the quick movement.

Half-crouched, rapt, and looking ready to bolt, Flea watched her. "Open it," he said with childish impatience.

Delanna cautiously pulled at a silver ribbon as if afraid it would explode. Within the wrapper was a small box. She opened it and removed some tissue and a small prescription bottle.

"Whatcha get, whatcha get?" Flea asked excitedly.

"Pills?" Delanna said cautiously, sounding more like a question.

"Yes! Well, capsules actually, but not just any capsules…those are special *Jesus* capsules. They'll take *all* your pains and worries away," said Flea. "And there are six of them, in case you're in the giving spirit. Sharing is caring! What a wonderful gift! I'll even open them for you."

He did so, setting the bottle and cap on the table before her.

"I really have to piss," Gwen said again.

"Me, too," added Miguel.

"Be my guest," Flea offered amiably, dismissing them. "Okay, who's next?" After a short silence, he patted his left pocket. "Number two-ooo. Zap!"

"Yup," said Shep. He crumpled the paper and tossed it to the center of the table.

"I'm so looking forward to you!" Flea gushed, enthusiastically clapping his hands.

"I'm sure you are," Shep muttered.

"Alright, Cowboy, make a choice."

Shep sneered at their twisted host and said, "The flat one."

"Ooooh!" Flea brought the chosen gift to Shep and set it down.

Shep slowly opened the package and from inside the slender box withdrew an old hacksaw with a black Bakelite handle and a rusted blue blade.

"Oh, what have we here?" Flea said. "It looks a little worn. I doubt it would cut metal, but in a pinch, it could still work for you."

Flea grabbed the saw from Shep and dragged it across the man's exposed arm, leaving an angry red gash. Shep recoiled and hollered in pain. He pressed his wounded arm against his abdomen, leaving a bloody streak on the denim. His jaw tightened and his face darkened as he defiantly tried to compose himself. Buttercup, in contrast, launched into another bout of squealing cries.

"Such a *handy* gift, if you catch my drift," Flea said.

Buttercup's wails escalated and Flea's head dropped while his shoulders sank. He set the hacksaw down before Shep and walked purposefully around the table to stand behind the squealing woman.

"You are ruining our *fun*," he admonished her. There followed a high-pitched report, like the snapping of a dry branch. They all jumped and Delanna yelped in surprise at the gunshot. Buttercup's body went rigid as her right eye blossomed red, then she slumped to her side, silent and still. Eyes wide, mouth agape, Kat watched Flea switch the small pistol to his right hand and pocket it. Despite her shock, she had the absurd realization he was left-handed.

"Why the fuck you do that, man?" Miguel demanded, disbelieving.

"She was such a party pooper," Flea said with embellished pathos. Recovering quickly, he clapped his hands. "Look on the bright side! We have an extra gift!"

Kat couldn't take her eyes off Buttercup. They had turned a

corner. Reality shifted. She knew the potential of death was present, but she had wrapped herself safely within denial until then. A series of panicked thoughts scrolled through her mind and the awareness that they had never found out Buttercup's actual name.

"So, Cowboy, are you keeping your gift, or do you want to trade with Delanna for her capsules?" Flea asked.

Shep stared coldly at him. "I'm good," he said. His arm was still pressed against his shirt, but judging by the stains, he wasn't bleeding much.

"Now we're back on track! Who's number three-eee?"

"Yo," said Gwen, holding the paper loosely between thumb and forefinger, trying to appear unfazed. The fast rise and fall of her chest betrayed her terror.

"Yo-ho-ho, Gweno!" sang Flea. "Pick a gift, Sweetie-pie."

Something in the way he said her name troubled Kat.

Yo-ho-ho, Gweno!

Gwen's eyes shifted to the goblin face and Kat thought she saw recognition in the woman's eyes. "*Frozen*," Gwen said, suspiciously watching the demon mask, searching.

"Adorable!" Flea clapped again, a frenzy of hand pats.

Gwen...Gweno, Kat thought.

Flea delivered the box to Gwen, his hip brushing Kat's arm. She recoiled impulsively, as if his corruption could leach through her clothing and flesh and contaminate her. Flea's head jerked toward her and Kat hoped he felt threatened, if only for two seconds. She sensed—or more so, smelled—a faint whiff of cologne. It was one she recognized...one she both loved and hated. It was so manly and stimulating on Vernon, so cloying on Randy, but downright nauseating on this piece of shit.

"Lacoste," Kat said.

"What?" Flea asked.

"Lacoste," Kat repeated. "Your cologne. You're wearing Lacoste Essential."

He froze for a moment and Kat knew she had shaken him and wished she could see his face behind the mask.

"Open your gift," he said to Gwen, a little less vibrant. She accepted the package, her frightened eyes never leaving the mask. He seemed to notice the scrutiny.

"Yes?" he asked her with a tilt of his head, his voice chipper, yet wary. Gwen didn't answer. "Open your gift," he repeated, his voice deeper under the gravity of threat.

Gweno. Gwen the Ho, Kat thought. Gweno...tattoo artist...Lacoste Essential...left-handed.

Gwen opened the package and removed a small Igloo cooler, inside of which was a single box cutter that, like the hacksaw, had a rusty blade.

Flea, returning to form, gasped with glee. "Isn't the cooler delightful, sticking with the *Frozen* theme that way? And a box cutter! It would work great on those pasty white wrists of yours. Now all three of you have an easy way out...if you so choose!" He compellingly put his hands to his chest. "See, I'm not a bad guy. You can't deny there's an element of generosity here."

"Oh my God!" Kat said with a sob. "You're supposed to be in Singapore!"

Shep looked confused and Delanna studied Kat like a scientist awaiting a chemical reaction. Kat's reality swooped and spun. The room seemed cavernous and then tiny, fading and sharpening, echoing and then stuffy, and Kat sensed she was on the verge of passing out.

"Excuse me?" asked Flea.

"You called her Gweno," Kat said. "Gweno the Ho. Gwench the Wench...the unfaithful ex. I know it's you, Vernon!"

"Vernon?" Gwen said in disbelief. A parade of emotions crossed her face starting with shock, then confusion, anger, disgust, and settling on fear.

Flea's shoulders fell and he pulled off the mask revealing his handsome face. Delanna's eyes widened but she remained silent. Somehow, she knew him, too.

"You miserable prick," Shep said.

"You always have to fuck things up, don't you?" Vernon said to Kat, his eyes cold and feral.

Gone were the elfin voice and ostentatious gestures, nor was there any sign of the tender man who had asked for her hand six months earlier; the man she had kissed in E terminal of Logan airport four days ago. Kat felt as if she were detached from her body, trying to make sense of the unexplainable.

"Vernon. Oh, Jesus Christ, how could you?" Kat asked, her words choked with emotion and snagging on her confusion.

"I didn't get on the plane. I didn't go to Singapore, you idiot…I've never been there," Vernon said.

How could that be? He left for a week every two months, had been doing it since she first met him more than a year ago.

"You fucking killed someone!" Gwen said, not comprehending. "You need help."

"She was a piece of shit. My asshole landlord. She deserved it." He gave a dismissive *oh well* shrug. "I planned to let one of you live. Not you," he said to Kat. "But since you let *this* cat out of the bag," he said, jacking both thumbs toward his chest, "no one's going home."

Disbelieving and fearful glances passed around the table, most pausing on Buttercup's still form. With surprising reserve, Shep asked Delanna, "So, what did *you* do to cross him, sweetheart?"

Delanna's lip curled as she spoke. "We worked at Hastings. He kept asking for a blowjob. He tried to drag me outside one night. I started screaming and he got fired."

"Hastings?" asked Kat. As far as she knew, Vernon had never worked there, but it seemed there was quite a bit she didn't know.

"In Waltham. We make heat sinks," said Delanna.

"*Made* heat sinks in your case, you frigid bitch," Vernon said with a mocking laugh. "Should have just done it, you wouldn't be here. You're still going to give me one…maybe more."

"So this is a grudge-fest?" asked Shep. "Punish those who hurt your little pussy feelings?" His reckless defiance concerned Kat.

"Exactly. They might be little pussy feelings, but who has the upper hand now?" asked Vernon. "Not a thing even a piece of shit Texas lawyer like you can do."

"What the fuck did I do, man?" asked Miguel.

"Sorry, guy, wrong place at the right time. I needed six players and you were convenient. Sucks to be you."

Players? Kat wondered. *This is all a game to him.* Who was this stranger? He was insane…evil. How had she planned a life with him? How had she slept with him, been intimate, and gotten pregnant by him and not seen this?

"I'm pregnant…with *your* baby!" Kat said.

He glanced at her abdomen and released a single, quick snort. "Number four," the man who looked like Vernon demanded.

"Are you fucking serious?" asked Gwen.

"Yeah, I'm fucking serious," mocked Vernon. "Number four. NOW!"

"I want to trade," Gwen said quickly, her scared eyes wide. "You said we could trade."

Vernon stared at her acidly. "Fine. With whom? How about Delanna's capsules? I'd love to watch you take one."

"Fuck your capsules," said Delanna. She flicked the bottle with the back of her hand, sending it spinning and scattering its contents across the table.

Rage contorted Vernon's face. He reached into his right pocket but stopped and forced composure. He smiled at his former coworker, and Kat could see it took every iota of his strength.

Disregarding Delanna, Vernon instructed Gwen to slide the

box cutter to Shep, which she did. He then told Shep to slide the hacksaw to Gwen. Staring blankly at Vernon, Shep gave the hacksaw a quick push and it sailed over the edge of the table. With barely bridled reserve, Vernon bent to retrieve it, his eyes locked on Shep's. Kat's eyes moved to the cutter.

"Watch yourself," Vernon said.

Kat wasn't sure if the warning was for her, Shep, or Gwen, but decided she'd rather not have any more of his attention than necessary. Vernon placed the hacksaw in front of Gwen and held her gaze. Kat saw the dare in his eyes, but they shifted warily and she thought, *He's scared, but he has to go through with this. He can't leave any of us alive, and he knows we're desperate.*

"Number four!" he demanded.

Staring blankly ahead, Kat set the paper face up on the table.

"Pick!" Vernon immediately responded, discharging the word like a bullet.

"The white box," said Kat.

Leaning close to Delanna, Vernon reached for the gift and slid it in Kat's direction. It fell over the lip of the table and dropped solidly into her lap. It was heavier than she had expected.

"Open it," he said impassively.

From inside she withdrew a wooden cigar box, the name *COHIBA* printed in thick black letters on the lid. A small metal latch held the box closed and Kat preferred it that way.

"Go on. Open it," Vernon said.

Kat considered throwing it at him but she'd never had good aim and it would only piss him off further. She slowly lifted the latch, opened the cover, and gawked at the box's contents. She quickly placed it on the table.

"That's a Ruger SR9c, but of course *you* wouldn't know that. It's also ironic *you* picked it, since you're too goddamned prissy to use it. For what it's worth, it's fully loaded, but I'm not concerned. How many times have you told me you'd never take a life, even to save your own? I guess we'll find out now just how honorable you really are."

She was confident he'd never give any of them a loaded handgun unless he was suicidal. He couldn't have known she'd be the one to pick that gift. But he'd already surprised her on a few accounts, so she couldn't really know. The bitch of it was that he was right. No matter her own shock and horror, she wouldn't kill. Couldn't kill.

"You're lying," she said.

"The clip holds seventeen rounds, check it out. Give it a try."

"Do it! What do you have to lose," hissed Miguel. "Shoot the motherfucker, man."

Kat couldn't. She didn't have it in her, but she could trade with someone who did. Maybe if... she again glanced at the box cutter.

"I want to swap with Shep," she said, and prepared to slide the box.

"Hold it!" Vernon said. Kat stopped and Vernon grinned. "Cowboy, slide the box cutter to Kat."

Kat's bleakness increased. She had planned to slide the gun over the edge of the table and divert Vernon's attention so Shep could use the box cutter on him, but Vernon was too attuned.

I'm so stupid! Kat thought. *Now I have a blade I'm afraid to use and Shep gets a likely useless gun.*

"Slide the box to Cowboy. Gently."

Kat did.

When Shep reached for the box, Vernon aimed the Ruger at him. "I'm watching your every move," he said. Shep slowly settled back, the chains rattling against his chair.

The gun might actually be loaded, Kat thought. Vernon's reaction seemed authentic. Vernon rounded the table and stood behind Buttercup's corpse, to Miguel's left. His eyes stayed trained on Shep.

"Two presents left, thanks to your neighbor here," he said to Miguel. He patted Buttercup atop her head.

Kat looked at the presents and then saw Gwen to her right. She sat with her head slightly lowered, breathing rapidly as if she had sprinted up a series of stairways. Kat wondered if it was a form of meditation to alleviate the discomfort from having to piss, but Gwen looked up, displaying the terror in her eyes.

"Oh God!" Gwen gasped and then snorted, desperate for breath. She tried to rise but the chains caught. She dropped back into the seat and started convulsing.

Is she epileptic? Kat wondered. A milky froth coated Gwen's lips and Kat understood what she had done. "No! Help her! She took the pills!"

All heads turned toward the struggling woman and pleading voices rose. Kat's attempt to rise also succumbed to the limits of the restraints.

Vernon walked slowly toward Gwen, watching her with profound interest. He squatted near her and studied her horrified eyes as she searched the room, her now shallow breaths creaking in and out of her.

"Not as quick and painless as you were hoping, is it?"

"Help her!" Kat said.

"Come on!" said Miguel.

Silent, Delanna watched Gwen, her eyes wide with shock.

"Nothing I could do if I wanted to," Vernon said, his eyes still searching Gwen's as if looking for some cryptic truth. Finally, gratefully, she fell unconscious.

To Kat's right, Shep snagged the box from the table. Vernon sprawled to the floor and scrabbled behind Gwen as Shep wrestled the gun free of the box and clicked off the safety.

"Stupid move, Cowboy!" Vernon said.

Shep aimed for Vernon's voice and the reemerging arc of his head as it maneuvered to either of Gwen's shoulders, popping up for a fraction of a second, and then disappearing.

"He's got his gun out, bro!" warned Miguel. The words no sooner left his mouth than a shot snapped, and a red star blossomed on Miguel's left cheek. He jolted upright in his chair, as if posing for a portrait, and then slowly slumped forward.

"You fuck!" screamed Shep, steadying the Ruger with both hands.

Vernon feinted to the right and then lunged left, putting Kat between them. Shep tried to draw a bead on him, but Vernon repeatedly bobbed from left to right over Kat's shoulders.

"Shoot him!" Kat, feeling certain she'd be the next to die, surprised herself by slapping hard at Vernon's gun hand. The little gun cracked a shot off before careening across the room and settling beneath the Christmas tree.

Taken off guard, his expression unreadable, Vernon stood with his hands slightly raised. Shep held the Ruger steady, aimed at Vernon's head, and pulled the trigger, but no shot rang out. Instead, Shep yelped in pain, threw the pistol to the ground, and brought his hand to his mouth.

A smile spread across Vernon's demented face. He walked toward Shep and stooped to pick up the gun. Holding it with the handgrip toward the ceiling, he pressed the trigger and a silver needle protruded from the handle directly behind the trigger.

"I'm proud of this one…it's an old trick, making the trigger a syringe, but I machined it myself." He patted Shep on the shoulder, though keeping safely behind him. "You're in store for an ugly, painful death, Cowboy, which kind of pleases me after the screwing you gave me. Ever hear of an eastern brown snake? Australia has the best critters. The venom is available on the black market, if you're willing to cough up the cash. I was willing, so you'll be dead within the hour." He set the Ruger on the table.

Gwen's body released a shuddering paroxysm and Kat hoped it was her last, for Gwen's sake.

"Three dead. Soon to be four. Two to go," Vernon said.

"They'll find you," Delanna said. "They'll make the connections."

"No, they won't."

His smug confidence disgusted Kat. She couldn't believe she had once found it appealing. She recognized the certainty of her death, but she couldn't accept the unfairness that her child would be cheated of a life. When she had announced her pregnancy three months earlier, Vernon had seemed so pleased and comforting.

Beside her, Shep jerked in his seat. A fine sheen of sweat had formed on his brow.

"Won't you help him?" Kat asked.

"Nope."

"And you're willing to let your baby die?"

Vernon gave a scoffing laugh. "That's the reason you're here…well, it was the final straw. I don't want no fucking kid, and I know you wouldn't let me walk away, like I wanted to. You'd demand money and other shit and make my life miserable, like the rest of these pricks have."

"Who are you?" Delanna said, the thought contorting her face. "You evil bastard. I hope you burn in Hell forever."

Vernon snorted. "Maybe if I believed in Hell."

"So you feel nothing," said Kat.

"Nada." He gave a sarcastic *sorry* shrug.

"And for me?" Kat asked.

"Especially not for you," Vernon said.

"Prove it," said Kat. "Kiss me."

"What?" asked Delanna, unbelieving.

"I can't even stand looking at you, why would I want to kiss you?" asked Vernon.

"If you really don't love me, kiss me and prove it has no effect on you. You know you still care."

Vernon searched her sad eyes and looked behind him. Gwen

was no threat. Shep sat across from them, staring blankly forward, his chest rising and falling rapidly. On the table, out of reach, were the Ruger and the box cutter.

"Fine," Vernon said, too arrogant to refuse the challenge.

Vernon pressed his lips to Kat's and she spit heavily into his mouth. She simultaneously dropped her left hand and drove her balled right fist into his throat. Even though the chains enfeebled the blow, it worked. Vernon stumbled backward, the impact of her small fist causing him to swallow both her spit and the little capsule she had popped into her mouth.

Vernon recoiled, shocked, disgusted, and clutching at his throat. He collided with Gwen, swerved around her chair, and staggered away, trying to cough. Leaning his left hand on the back of Gwen's chair, he glared at Kat who was spitting repeatedly onto the floor, praying she would be able to get rid of at least most of the residual poison.

Vernon reached to gain his balance, but Shep, rattlesnake-quick, grabbed his wrist and yanked, pulling him onto his lap. The Texan wrapped his arms tightly around Vernon, trapping him.

"Can either of you get to the blade?" Shep asked, his face contorting with the effort, his body shaking.

"Just hold him! He swallowed cyanide!" Kat said.

"No shit?" Shep asked, managing a grin despite his struggle.

"He's reaching for the stun gun!" Kat warned, noticing Vernon's fingers working at his jacket pocket.

Shep clamped his teeth into Vernon's shoulder and bit down hard. Rewarded with an agonized wail, he clenched harder and held Vernon until his breath became labored, his limbs twitched, and ultimately his body went limp. Shep let him slide to the floor.

"How in the hell did you pull that off?" he asked.

"I was counting on his ego and that he'd look to see if he could reach the box cutter, and he didn't disappoint. That's when I popped the pill." She spat on the floor again.

"I think you'll be okay. Those were capsules and the poison's inside," Delanna said.

Kat looked at the inert form of her fiancé sprawled on the floor and spit again. The betrayal, the emotions, and the utter horror of what had transpired finally grabbed hold of her and she burst into tears.

"Shep, oh my God, are you okay? Is it starting to affect you?" Kat asked, guiltily pulling herself out of her grief and back to the present.

Shep flexed his hand. "Got the nervous sweats and a little burn where the needle bit me, but feeling no worse for wear. I'm thinking Vernon got played by his black-market friends. Either that or I'm nastier than that old snake. 'Course, he said an hour, so maybe it just hasn't set in yet."

Kat pitched forward, bouncing her chair and herself toward the table in diminutive increments.

Shep watched her for a moment then asked, "Where you off to?"

"The hacksaw," Kat said. "Might not cut metal, but if it'll cut a bone, it'll cut wood. We got to get out of here and get you to a hospital."

The saw lay on the table in front of Gwen's slumped form, but at the rate Kat was moving, it would remain there a while longer.

Shep took up after Kat's lead, bouncing forward in small hops toward the table.

"Don't! You'll speed up your circulation!" Delanna warned him and started bouncing toward the table, too, but Shep was quickly within reach of the box cutter and Ruger. Delanna and Kat both stopped bouncing.

"I'm going to try to knock the saw closer to you, Kat," Shep said. He took aim and slid the box cutter across the table. It careened off the side of the hacksaw, only managing to nudge it closer to Gwen. Delanna rolled her eyes, and despite the nightmare they had endured, Shep laughed aloud.

"Well, that wasn't worth its weight in shit," he said. "Hang on."

"You're the one who needs hanging on," Delanna said.

"I'm good," Shep said. He repeated the process with the gun, which again missed the mark. "Fuck!" he shouted as the Ruger shot across the table, knocking the hacksaw even farther to the left.

The gun plunged over the edge of the table, but Kat hooked the trigger guard with the tip of her ring finger in an impressive display of athleticism. She was saved from tumbling to the floor by the arm restraints, but not without a substantial dose of discomfort to right herself. Shuffling a bit closer to the table, she set the gun flat, aligned her sights, and pushed. The gun hit the intended target squarely and the hacksaw ricocheted perfectly into Shep's waiting hands.

"Show-off," said Shep.

The saw was indeed dull. By the time Shep made the four cuts necessary to free him from the multiple binding points on the chair, his arms and hands shook and throbbed, and a clammy sweat covered his brow. He sat back to rest a moment.

"Still feeling alright?" Kat asked.

"Yeah." He flexed his hand again. It felt weak and was still vibrating, but he attributed that to the sawing. "Maybe Vernon's venom was a dud, after all."

"Clearly, after exerting like that," Delanna said. "You're a lucky guy."

Shep rose, flipped his chair, and freed the chain. Fighting a bout of vertigo from rising too fast, he gathered the restraint over his shoulder and asked, "Who's next?"

"Forget that! See if you can find a phone," Kat said. "Call the police."

"Maybe there's a better saw around here somewhere, too," said Delanna.

Shep looked at them and huffed. "Smart ladies," he said.

He headed for the kitchen; if there was a phone, it would be in there, he figured. Legs numbed from sitting too long, he stumbled through the doorway and scanned the room, which was cluttered in a haphazard way that was indicative of intrusion, not of residence.

A computer backpack lay open on the countertop beside an opened laptop. To the left, near the door, a landline phone was mounted to the wall, and to the right, two open clamshell containers, one of them still half-full of Chinese takeout food, an empty bottle of Corona, and a mostly full bottle of Diet Coke. Shep found this especially disconcerting.

Dinner for two.

He stood silently still and listened for evidence of another soul, then decided the best action was to get help as quickly as possible. As he reached for the phone, a sudden dizziness washed over him. He staggered to the counter, knocking the laptop's mouse to the floor and awakening the computer display to a disturbing split-screen image of the dining room from either end, one facing Kat, the other facing Delanna. The cameras were black and white, which gave everything an ethereal, indistinct hue. The women's eyes shone silver and Shep was taken by their vulnerability, chained to the chairs as they were.

With a shaking hand, Shep lifted the handset, which slipped through his numbed fingers and fell to the countertop. His left leg defied him next, folding beneath him and dropping him to his knees in front of the laptop. The strength in his legs had diminished with unsettling speed, but it wasn't his legs that stopped his effort to rise.

On the small computer screen, Shep watched as a

monochromic Delanna stood before Kat. Short lengths of untethered chain dangled from both of Delanna's manacles, dragging across the tabletop as she picked up the box cutter.

Shep corralled the phone handset closer to him and jabbed the break button. Once he heard the dial tone, he managed to depress 9-1-1 with barely responsive fingers.

Ringing...

On the screen, Delanna moved toward Kat. Shep's chin hit the counter, and as he fell to the floor, awkwardly clutching the phone to his ear, Kat's screams emanated from the dining room. He heard a voice that sounded miles away.

"911, what's your emergency?"

John McIlveen

TEACHER'S PET

In Noel's experience, few things compared with the first day of school, but root canals, third-degree burns, and amputation could be on the list. School held nothing redeemable for him; nothing to look forward to, for what was enjoyable about busting your hump to keep your head above water? He managed to maintain passing grades, but the phrase *skin of your teeth* was generous in his case. His parents accused him of being lazy and an underachiever. He figured, what was the sense in trying when even his best efforts were met with criticism?

"A ninety? Why, heck son, that's still ten away from a hundred! When I was a junior, a ninety would have been unacceptable because I was class president, captain of the debate team, and star quarterback on the football team..."

...and I could juggle six double-bladed chainsaws while running full throttle and carrying three unconscious mountain climbers to safety from the stormy summit of Everest, Noel amended bitterly.

In truth, his parents were average folk who cared for him deeply and wished him to achieve greatness. Truth was...Noel *was* lazy and an underachiever, but he knew that would all change once he escaped this crappy, mundane town. He thought if the world were to end right then, he would have wasted nearly his whole life in school.

His classmate Kyle Grainger was a bit of a waste, but he had the right idea. He'd hit the road earlier that summer and never looked back. Noel dreamed about doing the same.

He scanned his mindless classmates from his remote throne at the far back of the classroom. He had nothing in common with them and probably never would. Their juvenile ways irritated him, with their odd lingo and embellished gestures; it was all like some bizarre mating ritual that lowered the IQ. Sure, some of the girls were hot, with their overly made-up faces, artery-choking jeans, and skimpy tops that accentuated and manipulated their assets to the fullest effect... *making mountains out of molehills*. Besides, it was easier to hate them than to obsess over the reality that such girls wanted nothing to do with him.

At the far wall, Ben Molina jokingly slapped a girl's ass. The girl smiled prettily and fluttered cable-thick eyelashes, cranking up her feminine appeal. He could almost hear her pheromones kick into overdrive. If Noel ever tried anything *that* nervy, he'd be slapped right back. Hell, he'd be arrested.

"Morons," he mumbled.

"Who?" asked a girl seated beside him.

He recognized her from previous years but didn't know her name. She was on the pretty side of plain, but wore simple clothing and used no makeup. *Trowel on some Mary Kay, squeeze her into skinny jeans two sizes too small, and she'd go from not-so-hot to hot-to-trot,* thought Noel.

"Everyone. You're all morons," Noel sneered.

She searched his face for a moment, rose, and moved to another desk.

Good, he thought, tilting back in his seat. He was bored senseless. He wanted to be somewhere exciting, doing exhilarating things. He wanted adventure—anything besides whiling away another year in this abhorrent classroom, humiliated and hated...hating himself.

And then...school got interesting.

Everyone in the classroom went silent as she walked through the doorway, girls and boys alike. Even *Molina the Weena* stopped to watch her glide confidently past the teacher's desk to the whiteboard. With tantalizingly long and delicate fingers, she lifted a marker from the tray and wrote *Ms. Dewer*.

Oh, the implication of that name will be problematic, Noel thought. Sure enough, a few titters arose from the classroom. He wondered if her first name might be Ivana. Unperturbed, Ms. Dewer faced her new students.

"Good morning, Homeroom 544. You may have noticed the new name on your schedules. I am she, and I might be your history or social studies teacher, as well. Before moving here in June, I taught for four years at Gray-New Gloucester High School in Gray, Maine. Gray's sister town, New Gloucester, has only one claim to fame, the Sabbathday Lake Shaker Village, which is the last active Shaker village in the United States. Both Gray and New Gloucester combined have about half the population of Taylors Falls, New Hampshire."

"Nowhereville," someone said. Noel agreed.

"Has anybody here been to Fryeburg, Maine?" Ms. Dewer pleasantly asked. When no one replied, she said, "I was born in Fryeburg, where there are more people than teeth. Now *that* is Nowhereville." She smiled, flashing her perfect set of bright whites. Noel couldn't look away.

Her age was difficult to assess. She could be anywhere from twenty-five, to a youthful thirty-five. She had friendly, yet dark, penetrating eyes that demanded his undivided attention…as did the rest of her. She was an oddity, classy and exotic, unlike any teacher he'd seen outside of the idealistic realm of movies and television, and completely unlike any of those at Nottingham High. Thick black hair tumbled down her back in turbulent waves, contrasting nicely with her navy-blue dress, which was tasteful, fashionable, and subtly stimulating. The way the fabric sensually draped the smooth curve of her hips, accentuating her figure, was hypnotic; it beckoned notice but didn't scream for it. She looked Hispanic, could probably pass for Selena Gomez's big sister, but the name *Ms. Dewer* implied different.

Abrupt laughter caught Noel's attention and he noticed every eye in the classroom was on him. Humiliation warmed his face as he realized Ms. Dewer was talking to him.

"What?" he asked, sounding daft instead of the cool indifference he hoped to display.

More laughter.

"Welcome back, cosmonaut, I'm sorry to interrupt your reverie, Mister…" She waited.

"Knob!" someone said.

"Uh, Noel Keating," he said, ignoring the heckler.

"See? That was practically painless," she said. "It seems I'm having a hard time holding your attention."

"Got mine," someone murmured, loud enough to be heard.

"Get a napkin!" said another.

Ms. Dewer ignored them, keeping her eyes on Noel. "Move here so you can hear me better, Mr. Keating," she said, pointing to a seat directly in front of her desk.

Noel considered refusing, but the prospect of being in close proximity to her had a definite appeal. He moved, trying to appear unbothered. He was no stranger to targeting by teachers who considered him a troublemaker. He didn't think himself one, just a nonconformist, and a nonparticipant with zero desire to be present.

"Thank you, Mr. Keating," she smiled.

Noel didn't respond, which didn't seem to bother her in the least.

She was even better-looking from his new seat and he could smell her perfume, which was captivating to the point of irresistible.

Noel lay on his bedroom floor, his head resting on a pile of discarded clothing and his feet propped on his bed. The thunderous riffs of Mastodon traumatized his eardrums through his headphones, cutting off anything outside his personal universe. He tried to disappear within the thrumming bass and machine-gunning drums, but he couldn't drown out his fixation.

He'd had crushes before—realistic ones on girls his age —but this was over the top. Like Van Halen's video "Hot for Teacher," he had an all-consuming mega-crush on Ms. Dewer.

This is insane! I'm hot for my history teacher! It made him laugh, especially when he thought of his prior history teacher, Mrs. Hurley, who resembled the love child of a Shar-Pei and a toad, somehow retaining bulgy eyes through her profusion of wrinkles. Mrs. Hurley would often joke that she was the world's best history teacher, not because of her schooling, but because she had "been there," and by gosh, you could tell.

Noel removed his headphones, closed his eyes, and his thoughts immediately returned to Ms. Dewer. It was understandable. She was amazing, worthy of magazine covers or makeup ads. He fantasized about her clad in a minuscule bikini, lying on a beach beside him and sharing drinks in some tropical paradise.

Noel rolled over, trying to return to reality. He needed a more realistic obsession, one where he had a sliver of a chance.

Maybe if I toned up. I could stand to lose a few pounds, but I'm not bad-looking, he reasoned. Noel pressed his palms against the floor and pushed. No time like the present.

One... two...

When he reached his fifth pushup, he was nauseous and his

arms were shaking.

Not bad, he thought. Two better than last time.

He dropped to the floor and slammed his fist to the carpet. "Come on! Get over it, dude!" he growled. "Get real!"

But Noel didn't "get real." He got far worse as the end of the week rolled around, but something incredible was happening, something that worsened his obsession: as improbable as it was, it seemed Ms. Dewer was flirting with him. He wasn't sure if his overactive imagination was responding to his libidinous hopes, but her subtle smiles seemed meaningful, and whenever she walked past his desk, she'd pause slightly, letting her delicate scent engulf him. She would then move on, never faltering in her lessons.

On the third day, she returned an assignment with "Good Job!" and a winking smiley face on it. It was intriguing and probably meant nothing, but what occurred Friday convinced Noel her flirtations were real.

She had handed out their first test, an involved assessment she called a feeler exam. It didn't count toward their grades, but it gave her a good indication of where her students stood in their knowledge of world history. As the class labored silently, save for a few shuffling feet and a sneeze or a mumble, Noel chanced a look at Ms. Dewer. She sat at her desk holding a few papers, not reading them but staring directly at Noel with that slight, evocative smile. He returned her gaze, but her eyes never wavered. Twice more Noel looked at Ms. Dewer, her ebony eyes pinning him to the spot. They made promises and knew his deepest secrets. If someone coughed or lifted their eyes, she would casually avert her own, and then return them to Noel once the interruption was over. It made him nervous, but excited him.

He was out of her league in so many ways; could he really be attractive to her? It seemed so unlikely. If nothing else, it was a brilliant tactic to improve his attendance and grades. He needed to know if Ms. Dewer's flirtations were legit, but to do so, he'd have to get more enterprising.

He arrived at school Monday planning to stare brazenly and flirt with Ms. Dewer as she had with him.

It didn't work.

When he'd meet her eyes, she'd ignore him, dismissively sweeping her gaze over him or looking clear through him, but at other times, he'd catch her staring in that beguiling way. She seemed to be making a game of it.

During Wednesday's history quiz, she had run her hand softly over his back as she walked past his desk. He checked to see if anyone noticed, but all eyes were focused on their desktops. He wondered if she got off on driving schoolboys mad, or maybe she just had some weird kink that made her horny during exams. He'd heard stranger stories, like the woman who cried uncontrollably whenever she touched satin, or the man who became violent when he smelled cinnamon. But this was different...it involved him.

By Thursday, Noel was perplexed and nearly feverish with frustration. During homeroom, Ben the Goon walked into class, looked at him, and shook his head as if Noel were the saddest person he'd ever met. Noel returned a challenging stare, saying nothing.

"Hey, Romeo, do you have any idea how stupid you look drooling all over yourself?" Ben asked. His classmates laughed. "You're pathetic."

"Screw you," Noel said.

"You wish! No wait...I bet you're saving yourself for Ms. Dewer," the Goon went on, provoking another round of laughter.

Noel intended on doing nothing. He'd get no backing in an

altercation, and "Mr. Popular" needed only to blow his dog whistle to have the football team there within seconds, face-planting him to the floor. As Ben walked to his desk, he smacked Noel smartly on the back of the head. Noel sprung to his feet and gave the Goon a double-handed shove to the back, sending him comically sprawling over two desks and onto the floor.

"Stop!" someone demanded from the classroom doorway.

Ben the Goon jumped to his feet, his face contorted with rage, and whipped a textbook at Noel, who deflected it with his left arm.

"I said *stop!*"

They obeyed but held their positions as Ms. Dewer walked coolly to her desk.

"Your *pet* attacked me from behind," Ben the Goon said.

Ms. Dewer held up her hand, shushing him. "I saw, but I'm sure there's more to it than meets the eye...or *my* eye. I should send you both to the office, but that would waste time and could end up in suspension, which wouldn't please your little buddies on the football team, would it, Mr. Leeds?"

She aimed a well-manicured finger at Noel. "Since I saw you doing the shoving, I expect to see you in detention after school today."

"But..."

Ms. Dewer raised an eyebrow and said, "Do you have a problem with this, Mr. Keating, or would you prefer a visit to the office?"

"No," Noel muttered.

"Bring your bib, douche," said Ben the Goon as he walked to his seat.

"Enough," said Ms. Dewer, but the look in her eyes did the shouting.

Noel stewed in aggravation for most of the day, and his mood had reached rock bottom by the time he arrived at Ms. Dewer's class after school. She stood with her back to him, her body moving rhythmically as she erased the chalkboard. Noel watched, entranced.

"Sit," she directed, showing no indication that she had seen him.

Noel took the seat closest to the door.

"Not there. Your assigned seat, please."

Noel considered walking out, but as provoked as he was, he had finally gathered the gumption to ask her what her game was. He obligingly sat in front of her desk.

Ms. Dewer—always graceful, always smooth, always in command—walked to the door and gently closed it. She glided to her desk and sat—or, more aptly—drifted into her chair. Noel's resolve was slipping, but he held on, trying to look defiant and put out. She looked at him and winked.

"Well, Mr. Frumpy Face," she said, her voice silky, her lips playfully pouted. "You know, if anything is to become of us, we need to be careful."

Noel's every thought derailed and tumbled into a tortured smoldering heap. "What are you talking about?" he demanded, utterly confounded.

"Discretion, Noel. Pull out a notepad and look busy," she instructed. He did as she asked. "Okay, I like you, and unless I'm blind, you like me, but if you want this *thing* to work, we need to be discreet."

"What thing?"

"Who knows until we try, but we won't get that chance if you make it so obvious." She looked quickly to the door and back to Noel. "I'm a teacher who likes her job and wants to keep it, so if anyone finds out about us, my career is over. If you can keep us absolutely top-secret, this could turn into something fun and adventurous."

Adventurous! The word hooked him. It's what he'd been looking for.

"I…" he mumbled.

"So, are you *up* for it?" she asked.

The insinuation was blatant enough, but he had a hard time believing it. Could this…*goddess* really want him? No woman had ever shown interest in him, not for long, at least, and especially not like *that*…which posed another problem.

"Uh, yeah. Of course I am," he said. "But I've never…"

"Oh, I'll take care of that," Ms. Dewer reassured him, her promise departing her lips like a kiss.

Noel was thrilled—yet clueless on how to proceed. "Okay, where do we go?" he asked.

"The perfect place," his teacher said. "Nowhereville."

It took a moment before it clicked. "You mean where you were born?" he asked. "That town in Maine?"

"Yes, Fryeburg. My parents own a house there, but they're in Florida until April," Ms. Dewer explained. "We could spend the day and get to know each other without any interruptions. We'd be out of sight there."

It was mind-blowing, this conversation in the classroom that, to anyone who peered in, would be just a teacher and student having a discussion.

"The most important thing is we don't raise suspicions. Keep it quiet and don't act foolish. I'm thinking I'll want this to last a while."

Dozens of questions and concerns came to mind. "How will we get there? When would we leave? When would we get back?"

She smiled and said, "My car, Saturday morning, Saturday night…late. There's a wonderful deck and it's magical under the stars. Full moon, very romantic. Do you work this Saturday?"

"No," Noel said.

"Perfect! You live on Belknap Road, right?" she asked.

"Yes," Noel said, surprised and flattered she knew his address.

"Good, nine o'clock Saturday morning. Be walking on Ferry

Street toward Dairy Queen. I'll drive by. If it's safe, I'll pull over and you get in… quickly." She looked at the wall clock and again at the door. "If it isn't, I'll loop around until it is, all right?"

Noel nodded.

"Do us a favor. Pack some snacks and drinks, it's a two-and-a-half-hour drive," she said.

Noel nodded and she flashed her wonderful smile.

"Good, and remember, discretion is everything. Oh, and a little something to think about until Saturday…a vocabulary lesson of sorts. The word *pet* is both a noun and a verb." She gave him a teasing wink. "Detention is over."

Numb, Noel stood and left the room without looking back.

Noel lumbered along Ferry Street, eyes to the ground, trying to look inconspicuous. His backpack rode low, heavy with a variety of snacks. His normal snack preferences leaned toward Doritos, Starburst, and Mountain Dew, but hoping to appear more sophisticated, he brought a block of good cheese, gourmet crackers, apples, Lindt chocolate balls, two bottles of Coca-Cola, and two bottles of iced tea. He had showered, shaved, and splashed on his father's Drakkar Noir cologne. His hair was still wet and the cool morning breeze made it uncomfortable.

By quarter past nine, he was sure Ms. Dewer was playing him. He imagined her, the Goon, and rows of laughing and jeering faces, mocking the pathetic, love-struck boy. There would be no returning to school, he'd be the laughingstock! His only choice would be taking the Kyle Grainger route and hitting the highway in search of greener pastures. Maybe Los Angeles or somewhere warm like Tampa Bay. He'd start at the bottom, flipping burgers or cleaning toilets, since he'd never exceled at anything, or even tried. He'd live on the streets until he settled, but there had to be places he could hole up.

A car approached from behind but he didn't look, fearful it might be the police or some turd-cake intent on harassing him. If so, he wished he had a baseball-sized stone to hand so he could sail it through their windshield.

A gray Honda Accord pulled beside him. Ms. Dewer pushed open the passenger-side door. "Hey, lonesome traveler, going my way?"

Noel tossed the backpack on the back seat and practically fell into the car, his legs weak from nerves, and the acknowledgement that it was really happening. Mrs. Dewer had actually showed up.

She looked phenomenal in red casual jeans and a low-cut black top that validated the endowed figure Noel had fantasized about. She kissed him quickly on the cheek and accelerated onto Ferry Street. Where her lips brushed him burned with the reality of her touch and he buzzed in anticipation for what the day might bring.

This was too good to be true, he thought, and as they drove toward their promising day, he understood it was also probably too good to last. At some point, Ms. Dewer—or Isobel, as she insisted he call her—would tire of this and be through with him, but he decided he wouldn't let that happen. She had her job and her reputation, both of which he would soon have the power to destroy. This would provide him with enough blackmailing muscle to hold her captive; he could make her his veritable sex slave. If she protested, he would go public—and he was okay with that. In most cases of *hot teacher seduces student*, society vilified the teacher and labeled the student a victim, regardless of whether they were willing participants or not.

Who wouldn't be willing, with a knockout like Isobel Dewer? Noel wondered. Who wouldn't billboard that he was with her? It would be a badge of honor that even Ben "The Goon" Molina couldn't downplay.

They drove through Windham, New Hampshire, took I-93 to I-495 to I-95, which they seemed to stay on forever. About ninety minutes later, Isobel exited the highway and then drove farther. Each turn led to narrower roads, finally turning onto what, despite being little more than a dirt path, had a street sign. Blue Goose Drive led to a picturesque log home perched upon a knoll that overlooked a pond. It was nicely kept, with freshly painted trim, well-tended flowers, and a large, uncluttered farmer's porch.

They climbed from the car and Isobel looked at Noel over the roof. "Hey, boyfriend. Are you ready for an adventure?"

Noel smiled, feeling nervous, yet oddly confident. Isobel tapped a code on a keyless lock and led them into the house, which was *very* country. The house smelled fresh, the kitchen appliances looked new, and the counters were empty and spotless. Copper pots and pans and assorted utensils hung from overhead hooks secured into thick beams.

"You come here often?" Noel asked. He wondered if she brought others here, like Ben the Goon…a disturbing thought.

"Often enough, it's my childhood home. I'm very attached to it."

She took his jacket and hung it with hers on a coat rack mounted to the wall, across from which was an open doorway leading to the basement; it appeared nicely finished.

"Before we get to fun and games, how about if I make my signature turkey and Swiss panini? I'm famished."

"Sure," Noel said, a little disappointed, but considering his inexperience with all things female, he figured he'd best let Isobel lead.

"Do you prefer beer or wine?" she asked, pulling a panini press from within a cabinet.

Another thing in which Noel was inexperienced; wine was

more refined, but beer was what most guys seemed to prefer. He chose beer.

"Great! I'll have one, too." She opened the refrigerator and searched the shelves. "Huh, we're out up here. Be a dear and grab some from the media room refrigerator at the foot of the basement stairs. I'll have Sam Adams and you take whatever you like. We have about a dozen choices," she said.

The basement was the ultimate man cave, with a wet bar, couches, a pool table, and a sixty-inch widescreen.

Nice! Noel thought. He opened the fridge door and perused the shelves for his quarry, but it was empty, the shelves were warm, and the interior light hadn't lit. "Is there another fridge?" he called up the stairs, but the slam of the door silenced him and then he was thrust into total darkness.

Noel had no sense of time or place. He'd surely been there for hours, but he had no idea if it was three, five, or ten hours. When the door had slammed and the lights had gone out, his first thought was that Isobel had an odd sense of humor. He carefully worked his way up the stairs, feeling for a light switch, but found only a blank cover plate. Someone had removed the switch. The door was locked, as he had feared, and unusually solid for a basement door; his fists made little sound as he pummeled it.

He was in utter darkness, which convinced him this predicament was intentional... planned. There should be *some* light, the laser outline of sunlight around a curtain or shade, from the gap beneath the door at the head of the stairs, or from some kind of electronic device. There was nothing. His mind went in numerous directions, but when the true ramifications of the situation hit home, panic sank steely talons into him.

He hollered his way through a series of emotions, from a

light-hearted *okay, that was funny, now let me out,* to an angry, *let me out, now,* to terrified pleading, and finally tears. He had settled on the top step, his throat raw and his fists sore and bleeding, before he calmed enough to seek other routes of escape.

He blindly felt his way down the stairs and around the perimeter of the room until he found a doorway near the bar. He turned the knob and was surprised to find it unlocked. The door, like the one at the head of the staircase, was disconcertingly heavy, but it opened easily, allowing him entrance to another space as dark as the first, but dank and much cooler. He shuffled his way around the room, feeling for a light switch, windows, or anything he could use as a weapon, but it was empty, save for a pile of discarded rags against one wall. He found the outline of another door, which was steel and had no handle.

Anxious to leave the cold emptiness of the second room, he returned to the first. A complete search turned up nothing: no bottles or glasses on the bar, no balls or cues on the pool table, and not a single pen to stab with or a damned book to throw.

Distraught, Noel sat atop the pool table, waiting and praying he was the target of some elaborate prank. He would embrace the laughter and mockery if Ben the Goon and the rest of the class appeared.

Nothing occurred for hours, until he heard a loud *clack* and scraping from the other room. Noel tensed, frightened, yet willing Isobel to appear. He knew he could take her, and he'd revel in the chance to sock her a good one. The door near the bar opened and Noel leapt to his feet, backing away until he was up against the wall. Nothing moved within the room, but he heard the sound of something breathing, waiting.

...and then the lights flared on.

Noel raised an arm to block the light, squinting and blinking against the sudden glare, helpless if anything were to attack.

An outline appeared and resolved into the form of a man—an ordinary man, thirtyish, of average height and build, with commonly handsome features. He was leaning on the bar top. He waved cheerily to Noel.

"What do you want? Who are you?" asked Noel.

"Hi, lover boy. I'd like you to meet my husband, James."

Noel spun toward Isobel, who sat on the stairway, six steps from the basement floor. He hadn't heard her open the door or come down.

"Your husband?" He looked back at the man, who waved again and offered a friendly smile, similar to Isobel's. "I didn't know you...you didn't...." Noel sputtered.

"No harm, mate, I'm cool with it," said James Dewer in a British accent as thick as stew. He took a step in Noel's direction, which, despite his amiable demeanor, frightened the heck out of Noel.

"I think I should go," Noel said, edging away.

"Oh, you aren't going anywhere. We have plans for you," said Isobel.

That damned smile.

"Plans?" asked Noel.

"We 'aven't even eaten, yet," said James.

"I'm not really hungry. Just let me go, okay? I won't say a word to anyone."

"I don't think so," Isobel said.

Noel prepared to spring toward Isobel, but James Dewer, sensing his intention, had him in an armlock within seconds. Noel had never seen anyone move so quickly and *damn,* he was strong.

"Why are you doing this?" Noel asked, struggling fruitlessly to get free.

"You were easy," said Isobel. "So unbelievably easy."

"People know I'm here. My parents... my friends. I told them I was going to Fryeburg, Maine."

"No you didn't. Besides, you have no friends, Noel, that's one of the reasons I chose you," said Isobel. "And, well…I told you a little white lie. We're in Turner, Maine, fifty miles from Fryeburg, which, of course, *you* wouldn't know. All anyone back in Taylors Falls might know is that you were seen walking along Ferry Street carrying a backpack. Gee, it appears you ran away from home, Noel, unhappy boy like you. It makes sense."

Isobel strode to the outer wall of the room and slid what looked like a letter opener into a small slot. A spring activated and a small seam appeared. She slid back a panel, exposing a window. She repeated the process on another window and pulled a thin remote from her pocket. With a jab of her thumb, the lights in the room went dark, although the room remained lit by silvery spears of moonlight through the windows.

Noel thrashed wildly, but James Dewer's grip tightened and his breathing became a guttural growl. The man's arms thickened as he squeezed Noel's chest. The boy gasped in pain as his ribs compressed. He twisted, frantically trying to face his captor to reach for his eyes, but when he saw James Dewer's face, all strength left him. The man's mouth, now a gnarled maw, twisted and elongated. Long protuberances sprouted from within, curving into feral, ivory spikes. Hair sprouted from his crevices and pores, turning the ghastly sight beastly.

"Almost dinnertime," said Isobel. "The full moon makes my man hungry. The disadvantage of living in a small town is that everybody knows everybody's business. Too many missing sheep, cattle, or people, becomes painfully obvious. With small-town mentality and mass hysteria, hell, one person cries werewolf and next thing you know there's a lynch mob. I've had to find alternate means to feed my man when he gets hungry. Fortunately, full moons only happen about once a month." She smiled her too-pretty smile at Noel and winked. "I'll leave you men alone to get acquainted."

Hot breath moistened the back of Noel's neck as the beast

lifted him into the air.

"Oh, honey. Hold it a moment," Isobel said, pausing on the stairway.

The creature halted, long ropes of drool spilling from its maw. It snarled its hunger but held Noel suspended against the ceiling.

"Sorry, Noel, but there's only *one* teacher's pet for me." Isobel disappeared up the stairway, her exit finalized by the solid clack of the door closing. The now-moonlit room offered Noel a view of the creature, transformation complete. It resembled no creature he had ever seen.

It slammed Noel's body to the tiled floor, driving the wind from him and snapping a bone in his forearm. It dragged him into the back room and slammed the door. The pain was brutal and blinding as Noel's fractured arm flopped to and fro. Huge and terrifying, it leapt onto the schoolboy's back and embedded long, brutal tusks into his neck, severing Noel's spinal cord from his brain stem. All feeling fled from his extremities, and as the creature feasted, Noel opened his eyes one final time and saw the pile of clothing he had come across earlier in the darkness. Within the pile lay a maroon-and-gold jacket, the team colors of Nottingham High School. On the torn and blood-streaked sleeve was the name *Kyle,* embroidered in a fine white turned grey.

Kyle Grainger.

John McIlveen

FROM A PURR TO A ROAR

DAY 1

"Hey, dickhead, wake up!"

Greg heard the voice, demanding and condescending, but not loud enough to break through his hypnopompic bubble. He continued drifting in his semi-sleep oblivion until two rapid swats to his face carried him over to wakefulness. He opened his eyes, blinking rapidly as his vision wavered in and out of focus. He sensed something close to his face, but too near to identify in the shadowy room. He withdrew from the blurred entity until the image sharpened and a shape formed into the owl-eyed countenance of his cat, who was staring at him petulantly.

Kotik was a large Russian Blue, a bulky combination of solid and soft that pushed the twenty-pound mark, wrapped in a shorthair coat the blue-gray hue of a stormy sky. His broad, complacent face normally had an etched-on expression that said the world was his oyster, except for those nights when he took up sentry duty inches from Greg's face. It was a little disconcerting, awakening to staring eyes, but it seemed to be part of the intrinsic nature of cats, and in Kotik's case, a routine part, so Greg had learned to dismiss it.

He started drifting back to sleep, but two more swift whacks brought him back.

"Come on, man. I have to take a shit!" said Kotik.

Greg's eyes sprung open.

Did the cat just talk?

Kotik continued staring at him with a look that could be interpreted as anything from *I want to cuddle* to *your liver would be delectable.* He sat with one paw slightly raised, ready to dole out another serving of feline indignation.

"I'm not shitting, guy...well, actually, I will be soon if you don't open the fucking bathroom door."

Greg didn't move, but his mind was suddenly alive as his thoughts shot off in a thousand different directions. *No freaking way,* was his only distinct one.

"Okay, I warned you," said Kotik. He got to his feet and arched his back in the universal posture of impending defecation. "Okay, I'm in crap-stance! You got about five seconds before I drop a dookie, and with that third-rate gutter sludge you've been feeding me, I can't promise to do you a solid, if you know what I mean."

"No!" Greg cried. He quickly shimmied out of bed, stumbled to the bathroom door, and swung it open.

The cat leaped serenely to the floor and coasted past Greg, shooting him a glance that looked genuinely smug. "A little psyche goes a long way, especially with the simple-minded," he said.

Greg watched him saunter into the bathroom, where his litterbox was located.

My fucking cat's talking to me! he thought, trying to wrap his head around it, and then came the realization, *My cat's an asshole.*

Was it the knock on the head? he wondered, rubbing the spot where a 4" x 8" x 12' chunk of lumber had hit him while at work. Someone had left a stray timber atop the stacked skid when he had moved it from one rack to another. He had lucked out for the most part. Fortunately, the fork truck's cab cover had deflected the falling lumber so that it wasn't a direct hit, but it had careened off another skid and connected with him solidly enough to give him an egg-sized knot that was still tender to the touch three days later.

This was the only thing that made sense to him: a good shot to the head, three days for the brain trauma to fester, and now his cat was talking to him. He wondered if a crack to the pumpkin could turn someone psychotic. Maybe he should have gone to the hospital after all, but as was so often his way, not wanting to be a nuisance, he played it down.

He walked to the bathroom and peered inside. Kotik was standing inside the cat box, sifting a paw through the kitty litter as if searching for gold nuggets. He stopped and stared expectantly at Greg.

"Are you going to stand there and watch me dump? You got some weird kinks? How about some privacy?"

"Oh, sorry!" said Greg. He ducked back into the bedroom. "But you watch me all the time," he said defensively, feeling chastised.

"That's different, cats are curious by nature," Kotik said, grunting. "Oh, man, this isn't going to be pretty, better break out the Febreze. I'd do it, but you know… no opposable thumbs."

Greg coughed and moved farther away from the doorway.

"Hey, I warned you. It's your fault, amigo. I'm not asking for filet mignon, but fucking generic? Really? I mean, this has been weighing on me. This relationship feels one-way, bro. And you know I would deliver fresh game to your doorstep at least twice a week if you let me out, so how about a little fairness here, Judy?"

"Judy?"

"Judge Judy! Who do you think?"

"How do you know about Judge Judy?" Greg asked.

I can't believe I'm talking to my cat!

"You've got that boob tube going most of the time. You think I just lay around sleeping all day?"

"Don't you?"

"Fuck no! I pay attention and I have acute hearing."

"I thought it was dogs that had acute hearing."

"Dogs suck."

Greg heard scratching and the hiss of kitty litter hitting the bathroom floor.

"Could you try to keep the litter in the box?" he complained.

"Really? You're the douche-nozzle who decided I was an *indoor* cat."

Kotik emerged from the bathroom, sat on the runner in the bedroom and proceeded to lick his forepaw. Greg grimaced with revulsion.

"Hey, I don't exactly like it either, but my only other cleaning options are my water bowl or your toilet. By the way, you'd do well to learn how to use a toilet brush. You may think those swirls you leave behind are art, but they're freaking revolting."

"Why isn't your mouth moving?" Greg asked.

"What? Why would my mouth be moving?"

"When you talk to me...your mouth doesn't move."

"Of course my mouth doesn't move, you dumbass. Cats can't talk."

"But I can hear you."

"So? I can hear you when yours doesn't move."

Was this an elaborate joke? he wondered, scanning the room for hidden cameras or speakers. Battling a sudden sense of paranoia, Greg followed his cat as he strolled lazily out of the bedroom, down the hallway, and into the kitchen.

Isn't paranoia a symptom of schizophrenia?

"Are you, uh, saying you can read my thoughts?"

"Sure. Think of something," Kotik said, rubbing his head repeatedly against a chair leg.

Screw you, Greg thought.

"Nice!" Kotik replied. "Screw you, too, ass maggot."

"We can read each other's minds?" Greg said in wonderment. "This is fucked up."

"Why is it fucked up?" asked Kotik.

Greg hesitated, weighing what his cat had just told him. "This isn't new to you?"

"No."

"You've always been able to read my thoughts?"

"Well, yeah, speaking of fucked up. Haven't you?" Kotik asked, sounding incredulous.

"No. Not until today."

"Well, that certainly explains a lot," said the cat.

"Kotik!" Greg suddenly blurted.

"What?" the cat replied, watching his master search the room for evidence of a pranking.

Would Cheryl prank me? Greg wondered of his girlfriend.

"Most assuredly," said Kotik.

"But she has no sense of humor," Greg said.

"Pranks aren't always humor-driven. Some are hate-driven and she's a complete bitch, so I wouldn't put it past her."

"She's not a bitch!"

"The hell she ain't! And she's a cat hater, too."

"No, she isn't," Greg protested, nearly whining.

"Yes, she is, and you're either in denial, or just stupid," said Kotik. "I can read her mind, numb-nuts. She hates me and she isn't very fond of you, either."

"Oh yeah? Then why is she with me?"

"I've wondered the same thing. What do you see in each other? Both of you are about as sharp as pudding and she has the personality of paste. Plus, she's ugly."

"No she's not, she's gorgeous and built! Have you noticed her rack?"

"Dude, I'm a fucking cat. We have no more interest in *racks* than you have in…well, authenticity and intellect, obviously," said Kotik. "By the way, there are no cameras, microphones, speakers, or little magic genies hiding around the room. I would have seen her installing them. Though, maybe *you* should invest in a camera."

"Me? Why? What are you implying?"

"I'm implying nothing. I'm saying. She comes here when you're not around, Bozo."

"She does?" Greg asked, taken aback.

"Yeah. You're an idiot for giving her a key. You've been together, what, three months? Why don't you add her to your bank account, and while you're at it make her beneficiary to your life insurance and 401(k)."

In hindsight, it probably had been a little impulsive, giving her a key so soon in the relationship, but Greg couldn't figure out why she'd come here when he was at work.

"Maybe it's your inheritance," said Kotik.

"How would she know about that?"

"Don't know, but your mother goes tits up six months ago, leaves you a sweet parting gift, and Maleficent shows up shortly afterward. Do the math."

"That's rather harsh. Are all cats like you?"

"Yeah, sensitivity isn't exactly our forte."

Greg stared at Kotik, contemplating what he had just been told.

"Stop staring at me, it's B-movie creepy," said the cat, backing beneath the table. "Don't you have to get up for work soon? Shouldn't you get some sleep? Just think… maybe you'll wake up and find out this was all a dream."

It was an appealing concept since he was feeling confused and very surreal. "Yeah," Greg said. He turned for his bedroom, but he had a feeling sleep wouldn't come easily.

"Prick," Kotik murmured as Greg closed the bedroom door.

The alarm went off at 6:30 a.m. Greg had somehow managed to get back to sleep—if he'd ever been awake—but he awoke feeling hazy and sleep deprived, and the night's events all seemed obscured and miles away.

His mind was still on Kotik as he showered and dressed, though he resisted looking for the cat. Denial made it easier to grasp. He finally spotted him as he passed through the living room on his way to the front door.

Greg stood in the foyer, half expecting the cat to make a comment, but he knew it was foolishness. It had clearly been a dream. Kotik was blithely stretched across the top of the couch, seemingly oblivious to his presence.

"I'm off to work, Kotik. Hold down the fort, will you?" Greg said.

The cat lifted his wide head, looked at his master, and then lowered it back down, unimpressed.

Greg left for his job at Lumbertown, feeling a little better. He was still tired, which did not mix well with fork trucks and large skids of wood, but he'd somehow make it through the day.

Greg arrived home at five that evening. The workday had been long and miserable due to fatigue, but he concluded that his encounter with Kotik the previous evening had been a dream or some kind of mental aberration. Maybe it was simply voices in his head. Maybe he'd gone manic and took a header off the walls of sanity. Maybe he was just tired. He was certainly suffering the symptoms of sleep deprivation.

He kicked his shoes off at the door, made his way into the kitchen, and took a Diet Coke from the refrigerator. He grabbed the remote, switched the television on to truTV, and dropped onto the couch. Kotik was sprawled along the back, much in the same position as when Greg had left nine hours earlier.

On Fridays, Greg usually binge-watched *The Smoking Gun Presents: World's Dumbest...,* since the station ran several episodes in succession. Cheryl worked until closing on Mondays, Thursdays, and Fridays. Last call at The Kilted Keg was at two in the morning, and cleanup kept her there until three, so on those nights, she didn't come over.

Greg sipped from the soda can and glanced at Kotik, still dozing in place, or so he thought until the cat opened one eye inquisitively.

"You been lying there all day?"

"That's a stupid question," said Kotik.

"Oh God, really?" Greg let his head fall back against the cushion but regretted it as a bolt of pain jarred him, emanating from the welt on his head.

"What?" asked the cat.

"Okay, I'll play," said Greg. "You're fat, you're lazy, and you're a cat. Why was it a stupid question?"

"Because the answer makes no difference; it's a waste of words and isn't worth a thimble full of shit." Kotik climbed to the cushion and sat. "Is the bimbo coming over tonight?"

"If you mean Cheryl, no, it's Friday."

"Which doesn't mean diddly-squat to me. I have no idea what day it is, nor can I differentiate between one day and another," said Kotik. He raised his leg and proceeded to lick his balls.

"Do you have to do that?"

Kotik paused in his ministrations and looked at Greg

incredulously. "Don't think I haven't seen you and the demoness going at it. I've seen where you stuff your face, so you have no grounds to criticize where I put mine."

"Fair enough, I guess, but it's not quite the same. I don't lick *myself*," Greg said.

"Oh, I'm sure you would if you could," Kotik challenged. "Besides, you have your hag friend to do it for you. It's not as if I can just grab my dick and scrub it clean, or whack-off, like you do whenever *your* balls tickle, so give me a break. I'm an indoor cat in a single-cat house and it gets a little fucking lonely around here, bub, if you catch my drift." He continued his bathing.

"It's not the same now that you can talk, or whatever it is you do. It changes things, like you should know better now that I know you have intelligence."

"Says the ass-wad who plays air guitar to Adele."

"I don't air-guitar to Adele!"

"No…nobody *normal* air-guitars to Adele, but you do," Kotik said and then mocked, "I wish nothing but the best for you-ooh…."

Greg felt a blush heat his face.

Kotik stopped suddenly, appearing to concentrate on something. "Damn, I always have to take a piss after I clean myself," he said, and dropped to the floor. "That reminds me. When are you going to do something about my box? It's like trying to do a squat-shot in a minefield."

"I just changed it."

"You changed it Monday. It's been four days."

"I thought days didn't mean diddly-squat to you," said Greg.

"Bite me."

Greg figured it was a good time to go for a walk.

DAY 2

Kotik jumped onto the bed and bumped the tender egg on Greg's head and started kneading the pillow.

"Scratch my rump," the cat said.

"No," said Greg. Ever since he had started communicating with the cat, he found that many of the affections he used to give Kotik without a second thought now caused a sense of aversion—one that even crossed into revulsion.

"What the hell? Did you eat an ass muffin for breakfast?" Kotik complained, jerking his head back.

"You never complained before."

"Yeah, and you used to scratch my head and rub my tummy, crap like that. Why don't you ever pet me anymore? It's not like I'm asking for a blow job, for Christ's sake."

"It's just freaking weird."

"No, *Duck Dynasty* is weird. The crazy sex shit you do with Annie Wilkes is weird. Petting your cat is natural and relieves tension."

"It's different now. It's kind of disturbing, actually," said Greg. He sat up and swung his legs to the floor. "Okay, get up. I have to change the sheets."

"Why, is Lizzie Borden coming over?"

"She's hardly Lizzie Borden and yes she's coming over, it's Saturday. You're jealous!" Greg said.

"Of that knob-jockey? Yeah…I don't think so, but she's got you totally whipped," Kotik said, leaping to the floor.

"How so?" asked Greg. He rose and then steadied himself on the bedside table as intense vertigo washed over him.

"You clean the house and change your sheets every weekend."

"So? Cleanliness is next to godliness." Once the wooziness eased, Greg pulled the sheets from the bed, balled them, and tossed them near the door.

"Then you must have been the fucking devil my first two

years here. You had tumbleweeds behind the couch—trust me,
I know—and those sheets probably got changed twice a year
until Broomhilda showed up." Kotik jumped back onto the bed
and sat. "It would make more sense to change the sheets after
you and *The Repugnant One* defile them with your spunk and
junk, but no, you let them fester for the week."

"I never realized cats were such hypercritical dicks." Greg
picked up the bedding, a scattering of discarded clothing, and
left the room. He was anxious about Cheryl coming over.

Kotik had been following him for the better part of the day,
hounding him about everything. He supposed the cat wasn't
around any more than he'd been before, but the continuous
banter was beginning to rattle him. At one point, he offered to
let Kotik outside, holding open the door while the cat stood
poised in indecision.

"What the hell's wrong with you? Why won't you go outside?"

"Who said I wanted to go outside?" asked Kotik.

"You did."

"When?"

"Last night you complained that I'd made you an indoor cat."

"No. I said you were the dip-wad who made me an indoor
cat. Never once did I say I wanted to go out."

Greg supposed that was true, but it only aggravated him
more.

"You're missing your opportunity. I'm closing the door in
three seconds."

"Are you really going to try that psychology crap with me,
you condescending turd-handle?" Kotik turned dismissively and
returned to the kitchen. "It may have worked for your mother,
but not for you."

How in the hell did he know that? Greg wondered, recalling
his mother's continuous requests for him to "just go out and
play" or to "get out of my hair for a while". The cat seemed
especially good at hitting Greg where it hurt, almost as if he

knew his weaknesses and insecurities. He'd always been a little paranoid, and Kotik played on it with little insinuations about Cheryl's fidelity and his penchant to "relieve his itch" maybe a little more than was probably healthy. The cat seemed to know his innermost secrets and fears, which amped up two major concerns. If his communication with the cat was a result of the knock on the head, it showed no signs of diminishing and was, in truth, increasing. If not, and it turned out Cheryl could hear Kotik, it could be disastrous.

Holy shit, talk about a catfight! he mused.

Cheryl showed up at four that afternoon, walking into the kitchen unannounced and carrying a large, brown paper bag.

"She didn't even knock," Kotik complained. "She thinks she owns the place!"

Greg bristled and waited for Cheryl to freak out, but was astonished she seemed not to hear the cat. To him, the voice was loud and centered in his head as if he had earbuds in.

Cheryl set the bag on the kitchen table and planted a soft kiss on Greg's cheek. "Hi, baby!" she purred, her voice so silky he wanted to take her right there on the table.

"Hi, sexy. You look absolutely delicious," said Greg. He gave her a long hug and returned the kiss. He glared at Kotik.

"What the hell!" hissed the cat. "She just sashays right in and that's it? Hi, sexy? Give her hell, for fuck's sake!" He jumped to the floor from the couch and regarded Cheryl. "Wow, you splurged and went with the ten-dollar whore?"

Greg refrained, barely, from kicking him.

"Christ, you make me sick," Kotik went on, and then proceeded to hack up a hairball on the living room rug.

"Eww," said Cheryl.

"Nice," complained Greg. He pulled a length of paper towel from the holder and cleaned up the mess.

"That's right. Now you're learning the natural order of things," said the cat.

Greg shooed him away with the wad of paper towels, returned to the kitchen, and noticed Cheryl's lip curl in distaste when he tossed the Bounty-wrapped hairball into the wastebasket.

"Not much of a cat fan, are you?" he asked her.

"No, they're gross. They puke and spray everywhere, and they stink," she said.

"Told you she's a cat hater! And she stinks, too!" Kotik complained indignantly from behind the couch. "She's pickled in perfume and smells like a brothel full of geriatric hookers."

"Does Kotik smell?" asked Greg. "Can you smell him now?"

He had dumped the litterbox earlier that morning and used Fresh Step litter, which was supposed to send out a poof of freshness every time a cat sifted through it. He'd also sprayed the shit out of the house with disinfectant.

"Yeah, pretty bad," said Cheryl, scrunching her nose again. She withdrew a bottle of wine and a white pastry box from within the bag and set them on the table. "Don't you notice it?"

"Oh, up yours, you prima donna," growled Kotik. "Will you get rid of her already, before I cuff her a good one?"

"I guess I've gotten used to it," Greg said. He took four filet mignon portions from the fridge and set them on the counter near the stovetop.

"Sure, *you* get filet mignon," grumbled the cat.

Greg shot a scowl toward the couch, hoping his miserable pet would see it. "I have been thinking that cats might be more trouble than they're worth, lately," he said.

"Are you fucking kidding me?" Kotik railed, his voice echoing inside his master's head. He bounded out from behind the couch, launched himself over the armchair, and slid across the end table, dragging the remote, a magazine, and a short, squat candle to the floor with him in a fury of scrabbling paws.

Composing himself, the cat leaped onto the chair, successfully this time, with exaggerated aplomb and glowered balefully at Greg.

"He's kind of disturbing, and dumb, too," Cheryl added, watching the cat dubiously. "And what kind of name is Kotik? Does it mean anything? It reminds me of Kotex."

"You remind me of Kotex because you're a bloody twat!" Kotik said, and then proudly added, "Hey, that was pretty good for an unintentional pun."

Greg chuckled. "I don't know. I didn't name him."

"Well, it's a stupid name," said Cheryl.

"What? What? Are you for real? It's Russian for *cat,* you buffoons! It's the most appropriate name ever!"

"Oh, I guess it means cat in Russian, which kind of makes sense since he's a Russian Blue." Greg flashed his cat a glance. "It was his name when I got him from the SPCA."

"Wait a minute...I'm adopted?" asked Kotik, sounding forlorn.

He sat and groveled for more than an hour as Greg and Cheryl prepared dinner and then proceeded to wolf down their meal along with two bottles of wine. Small talk turned to flirting, flirting turned to fondling, and soon they were entwined on the couch, petting, panting, and shedding their clothing.

Detaching long enough from the heated make-out session to catch his breath, Greg opened his eyes and noticed Kotik raptly watching them. Without interruption in their shameless groping, Greg rose from the couch, Cheryl's naked body adhered to his like a leech, and moved to the bedroom as a single, eight-limbed entity. He closed the bedroom door with his rump and then dropped Cheryl onto the bed. He kissed a trail from her shoulder, down to her ankles and halfway back again, finding the central focus of his interest.

Grabbing Cheryl around the waist, he rolled onto his back, pulling her on top of him... and then he heard the sound of the door latch springing and cursed his procrastination at getting the door aligned so it would close properly.

"Holy Christ, you're doing that sixty-nine thing again?" Kotik said from somewhere behind him. "I don't get it. Why are you so fascinated by something that almost suffocates you both to death?"

"Shut up," Greg warned him mentally.

"Holy crap, she shaved that puppy clean as confession," Kotik persisted. "Reminds me of this Sphynx I once screwed, not a hair on her, tail like a rat. It was different... kind of freaky, but not for me."

Greg tried to ignore him and focus on his objective, but he heard the cat leap onto the dresser opposite the bed.

"Shit! Look at the meat wallet on her! I've never seen it from this angle before. That's fucking frightening!"

"You're a cat, you idiot," Greg said, in his head. "Your pecker's probably the size of a Mike and Ike. You're obviously in no position to critique."

"Man, that's cold, criticizing the size of my dick. I was just saying it's evident that yours wasn't the first paddle in that creek."

"Will you just shut up?" Greg pictured himself throwing the thought at the cat. He doubled his efforts with Cheryl.

Kotik remained silent...but not for long. "Sounds like you're slopping a pig in there. Aren't you afraid you might catch something with all those body juices going everywhere?"

Greg pulled Cheryl's legs tighter to his ears to block the cat out, but to no avail; the voice was inside his head.

"How do you know they're only *her* juices? Like, they could be leftovers, like from that guy she had here when you were working."

What the fuck? Was Kotik telling the truth, or was he just talking shit because he was jealous of Cheryl?

"Now they do it right," Kotik said. "Doggy style, just like we cats do it. I know that sounds fucked up…"

"Why would she bring a guy here when she has her own apartment?" Greg challenged.

"Why do people screw in a full-to-capacity Fenway Park? Why do we cats screw on the tops of cars in the middle of the night? It's the thrill of the ride, and the boner you sprout getting away with it."

"You're lying."

"I don't know, am I?"

"You're an asshole."

"I guess you'd know, considering your trajectory."

"You okay, baby?" asked Cheryl.

Greg, unaware of it, had begun growing limp.

"One minute," he said, rolling her off him. "I can't get into it with that cat staring at me."

"He is freaky," she agreed.

He grabbed Kotik from the bureau and tossed him down the hallway. He closed the door and wedged a chair under the knob.

"Okay, where were we?" he said, climbing back onto the bed, anxious to get back to the action, but a little seed of doubt had sprouted.

DAY 3

As Greg slept, the seed of doubt flourished into a Sycamore of suspicion. His night was wrought with dreams of Cheryl in his home and in his bed, hosting a multiplicity of men while he worked. Each dream was more perverse and explicit than the last, culminating with a most disturbing one where Kotik mocked him and explained that even *he* was putting it to her.

Greg sat up in bed, the sheets twisting awkwardly around both him and Cheryl, who was sleeping soundly despite his restlessness. He watched her in the dim light cast by the alarm clock and wondered if the suspicions were true. It wasn't beyond belief. She was certainly beautiful enough. Maybe not in the classic Elizabeth Taylor sense, but in a voluptuous, contemporary way.

While this aroused him to no end, it also aroused his concerns to the point that he could think of little else. It was unsettling. He'd always had a lower-than-average self-esteem, which fostered his fair share of insecurities, but never this deeply. He'd never become obsessive about it.

A dull throb thrummed at the back of his head. He kneaded the knot, wondering if it were the cause of his elevated anxieties. It seemed a lot had changed or been generated since he had taken the hit. Although the swelling was mostly gone, it was still tender to the touch and centralized pressure caused queasiness and sent a bolt of pain that nested between his eyes and made them water. It was a familiar feeling that foretold of an oncoming migraine.

"You okay, baby?" Cheryl asked.

"Headache," Greg said flatly.

He couldn't shake the image of her lying in the same bed they were now in, but with another man…or two…or three. He squeezed the sides of his head with his hands, trying to drive the thoughts away, but it only fueled his headache.

Kotik never said there was more than one, he mentally reasoned. But even one is unacceptable, he counter-argued.

"What is it, honey?" Cheryl sat up and put an arm around him, her brow furrowed with concern. She looked and sounded sincere, but…

"Fuck!" he growled, and stood. He went into the bathroom and brushed his teeth, rinsed and stared at his rheumy, red-rimmed eyes in the mirror. *Ask her, you coward,* he berated himself before returning to the bedroom.

"What's going on? You're very riled."

I need the truth. I need the truth. The thought drilled into his head, an apt companion to his budding migraine.

"Did you come by here when I was at work last week?" Greg asked. He tried to smile and sound casual but failed miserably on both accounts.

"What?" Cheryl asked, taken aback. "Why would I be here when you're not?"

"I was just wondering, because…" *Think, think!* "…because someone said they saw a woman coming into the house last week and I wanted to make sure it was you," Greg said, sitting on the edge of the bed.

You pathetic ass!

Cheryl looked a little uncertain, so Greg gave a little nudge.

"I don't know anyone else with a bright red Prius, but you never know," he said, standing again.

"Oh yeah!" Cheryl said with an uneasy chuckle. "I did come by to … to look for my nametag from work…I forgot. I've lost a few of them and my boss got upset the last time."

"Did you find it?" Greg asked.

"No."

He had a sudden urge to slap her and had to move away. He had never hit a woman in his life, and the feeling was distressing, so he left the bedroom and headed for the kitchen.

"Well, it's about fucking time," Kotik's voice trumpeted inside Greg's head as soon as the cat was within sight. "What kind of pet owner are you, leaving me locked out here with no food, no water, and no access to my litterbox?"

"Don't start," Greg said. "And get off of the counter."

"Don't start? Hell, I was running for cover last night. I thought there was an air raid." Kotik leaped onto a chair at the table. "What do you do to the witch to get her shrieking like that? Christ, anything goes full banshee on me like that, I get far away."

"Will you just shut up?" Greg insisted.

"Are you talking to me?" Cheryl asked from down the hallway. She sounded like she had a mouthful of toothpaste."

"No...the cat!" Greg yelled back. He went into the utility room and pulled his other set of bed linens from the dryer, returned to the living room, dropped them on the couch, and started folding them.

"Man, I hope you bleached those, after what she and her *man* friend did on them," said Kotik. "I mean, I made the mistake of going in there when they were going at it and it was like the day I was in the shower and you turned it on."

"Enough!" Greg roared, and the pain in his head did as well.

"What is your problem?" demanded Cheryl. She stood in the archway between the kitchen and living room staring disapprovingly at him. "Why are you so upset? I figured it'd be okay. You gave me a key."

"I'm not upset about *that*." Greg pulled a pillowcase from the pile and started folding it, wondering if her head had been on it while some guy knelt over her chest, pressing between her pouty lips with his..."

STOP IT!

ZING! went the pain behind his eyes.

"My god, then what?" Cheryl persisted. The anger in her voice...

"Tell her, you pussy!" Kotik insisted.

Greg looked questioningly at the animal. "Really?"

"What? Pussy? It's like this." Kotik leaped onto the top of the couch. "I'm a cat, but you, pal...you're the real pussy! Tell her you know she had a guy here!"

"I know...I..."

"What?" Cheryl prompted.

"Say it, asshole!" Kotik demanded.

Greg held his head in his arms and squatted near the couch, feeling seasick and wanting to escape the onslaught.

"What is with you?" asked Cheryl.

"Pussy!" said Kotik.

"I know you had a guy here," Greg said, whining.

Cheryl was silent for a moment. Greg couldn't look at her, afraid to either hear the truth or confront her anger. Afraid his head would fall off his shoulders if he moved.

"Are…you…kidding…me?" she finally said, her words like metronome clicks. "Is that what this is all about? It was my brother, Chris."

"Liar!" charged Kotik.

"Chris lives in New York," Greg said. He had never met Cheryl's family, but she had spoken of them.

"He's visiting. He got here Wednesday," she said with growing annoyance.

"You never said anything about him visiting," Greg said dejectedly.

"It never came up. Damn it, Greg, you should have just asked," Cheryl said softly…sympathetically.

"You don't screw your brother! She's a liar!" Kotik roared.

"No, she's not!" Greg yelled back…and the room quickly went still.

Greg stayed kneeling on the floor; the only sound was the whoosh of his pulse sending a sledgehammering misery through his arteries and up to his head where it crashed inside his skull like arrows. He wanted to shrink into the carpet fibers and hide away from everything. He knew he had gone too far. He felt like a child—a lonely, lost, child.

Cheryl stared at Greg uncertainly. "Did you just yell at the cat?" she asked.

"Imbecile," said Kotik.

Greg had no idea how to handle it, how to fix it, how to stop the pain, so he started to cry.

"Wimp!' accused Kotik.

"Oh," Cheryl said, her hazel eyes softening compassionately. She stepped toward Greg, ready to comfort him, but froze. Then she transformed, the rage turning her pretty face ugly. "God fucking dammit!" she bellowed.

"Oh yeah. I took a shit near the chair," Kotik said indifferently.

"Oh, this is so fucking gross! I can't…" Her words were interrupted by a gag.

She hopped to the lounge chair and dropped down into it, her foot extended away from her. A wad of shit was adhered to the bottom of her foot and had squeezed up between her toes, forming little scrolls. The smell soon followed and she started gagging.

"Serves the cheating harlot right," said Kotik.

"Oh, get me something to wipe it!" she said, and gagged again. "I hate that fucking cat!

"Told you she's a cat hater!" Kotik said. "This wouldn't have happened if you hadn't locked me out."

"It's either him or me!" said Cheryl.

"Good! Tell the bitch goodbye!" said Kotik.

Each word felt like a nail entering his head. It had to stop. Stop it!

"It's your fault, you fuckrudder!" said Kotik.

"Stop," said Greg.

"I said, get me something, NOW!" said Cheryl.

"Stop it," said Greg.

"You'll be better without her…just us," said Kotik.

"…kill the fucking cat," said Cheryl. She grabbed one of the clean pillowcases and started working at the wad of shit on her foot.

"Stop it!" Greg demanded.

"Fuck you!" said the cat.

"Fuck you!" said Cheryl.

With a primal scream and the pain of a million knives, Greg sprang to his feet.

"Good! Kick her ass out of here!" cheered the cat.

Greg grabbed the remaining clean pillowcase, shook it open, grabbed Kotik by the scruff of the neck, and shoved him inside. It wasn't easygoing. The cat fought diligently.

"What are you doing man?" spat Kotik. "Wait! I'm your cat, dude!"

Greg ignored the wasp-like buzzing in his ears that swelled and receded with the thumping of giant feet in his head. He knelt on the opening of the pillowcase and slid his leg down, pushing the cat far enough inside so he could tie a knot in the top with relatively few scratches.

Cheryl finished wiping her foot clean, dropped the soiled pillowcase, and inquisitively watched Greg walk into the kitchen. She stood and followed him.

"Come on, guy...I'm your fucking puddy-wuddy, you ass-flap!" Kotik pleaded, sounding desperate for once. "Tell you what...I can be the pussy, okay?"

Greg looked at Cheryl and the beginnings of a knowing smile grew on her face.

"Humane Society?" she asked, and then flinched as Greg swung the pillowcase against the side of the refrigerator with all of his strength.

Greg stood still, relishing the blessed absence of Kotik's voice. He looked at the now-still pillowcase, then the refrigerator with its telltale dent. Cheryl stood in stunned silence, also staring at the pillowcase.

She wasn't expecting that, Greg thought sardonically.

Neither was she expecting it when the pillowcase caught her on the side of the head. A twenty-pound cat can be quite substantial, and can even snap a neck, with the proper force and accuracy.

Greg's force and accuracy were dead on.

DAY 4

Greg slept late…past noon, in fact. It hadn't occurred to him how much the cat and Cheryl had demanded of him. He woke with no voices in his head, no paranoid thoughts, no guilty feelings, and the sense that he had taken a positive step in rebuilding his self-esteem.

It was refreshing how clear his thoughts became immediately after he'd quieted the madness created by the other two. He had launched right into rectification mode; he knew immediately what he had to do and how to do it.

Disposing of Cheryl, her car, and the cat had been easy. About a mile from his house there was an indistinct dirt road that hunters and fishermen (or women) used occasionally, and more often by high schoolers out for a quickie. The first two usually employed the road in the early mornings, and the latter, usually after midnight. It ran half a mile into the woods, ending at a steep, makeshift ramp that swiftly dipped into the Merrimack River.

Saturday evening, when it was nearly dusk, Greg pulled the red Prius to a stop about a hundred feet from the ramp, Cheryl and Kotik tucked snuggly and unseen in the hatchback. With the car still running and all four windows lowered for better *sinkability* (a word Greg created just for this occasion), he positioned Cheryl in the driver's seat, her body sloughing toward the floor, and her foot wedged against the gas pedal. Reaching into the passenger-side window, Greg depressed the shift-lock, jammed the car into drive, and jumped clear as the car accelerated forward and launched from the ramp like a little rocket, landing a third of the way across the river. It took less than a minute for it to sink out of sight.

Greg threw the pillowcase containing Kotik's dense body into the river well downstream and then walked the rest of the way home.

Greg felt it was a sign of his imminent good fortune that it had all happened on Saturday. Neither he nor Cheryl had work scheduled for Sunday, and if all went well—and he knew it would—no one would miss her until Monday night. With the way he was thinking and feeling, with all the newfound clarity and confidence, he was sure he could have easily handled it on any other day, as well.

He had a few chores to do: first and foremost getting rid of that stinking litterbox. Invigorated, he jumped from the bed, quickly dressed, and then brushed his teeth. He retrieved a package of Hefty trash liners from within the bathroom vanity, doubled two together, and slid the complete litterbox ensemble inside the bag. Knotting it closed, he lugged it through the kitchen, then outdoors, and dropped it into a large barrel outside the garage.

In silent celebration that he would never again have to scoop Kotik's shit, he whistled an anonymous tune and returned to the house. As he opened the storm door, something dark shot past his legs and inside, startling him. His first fear was that Kotik had somehow escaped his watery fate...until he saw it sitting on the kitchen counter to the right of the sink.

It was another cat, but this one was midnight black, with a long, sleek body. Its tail swished and swayed hypnotically, like slow-rising smoke. The cat raised a fine paw and licked it with a small, pink tongue. Its movements were smooth and almost sensual, its face delicately featured with eyes that turned up ever so slightly, and Greg had no doubt that this cat was female. He stood in the doorway, unsure of how to handle this new situation. It seemed ironic and a little bit spooky that a cat would show up inside his house the day after...

He became aware of a slight pinging ache starting in his head and raised his hand to touch the spot, but then thought better of it.

"What are you looking at, psycho boy?" it asked in a decisively female voice that seemed to emanate from inside his head. It was suave and suggestive…Cheryl's voice, he realized. "What's wrong, killer, cat got your tongue?"

Greg lunged toward the table, grabbed an apple from the fruit bowl, and whipped it at the cat. The fruit exploded against the wall behind the sink and wet shrapnel rained throughout the kitchen. The cat seemed to have anticipated the attack; she had moved so quickly it looked as if she had disappeared. He scanned the kitchen and living room and snagged another apple. He cocked his arm, prepared to let fly at any sign of movement, when the cat buried the claws of her forepaws deep in his calf.

"Son of a bitch!" yelled Greg, grasping at the flaring pain in his injured leg. The cat tore into him again, lacing his hands with red-hot furrows, and then she charged up the hallway and into Greg's bedroom.

Greg gave chase as a searing rage enveloped him, awakening the beast inside his head. He slammed the bedroom door behind him and wedged the chair beneath the knob, making sure the cat couldn't escape. A quick scan of the bathroom verified that it was empty, so he closed that door as well, leaving only the bedroom.

"Okay, where are you, you little bitch?" Greg said, sneering.

"Wrong breed, lover boy," she said, but he couldn't locate her; the voice was muddled by the pounding in his head.

She could only have been hiding in one of a few places, most likely under the bed or under the dresser. He pulled a tee shirt from a dresser drawer and wrapped it tightly around his hand for protection, then took a pillow from the bed and shook it, freeing it from the pillowcase. It had worked well with Kotik, and this cat was a lot smaller.

Kneeling beside the bed and then dropping to his belly, Greg lifted the bed skirt and peered underneath, tense and ready to strike. It all seemed clear, from the headboard to the footboard, and then she was suddenly there. She hissed, cuffed the side of his face, and then darted from beneath the bed to underneath the dresser.

Greg roared his outrage.

Damn, she was fast!

He snatched the pillowcase and slid to the bureau, under which the cat was easily visible. Greg swiped with his wrapped hand. The cat hissed and backed up. He swiped again, missing the cat, but dragging something small and white out from beneath.

He picked it up and turned it over to reveal the checkered plaid of The Kilted Keg, and the name *Cheryl* in neat script within the provided block.

Cheryl's nametag. *Was she telling the truth?* He wondered.

"Good deduction, Romeo. You killed an innocent woman," said the cat.

"This doesn't mean anything," Greg said, weakly. "She probably planted it before she came out of the bedroom yesterday. She knew she was caught."

"No, she loved you," said the cat with Cheryl's voice. She slowly came out from beneath the dresser.

"She was here with a guy!" Greg murmured, slowly turning the name badge over.

"She explained that."

"But she...on my bed."

"Wow, you really are a fucking idiot," said the cat.

Greg looked at her sitting before him. He was confused, and feelings of remorse and sorrow started seeping into his armor, pushing away the confidence he had woken up with. It was a terrible feeling that amplified the slamming in his head, and he didn't like it at all.

Greg lashed out like a rattlesnake and grabbed the unsuspecting cat by the throat. He shoved her into the pillowcase, ignoring the condemning words and belligerent claws that tore at him. He ripped the chair away from the door and stomped into the kitchen, delivering the same punishment as the day before.

As the noise and the pain ceased, Greg slumped to the floor in relief, the limp pillowcase at his side. "Kelvinator two—cats zero," he chuckled.

Greg disposed of the black cat close to where he had thrown Kotik. Upon returning from his walk riverside, he was startled to see a man standing in his driveway close to the porch. He was young, barely twenty, Greg figured, and he was holding a bicycle upright. Greg approached cautiously but tried to appear confident and friendly.

"Hello. Can I help you?" he greeted. Greg noticed the man's dark hair, hazel eyes, thick lips, and a chill ran through him. *Son of a bitch...it was him,* he thought.

"Uh, hi," said the young man. His eyes locked momentarily on the four parallel gouges across Greg's cheek. "Are you Greg Fourtier?"

"Yes," Greg said, composing himself. He offered his hand, and they shook. "You must be Cheryl's brother...um...."

"Chris," the young man reminded him, glancing at the bandage wrapped around Greg's right hand.

"Yes! If you're not, then you have a female doppelganger."

Greg was sure Chris Kairns had no shortage of women vying for his attention.

"I'm looking for Cheryl," said Chris, forcing a smile. "She said she'd be staying here with you Friday night, but we were supposed to meet up for dinner last night. I've called numerous times and she hasn't answered her phone, either."

"She never showed?" Greg asked, hoping to purvey the proper amount of surprise and concern without overacting. "She left here yesterday about three in the afternoon. I only..."

Greg was interrupted as an enormous Siamese cat bounded

to the porch railing and then vaulted onto the porch swing. He faced the two men and sat, statuesque, sleek, and not just huge…he was bobcat huge and solid.

"Whoa! What the heck?" Chris said, taking a step away from the fearsome-looking animal.

The cat looked at him dispassionately and yawned.

Fucker must weigh fifty pounds, Greg thought, trying to appear unfazed, but the cat had shaken him to the core. His ears started buzzing and someone was whacking the welt on his head with a baseball bat, or that was how it felt. The cat turned his attention to Greg, and he could swear it was smiling smugly at him.

"Oh, that's my cat, Buttercup," Greg said. "Say hi to the nice man, Buttercup."

"Fuck you," the cat said to Greg.

Greg snickered and turned to Chris. "I only tried calling her once, but I figured she was busy…maybe with some guy. Did you check her work? There's a lot of them there." His right eye began twitching and welling with tears.

"That's where I'm heading next," Chris said, looking at Greg oddly. "What happened to your face and hand?"

Greg jabbed a thumb toward the cat behind him. "Buttercup plays a little rough at times," he said. "He likes it rough."

"You're meat," said the cat.

"I'm supposed to go to work tonight," Greg lied. "But I'll tell you what I'm going to do." He nodded to Chris and smiled like a televangelist. "I'm going to call in sick and then take a ride and see if she's at any of her hangouts. But I want you to call me if you hear anything from her work."

He gave Cheryl's brother a false phone number, stepped onto the porch and watched Chris bike away. *This guy's going to be trouble,* he thought to himself.

"Not for you," said Buttercup.

Greg held the door open and then followed Buttercup inside.

FRONTRUNNERS

"Eyes up, off the ground. Half a second's preoccupation could be your death," the voice said.

"Yes, sir," Franky responded and looked straight ahead.

Admiral William A. Rancourt wasn't a particularly large man at 5'10" and 175 pounds, but, garbed in his impeccable service blues, combination cap, and the compacted confidence of a career officer, he seemed like a ten-foot-tall wall of granite to Franky, even from a hundred yards away. He appeared to speak into his collar.

"See the big picture at all times. It will save your life," his words shuttled into her earbud.

"Yes, sir."

Navy commanders hadn't always been this militant, not in such a boots-on-the-ground way. Neither had training, but changing times necessitated transformed mentalities. Admiral Rancourt was SEAL trained, morally driven, and a time-forged patriot. But, since what he referred to as *The New American Regime* took over, his patriotism had faltered. He was a changed, but now-controlled man.

Franky walked forward, hugging the side of the street, her eyes forever scanning left, right, quick checks over her shoulders. The replicated townscape was nondescript and anonymous, aptly named Anytown, USA. Two-story residences interrupted every couple of blocks by storefronts, a faux motel, and a church that someone with a dark sense of humor had named Abandoned Hope Ministries.

Scanning left-right-up-down to match her hut-two-three-four cadence, a furtive peripheral movement caught her attention. She dropped low to the ground, pulled her weapon from the holster at her side, and logrolled behind an early-model Jeep Cherokee parked parallel to the sidewalk. She scanned for other movements that could open her to harm, ready to pull herself beneath the vehicle. It was not her preferred shelter, but safer than lying out in the open. She eased slowly to her knees, estimating the location of the movement at approximately eight o'clock, and belly-crawled alongside the Jeep. She peered through dirtied vehicle windows, and a round of gunshot echoed along the street.

Franky dropped to the ground, her gun flat in front of her and accessible, as she had been trained. She removed a small device from a hip pouch and urgently whispered into it. "Active shooter Ventura and Memphis, motel second floor."

"Copy, F.R. Do you have visual? Verify and report back at once," the admiral's voice replied.

F.R. was an acronym for a fairly new station, standing for *Frontrunner*. It had first been adopted six years earlier, in 2027, when it had become clear there would be no political compromise and that a bipartisan nation was a thing of the past. The rift only widened, the parties became more extreme in their agenda, and hatred had reached a level not seen since the Holocaust and Civil War, and made even worse by modern technology. There was no place to hide or to communicate without being seen or heard. Big Brother was indeed watching, terrorism was seen as the great equalizer by the extreme radicals, and sadly, protests, logical conversation, and outright pleading were hopeless. It had reached a point where the only avenue to self-preservation was to fight fire with fire.

Franky was a second-level FR, or FR2. Once she became an FR3, she would be able to go live—citizen protection level.

Schools had closed their doors for good in 2021, amidst the pandemic and post-election rise of the gun-wielding radicals. Active shooters became almost as common as students, culminating when one of the victims of a slaughter in Adelphi, Maryland, was identified as the child of a senator. All children were now web-schooled.

FRs were to populate a distinctive military-backed force to protect civilians from an ever-increasing list of dangers, including the mostly corrupt police forces still staffed by those who hadn't decamped, feverous mercenaries, and a small army of NRA disciples. To become an FR3 was a rite of passage, a high honor that was cause for celebration. One only became an FR3 once they had earned the full confidence of the commanders they were assigned to. Some made F3 quickly with a show of dexterity and commitment. Some were awarded F3 after displaying smarts and courage in a real-life event. Some never made F3. Franky was determined to make it by August 28—her thirteenth birthday.

Franky again crawled alongside the Jeep, the Kevlar vest slowing her progress, but a necessity, despite this being a drill. Not wise to get too comfortable during a drill. Need to be as real-time as possible, or the unexpected variance could be fatal. Leveling her head to the ground, Franky looked beneath the vehicle, across the street toward the motel. She could partially see the first floor, but no higher.

"Shit," she hissed. Scanning to her left, just outside the storefront, a woman—a mother—lay prone over a small child. Blood ran from the mother's hip and the left side of her ribcage. More ran from the child's head to the pavement, a kill shot. Though these people were 3D laser-generated, it never failed to nauseate Franky and fill her with an abysmal sense of dread. She felt responsible.

"Casualties. Adult woman," she said into the small transmitter. Then she paused and added, "One child, toddler," her voice cracking.

More shots.

Franky crawled toward the front of the Jeep and cautiously peered around the bumper. Fear and realization jolted her when the shooter darted across the motel's second-floor exterior walkway, raising the assault rifle to his shoulder. He was aiming at her.

She launched herself backward as three more rifle shots rattled the air and three red, laser-generated dots flashed on the ground inches away from her. She fired a wish-shot over the hood of the Jeep and scuttled back to the full safety of the vehicle.

She had to be wise and shoot sparingly. Her bullets, though only laser shots, were limited to thirty, as would a FR's lethally loaded Heckler & Koch. During drills, both FRs and shooters wore a full-body form-fitting undergarment they referred to as "onesies." Unlike the nightwear from which they had borrowed the handle, these onesies were Lycra, infused with a laser-sensitive mesh that interacted with your firearm, which would become disabled if the Lycra onesie sensed a hit.

She was breathless but feeling the buzz, the invigoration that came with these "games." She spoke into the transmitter again, "Shooter, white male." *Of course,* she mentally added. "Mid, maybe late-twenties. Assault weapon, too distant for identification but maybe a Vektor."

"Are you concealed?"

"Affirmative, but seen and fired upon by gunman. Will attempt a takedown."

"Copy. Proceed with caution."

Franky scuttled carefully to the rear of the Jeep, hoping not to be detected. She had a plan...a double-diversion tactic she was confident would work. An old Mini Cooper was parked about twenty-five feet in front of her and the Jeep, and across the street was the store. She found a plum-sized rock on the street edge and palmed it.

Franky's takedown of the shooter followed in a series of unexpected occurrences and reactions but transpired in a matter of seconds. As she reared back to throw the rock at the Mini, a blue, late-model Hyundai SunVolt rounded a corner behind her, driving toward her and the shooter, who rattled off a volley of shots.

Without knowing who was in the Hyundai, Franky scurried to the side of the Jeep, seeking cover. She reached for the transmitter but abandoned it. She'd worry about reporting later. Right now, she needed to be wise and perform efficiently.

A quick glance over the hood revealed the shooter lining his sights with the moving vehicle. She couldn't let him shoot.

"Shit-shit-shit."

Franky launched the rock at the Mini. Whether sensing the motion or reacting to the rock-on-metal concussion, the shooter turned and fired, but Franky was already rolling to the rear of the Jeep. Quickly to her belly, she fired a shot through the storefront window, an upward trajectory aimed at the top of the pane to minimize the chance of civilian harm. The window exploded with a loud crash and an impressive display of falling computer-generated shards.

Wasting no time on admiring the theatrics, Franky stood to see the shooter looking toward the store. Employing the rear bumper of the Jeep, gun at the ready, she raised her sights above the roofline and fired. Two red laser-dots flashed off of the roof close to her and she threw herself backward, landing behind the Jeep with a jarring impact that knocked the breath from her.

Damn, he's fast, she thought, forcing herself to move despite the pain. She settled her back against the Jeep's rear bumper, not thinking about the shooter, but what she saw in that half-second before she fired—the people in the blue Hyundai as it idled past while she climbed onto the jeep. The image of the man hunched over the steering wheel, and more so of the girl in the passenger seat, her head against the side window, her lifeless eyes searching the skies as blood blossomed like a large geranium across her chest.

Finally able to breathe, Franky lifted her gun, eased to the edge of the Jeep, and looked up to the second floor of the motel. The gunman, at the ready, aimed at Franky. She dropped back. There were no shots.

Was his gun disabled? Had she got him? Everything had been moving fast—a whirlwind—and she wasn't sure if she had gotten a clean shot off. He could be bluffing. She could wait it out, but that could mean more civilian casualties. She lifted the gun and waved the stock above the roof of the car.

Nothing.

Franky dropped back to the ground and triggered the transmitter. "Casualties. Two. Adult male, age N/A." She envisioned the girls' unseeing eyes and shuddered. She recognized those eyes. They looked at her every morning and evening from the bathroom mirror in her barracks. "Adolescent female," she said. "Age, twelve."

Franky waited for the response. When none came, she approached the rear edge of the Jeep to check on Admiral Rancourt's location and saw him walking toward her, rigid and swift. This was a certain sign the conflict was over, but his expression was livid, which confused and terrified Franky.

Did I blow it? How? The thought was soul crushing. It would mean either a one-year setback or disqualification. Franky stood and waited for her commander to reach her. She had to remain silent until he spoke.

Admiral Rancourt stopped inches in front of Franky, his eyes drilling into hers. "What the hell happened, Francesca?" he asked, his voice elevated, but not quite yelling.

God, she hated her formal name, and that he was using it was not a good sign. Some stiff collars in Congress felt the FRs under eighteen would be referred to by name instead of rank out of sensitivity to their ages, though the admiral often did. "But they'll let you die in fucking battle," her tearful mother had said the day they'd pulled her daughter from her in the immigration detention center two years earlier.

"I took down the shooter," said Franky, unsure to what he was alluding.

"Fire your weapon," Admiral Rancourt demanded.

Franky raised the barrel to the sky and fired. Nothing happened.

"You're goddamn dead, Francesca. You may have hit your mark, but he hit you first."

The truth in his words numbed her, and although it was severely frowned upon as weakness, she felt her tears threatening. This would set her back, maybe even disqualify her, and that utterly petrified her. Nobody seemed to know what happened to disqualified FRs.

The admiral studied her, his head slightly cocked as if listening for an air leak. "You hesitated climbing onto the car. That was your demise. Why did you hesitate, Francesca?"

She considered her answer and then decided that anything she said would be of no help. What was the use? "The girl in the car, the image was of me. I didn't expect it."

"That is no answer. You must be ready for *anything* at all times," he said.

"It's...." Franky started to say but stopped.

"It's what, Francesca?"

"It's not fair."

"It's a god-damned fight for your life and the lives of civilians. It's a war. Nothing is fucking fair!" he bellowed. The admiral turned to walk away, and Franky saw a flash of disappointment cross his face, and she knew it was because she was one of his most hopeful FRs. Now she was his failure. Tears welled and then rolled down her cheeks.

Admiral Rancourt stopped and turned back to say something. The red dot that appeared on the corner of his eye shocked her. There had been no sound to accompany it. As the red dot gave birth to a rivulet, Franky screamed and dropped to the ground.

Silencer, she thought. This is no game!

She rolled beneath the Jeep as Admiral Rancourt hit the ground like a sack of stones, his wide blank eyes staring at her like an accusation, or maybe a plea. The pain was brutal, and she knew she had at least a broken rib, maybe more, but the Kevlar jacket had saved her.

Swallowing the agony, Franky shot out from and then retreated under the Jeep like a snapping turtle, Admiral Rancourt's Glock 17 tightly gripped in her hand. She spun, trying to calculate the direction the shot had come from and thought, *Maybe I can still make F3.*

John McIlveen

TRIGGERS

Nightmares have tormented me throughout my life, they are part of this darkness I live in. But for maybe the tenth time in the last two weeks, I've awakened from one in utter panic. I spring upright, choking on a scream and gasping away the claustrophobic ether that propels me to wakefulness. I sit with my arms wrapped around my legs, my head on my knees, trying to find logic in this recent onslaught of dreams. They are brutally menacing and mysterious, yet somehow familiar. The sweat-soaked sheets, pungent with the smell of my fear, cool beneath me. I have stopped changing them, an act that has become futile with the cyclical nightmares. Instead, I shower each morning, and at night slip between the fouled sheets, knowing what is to come, but too exhausted to fight it.

Each night presents varying versions of the same dream. They are visions of darkness and of light. Both are terrifying, yet it is the appearance of light within the dream that awakens me; it is the light I dread most. My fear is complete yet childlike, for I am a child in these dreams. And there are others, other children like me. I haven't seen them within these dreams, yet I know they are there. Their voices are genderless, the cautious whisperings of incomprehensible words, and, like me, they fear the arrival of light. Alternately, in the waking hours, I fear the coming of night and the need for sleep nearly as much.

On the other nights, I do not dream. Or maybe I do, but I'm too drained to recall them.

The clock on the nightstand tells me that it's slightly after 4 a.m., which seems to be the calling hour for these nightmares. It is set for 5:30, and, despite the weariness that weighs on me, I know falling back to sleep will be fruitless. Not particularly wishing to return there anyway, I press the plunger.

So I shower, dress, and sit at the kitchen table with a cup of coffee, a bagel, and the latest Lee Child novel, the latter two of which go untouched. Reading is my lifeline, but through the current string of nightmares and insomnia, we have become estranged. Not to read two or three novels a week, even simultaneously, is alien, and despite my appreciation for Mister Child's dependably entertaining Jack Reacher series, I haven't had the attention capacity to make it fifty pages in the last two weeks. I had fared no better with the new Walking Dead graphic novel, which lay opened and facedown on the living room couch, a position I envied.

This fatigue does not bode well, being that I am an electrician, a profession I more fell into than chose. Nevertheless, fifteen years later, it pays the rent and keeps me fed and well stocked with books. I learned my trade from Henry Kinney, he and his wife Erica being the last in a line of foster parents and the first who wished to adopt a solemn, chronically depressed eleven-year-old son of a drug-addled mother and unknown sire.

When I was eight, I had turned up near Rockingham Park in Salem, New Hampshire, about twelve miles from my *then* home in Lawrence, Massachusetts, and coincidentally, about the same distance from my *now* home in the refurbished mills of Haverhill.

I had never been reported missing, nor could I tell them where I had been. I had had no answers for the Salem police, except that I was Raymond Bassett from Lawrence and my mother's name was Nadine. Years later, I would learn that they had found my mother in her apartment, four days dead of a heroin overdose.

For three years I disappointed a series of foster parents—four couples in total—whose hopes for an idealistic and upbeat son had been dashed by my morose disposition. The Kinneys took me in when I was eleven, and there I stayed as an only child. Maybe I fit in well because, due to an early hysterectomy, adoption was Erica's only chance at motherhood. Or maybe it was because they were about as unexceptional as I was. In all fairness, they treated me well when no one else would and they seemed to understand my gravity. They schooled me, clothed me, and kept me safe—things my own mother and father failed to do.

I still work for Henry Kinney. I've inherited his surname and if I manage to make it through these recent trials without electrocuting myself, I will be inheriting Kinney Electric once Henry retires, which he says will be soon.

The buzzing from my cell phone on the countertop startles me: "Steve Everett" blinks on the display.

"Hey," I answer.

"Well, a fine howdy-do to you, too," says my friend. "Reading Nicholas Sparks again, are we?"

"Funny guy. No, slept like shit."

"Does shit sleep?"

"You do," I say. I have my witty moments.

"Who's the funny guy now? Still having nightmares?"

"Yeah."

"Same one?"

"Yeah."

"Maybe you should see a psych or something," Steve says, more concerned.

"Maybe...if it continues much longer. I've seen enough of them for two lifetimes." Therapy had been mandatory until I was eighteen, voluntary (but still necessary) afterward. I've had a steady diet of nearly every anti-depressant the psycho-pharma industry has to offer and systematically built a befitting immunity to each.

"You working today?"

"Yeah."

"Electricity plus zero sleep equals not good," he reminds me.

"I know. It's a mindless job today. Residential. New construction." I look at the clock on the oven. Time to leave. "Need to wrap it up today. Drywallers come on Monday."

"Emily's asking about you," he says.

I knew it was coming. Emily is a good friend to Steve and Becky; she was her maid-of-honor. She is bubbly, doe-eyed, and as cute as a kitten. After an ugly divorce from a disloyal husband and two years of healing, Steve and Becky conspired to hook us up. Emily and I dated for nearly a year, but I would never allow myself into the relationship and broke it off about four months earlier before Emily or her daughter Cassandra could become too attached to me.

Like Steve and Becky, and like Henry and Erica, Emily holds a better assessment of me than I do of myself and she still hopes I will reconsider the relationship. I assure you, there is nothing wrong with Emily. She's stunning in every way and would be the pride of any sane man. The problem lies in my self-worth. I'm thirty-three, never married, and childless...it isn't rocket science.

"She's the ultimate catch, Ray," Steve says. "Men would offer their kingdom and select body parts for a woman like her."

"That was never my argument."

"I love you, brother, but you're an idiot."

"No argument there, either," I say.

"Come for dinner after work," he says.

"I would, guy, but I'm wiped. I need to sleep."

"Take a couple sleeping pills," Steve says.

"I might try that."

"Try not. Do or do not, there is no try," Steve says in an excellent Yoda impression.

"Okay, Fozzie Bear," I say.

"You get a pass on that. Call me tonight."

We hang up and I head to work which, despite (or due to) the tedious simplicity of the job, seems an eternity. By the time the shift is over I'm floating in a gauzy haze, a sharp pain is settling in behind my eyes, and Kyle, my apprentice, is observing me with concern.

"Sleep, dude!" he says.

We head in separate directions—he most likely toward wine, women, and song, and me to Buy the Book, and then home. Buy the Book is one of very few bookstores on the North Shore, and one of even fewer privately owned ones dealing in new and used titles, the kind of store I prefer to support. I stop in like clockwork on Fridays to browse the newly received used titles, and to pick up whichever of my pre-orders have come in. But the way I am feeling, I won't be browsing tonight.

"Hey, Sparky!" Tom greets from his station behind the counter, which is a cityscape of piled books that looks ready to cascade should he risk adding anything more.

Tom Bossey is the only person who consistently calls me Sparky, my nickname for obvious reasons. Henry has told me on a few occasions to beware of people who give other people nicknames, but Tom seems harmless enough. Tom started at Buy the Book eight or so months ago. He's fiftyish but appears older. Large and untoned, he looks soft, like someone who spends far too much time sitting and snacking. His ovoid head is devoid of hair aside from scant eyebrows, and nests into his shoulders as if he has no neck. As a whole, he looks quite like an egg. As you can imagine, he is not an attractive man, but he is amiable and knows his books. Seeing me up close he scrunches his nose in distaste and it dramatically transforms his face.

"Whoa, you look like shit!" he says, and then hunches his shoulders, realizing he has cussed aloud. A young woman chuckles from a couple of rows away. He cups a hand near his mouth and whispers, "I hope she was worth it."

The woman comes to the head of the aisle, looks at me, smiles coyly, and returns to browsing. She is bookish and pretty, but, as I am wont to do, I dismiss her, assuming she is judging me or is displeased by what she sees.

"Hi, Tom," I say, and smile apologetically. "Yeah, I've been under the weather lately. Won't be doing much in the way of shopping today, but I'll pick up my orders."

"Can't say I blame you," he says. He turns laboriously in his chair to scan the towering stacks on the shelf behind him. "Three this week. New titles from Jonathan Kellerman, Tawni O'Dell, and that Christopher Golden fellow who lives in town."

He deftly slips the books from the stack without spilling the works and places them on the counter. I pull four twenties from my wallet and lay them on the counter as Tom rings it up.

"Oh!" he says, recalling something. He stands and shuffles to a nearby shelf, removes a book titled *The Hidden Meaning of Dreams*, and tosses it on the counter. "This just came in. Thought it might interest you since you asked about dream books last week."

"Thanks! How much?" I ask.

"On the house," he says. "Our *thank you* for sticking with us and not buying online for a fraction of the cost."

"I wouldn't dream of it," I say, although I have. "You sure?"

"Yes. Cost us nothing. It came from a box of books an old

lady gave us. Get out of here. Go home, pop a couple Nytol, and get some sleep."

I arrive home around 5:30, put a frozen pizza in the oven, and stare uncomprehendingly at the television until the smoke detector protests. I throw the charred gluten Frisbee into the trash and settle for three Kraft singles, chased with a glass of water and two Sominex tablets from a travel pack I purchased from a convenience market.

I embark on a drawn-out session of page flipping through *The Hidden Meaning of Dreams*, trying to decode my nightmares until my eyes burn, and my head-drops justify the threat of whiplash. I remove myself to my bedroom, strip, and slip between my grimy sheets, too drowsy to let the smell bother me. I ask a short, silent prayer that the Sominex will help me sleep soundly and nightmare free.

It doesn't work. I don't fall asleep...I plummet into it, entering my night-world headlong.

Utter darkness.

Beneath me the surface is unforgiving, cold concrete. The space is tight, box-like, and sloped overhead ... a staircase. It reeks of urine and waste. I can feel the dampness of it on the floor. There is no escaping from it. I sit with my back against a wall, my legs extended. My foot is touching another bare foot. A child's. A third child sidles a little closer to me until our shoulders touch.

A door slams somewhere distant above us and we all gasp in unison. Footsteps traverse overhead, concussing like kettledrums. The boy closest to me starts crying, a soft mewling that makes me feel sorry for him, but also irritates me. We are all boys, this I know for some unknown reason.

Something small and furry skitters across the floor, over our legs and away, causing the boy to mewl louder.

Kenny...his name is Kenny, and the other one is Paul. We had disclosed this earlier through whispers. Kenny is the newest here, then me, and then Paul. Paul doesn't cry anymore. Glen was here the longest, but he isn't here anymore. I hope he got away. Like Paul, Glen didn't cry either.

Above us thunders the cannon-shot pounding of feet as something huge descends the stairs, and then it becomes comparatively silent as they contact the concrete floor. Metal clacks, clicks, bullwhip loud, and the three of us retreat, afraid of the light we know will come.

Then it comes—a blinding portent—and I, too, cry.

An arm, freakishly long and thick, reaches in, piercing the intense light. The pale skin is matted with bushy dark hair and riddled with a host of dime-sized scars, long healed. It swipes the air, missing us, then returns. It grasps my hair and pulls me through the opening into a dimly lit basement, crowded with cast-off domestic items from an earlier generation. It is a man, a fat shadow-giant; he blocks the brilliance of the light bulb, leaving him featureless in shadows. I fight with my thin arms and try to escape on adolescent legs, to no benefit. Metal clacks and clicks again; a lock engages. I am dragged up the stairs, down a hallway, into a bathroom.

I see him: a man, but a hallucination, a creature of nightmares. He is made anonymous by a full beard and mustache, copious amounts of hair, tangled and falling to his shoulders.

"You stink," he says, and grimaces with distaste.

He looks feral, a sneering wolf that terrifies me and I'm not certain he won't attack me, sink his teeth in, and rend pieces of flesh from me. He orders me to remove my shorts and tee shirt; I know better than to contend. He twists the shower faucet, pushes me inside, and orders me to wash. The water is frigid and I turn from him and stare at the missing tiles and the creases of thick, black mold.

He throws a towel at me and pushes me into a cluttered bedroom, a hoarder's bedroom, where he makes me do hideous and painful things. I close my eyes to hide from him and his sickly slug-like skin, all that black hair and countless dime-sized scars...rings upon rings...that ring and ring like a phone rings...

I shove the covers off and scramble out of bed, yelling my anguish and disgust. I am soiled by the imagery of the dream. I want to vomit. I need to shower, to cleanse myself of such filth. I can't breathe.

My cell phone rings again and the image of the little circles return. *Cigar burns*, my mind reasons, and I know it's true. I grab my cell phone from my nightstand, sending my glasses to the floor and nearly toppling the lamp.

"Hello!" I gasp, still breathless, still wanting to vomit.

"Bonjour, amigo! You never called last night, dickhead!" says Steve in his too-loud and buoyant voice.

"Yeah. Parlez-vous fuck you," I croak in return. I weave my way around the bed and into the bathroom, feeling my bladder will fail. I look at my bathtub, the tiled wall, and although it's clean—well, bachelor clean—I feel my gorge rise.

"You still sleeping, man? It's past noon!"

"Bullshit," I say, but look at the face of my cell phone. He's right. I sit on the throne, too unsteady to risk misfiring.

"Kicked the insomnia thing, it seems."

"Maybe, but the nightmares went into hyperdrive."

"Really? That sucks. Come for dinner today. It's at six, but come at four, or earlier, I don't give a shit."

"I…"

"Have no choice in the matter, asshole," he interrupts. "Becky's making your favorite, American chop suey."

I think to myself, *I hate American chop suey* and he knows that.

"Fucking with you," he says. "Steaks, fried zucchini, summer squash, and copious amounts of beer."

At dinner with Steve and Becky is where I get my first inkling of why I'm having the nightmares. Emily is here, too. Steve insists it is totally innocent and unplanned. I believe him. She *is* Becky's best friend.

I explain the dream in detail and receive a lot of speculation in return, most of which I'd rather not consider, but Becky makes a comment, highlighting a single word that changes my approach.

"Trigger," she says. "Something must have triggered you to initiate all these nightmares. Do you remember anything happening, or is there something in the dream that triggers you?"

"Everything," I say, but the light, the cigar burns, and that wolfish sneer stand out.

Emily notices my discomfort and asks, "What is it? Do you think it happened to you?" I sense her concern and I'm torn between appreciation and irritation. "Do you remember something?"

"Trigger," Becky says knowingly.

"That would cause depression," Steve offers. I glare at him.

I shake my head in denial as they try to delve deeper into my darkness. I tell them I recognized nothing until they finally dismiss it, but I do remember *something*. I'm not certain what or who, but it lingers with me like a bee sting, burning at my conscience until it slowly emerges…a possibility.

I dismiss myself, proclaiming exhaustion, but my senses are reeling. I'm going to look for cigar burns and a sneer I think I've recently seen. We exchange hugs, Steve, Becky, and then Emily, who quietly whispers to me, "I miss you."

I smile at her, not sure how to respond, feeling inadequate because of it…feeling helpless and like an asshole.

I open the door and carry a box into Buy the Book.

"Hey, Sparky," Tom says from his post behind the counter.

"Thirty or so hardcovers for credit," I say, and set the box in front of him.

"Any more credit, you'll own the store," he says, pulling the box to him.

The store policy is, return credit can only be applied to used titles. I buy primarily new unless something rare or unusual shows up. My credit passed the eyebrow-raising point a couple years earlier. I know I'll never use it but consider it support for the small business.

"Maybe you should have taken the dream book off," I say, and Tom chuckles.

"Did it help you any?"

"Not yet. Had nightmares again last night, but I was too tired to read it."

He lifts a stack of books from the box and sets them on the counter. Despite the summer heat, Tom is wearing a long-sleeve dress shirt, fastened one button short of his neck. *Has he always worn long sleeves*? I wonder. I never had reason to consider it before.

I wander down the fiction aisle. "Any old Harry Crews come in?" I ask, watching Tom through the gaps in the shelves.

"Doubt it. Not on my watch. Just the standard crap," he says.

"Did you just refer to Harry Crews' literature as *crap?*" I ask, trying to sound playful. I pull a random title from the shelf and pretend to read the back cover.

"I suppose I did," he says.

He reaches into the box and recoils, his face crumpling in disgust. It's difficult to tell with his lack of any hair, but to me the sneer looks savage, quite possibly wolfish, quite possibly the sneer of my nightmares…but maybe not.

"There's something dead in here," he says, stepping back from the box.

I walk to the counter, place the novel down, and look inside the box. I feign surprise at the offending field mouse, although I had put it in the box that morning.

"Well look at that," I say, picking up the minuscule creature by the tail. "No credit for this?"

"I'd say not," Tom says, cowering as I toss it into the trash barrel behind the counter.

"Is that a new Howard Schatz?" I ask, pointing to a tall book on the top row of the orders shelf behind Tom. I pray that it's an art book. It looks like one, and it is the only book on which I can read the author's name clearly.

"You're into photography?" Tom asks.

"Schatz's photography," I say. "Can I have a look?"

"Sure, but it's a customer's copy." Tom turns and reaches for the book and I have to calm my reaction when his shirt cuff drops back enough to expose a set of dime-sized burn marks.

(Trigger)

Tom notices, too, and adjusts his sleeve, but he also sees the change in my expression.

"What's wrong," he asks cautiously, slowly setting the large book on the counter between us.

Think fast…think fast.

"Were you a welder?" I ask. "My dad was a welder and he had similar marks on his arms." It's a bold lie, but not unfounded; I had seen similar marks on welders.

He watches me and I can almost hear the thoughts and questions shuffling about inside his head. "Yeah," he says, studying me. "Thirteen years at the Portsmouth Naval Shipyard." I can tell he is lying, too.

"Wow, that must be painful," I say, thinking, *pamper his ego*. "My dad never complained, either, but I can't see how that didn't hurt. You have to be pretty tough."

Tom watches me for a moment and then smiles, buying my story. "Won't say I enjoyed it," he says less suspiciously, but I can tell he's still wary.

He totals my credit as I skim through the Schatz book. The work is impressive. I return the book to him and he points at the novel I had set on the counter.

"You want that?" he asks and I nod, having no idea what it is. "Use credit?" I nod again.

I can feel his eyes burning into my back as I leave the store, and it is all I can do not to run. I climb into my car, my mind reeling and my nerves afire; any feelings of exhaustion are obliterated. It's surreal…unreal. The probability that he is the man in my nightmares is distressing, but not nearly as distressing as the possibility that the nightmares might be due to something that really happened, some repressed memories. I recall the pasty, slug-like blotted skin touching me in the dreams as he forces me to do the unspeakable.

I feel nauseated. I drive to a crowded parking lot at a strip mall that is cattycorner to the bookstore. I park near a hedge in case the need to purge becomes overwhelming. I want to go home and overdose on Paxil and sink into a comfortable pillow of numb detachment, but I stay. I want to know the truth, need the truth, but have no idea how to get it.

I watch Tom's cumbersome form slouched behind the counter—for how long, I'm not sure. My dash clock reads 9:02 p.m. when the bookstore lights go out, shaking me from my stupor. Five minutes later Tom emerges, locks the door, and then walks to his car. He struggles into the old Honda Accent, which sinks dramatically beneath his girth. All is still and I wait until the lights flare and the car backs from the curb. The driver-side taillight is dimmer than the other and it occurs to me this would make following him easy. So I do. Through downtown Haverhill, onto Route 97, and clear into Salem, New Hampshire. I follow, staying well back. He drives a couple miles onto Lawrence Road until he slows and turns left near the wetlands. I drive slowly past the barely detectable dirt path Tom had turned onto and look for somewhere close but unobvious to park. The front lot of a neighboring auto junkyard offers me exactly that.

I am terrified by what I'm contemplating.

Would he even live in the same house, if it is truly him? I wonder.

What about the hair? my inner coward asks.

He shaved his head, dipshit! my inner rebel responds. It's called a disguise.

As is typical of me, I start to doubt myself and consider driving home, but I look in the rearview at my tired eyes and I fight the urge. The burns, the sneer, it's too much for simple coincidence. I need to know.

I leave the car and enter the dirt road, a dual rutted path that extends into tree-shrouded darkness. In the oppressive heat of the night, the swamp smell is acrid and cloying and within seconds, swarms of mosquitoes discover me and start to feast. I keep to the edge of the path, ready to duck into the trees at any hint of movement. In the near distance I can make out the lighted windows of a house, and in the driveway, I see Tom's Honda.

Once I'm close enough, the old New England saltbox comes into view. Its details are muted in the moonless night, but it is white and weatherworn, years, maybe decades, in need of new paint.

I circle around the left side of the house, furtive, staying nearer the path...and the mosquito-infested water. As I approach the back yard, the shape of a shed emerges, decrepit and sagging under the weight of years and neglect, and likewise, the drooping roof on the back porch.

A sense of déjà vu assails me. I freeze and stare.

The porch...

(Trigger)

> *Pillars formed of mortar and baseball-sized stones support the porch and roof, rising up from the ground. Behind them, under the porch, a crawlspace cloaked in blackness, a child's face peers out from beneath.*

The yard overflows with blazing light and I freeze, unaware that I have been walking toward the house. Sensitive to my vulnerability, I dash ten yards to hide behind a large oak. I wait, expecting the worst, but realize that a pair of motion-sensor flood lamps has fooled me.

"Who's out there?" Tom's voice rings out from the direction of the back door.

I wait, unmoving until the lights die, and a moment later, I hear the sound of the closing door. I back away from the tree, cautious, trying to keep it between the motion sensors and me.

TRIGGERS

I see the porch again, the dark crawlspace beneath, and I remember…

(Trigger)

Light spears into the darkness. Blinded, we recoil as the scarred arm reaches in, grabs onto Paul's hair, and drags him toward the light. There is something different this time. Paul fights. He is savage. He kicks and latches onto the arm with his teeth. A man roars in pain. Paul is torn from the space and thrown against a wall. He screams in protest as two sets of feet slam and scrape up the stairway above our heads.

The hatch is still open, forgotten in the struggle. I grab Kenny's arm and drag him out the opening, away from the stairway and toward a door on the far side of the basement. The door opens easily and we push our way up through the bulkhead, which slams a loud betrayal that echoes across the yard and garners another scream of rage from within the house.

In our panic, I dash for the woods. Kenny dives for the crawlspace under the porch, but the fat shadow-giant bursts onto the porch and sees Kenny's wriggling legs.

I hide behind a large oak, the same oak I would hide behind twenty-five years later. The fat shadow-giant lunges toward the shed and I retreat farther from the house, stopping behind another large oak. The fat shadow-giant returns carrying a long spade.

Kenny's pale face peers from beneath the porch and then retreats into darkness as the fat shadow-giant kneels and stabs the shovel into the blackness beneath. I avert my eyes as Kenny's anguished shrieks cut the night, and I cower in the darkness when, minutes later, the fat shadow-giant walks past me toward the wetlands,

Kenny's lifeless body draped over his shoulder. When he returns and enters the house, I run as fast as I can, away from there.

I am numbed by the memories, so anesthetized that I don't hear Tom approach from behind until the lights come to life and I feel cold metal behind my ear.

"What the fuck are you doing here, Sparky?" Tom asks, confused and guarded.

I look at Tom, the fat shadow-giant, the monster in my nightmares, and all I can say is "My name is Raymond." I feel weak, helpless, and totally defeated.

Tom lifts his right hand and shines a flashlight in my eyes. "Was that you following me tonight? What are you up to, Sparky?" he asks.

"You killed him," I say. "You…"

A light fills his eyes—recognition. "Son of a bitch, that was you?" he says, sounding almost reverential, but there is no sign of fear or remorse, and I knew there wasn't just Kenny.

"You killed Glen and Paul, too."

"Oh, they had names? I don't name my toys. Never did, never will," he says, and it occurs to me that there were more, possibly many. I glance toward the house. "Two more in there," he says. "Want to play, too?"

The rage in me builds and I yell, "We were just kids, you sick fuck!"

A sharp pain lights up my jaw as he whacks me with the flashlight and then puts the barrel of a handgun against my ribs.

"Oh, you never complained," he says. "Give me your car keys."

It dawns on me that I won't be leaving here alive. My legs

loosen beneath me, blackness fills my head, and I struggle against passing out. I tell him they're still in the car. The fat shadow-giant looks at me, a blend of anger and humor fighting in his expression. He chuckles.

"Let's go for a walk," he says. He pushes at my back trying to steer me toward the water. I resist and he shoots me in the hamstring. The pain is brutal, fiery glass shards that override all thought and bring me fully to the present. I fall to the ground grasping at the wound.

"The next one hits your kneecap. I don't want to carry you, but I will if I have to. Now get up and move. Let's be reasonable."

I struggle to my feet and he directs me. I hop about two hundred feet into the woods that skirt the wetlands. When we stop, my leg is throbbing and blood-soaked. He aims his flashlight at a large pile of rocks and I'm sure he's going to tell me this is where he buried his victims, but it is worse. He redirects the light to a pool of blackness in the rocks and the light disappears into its depths.

"Pit cave," he tells me straightforwardly. "Natural shaft. It goes straight down, but I don't know how deep. Never heard a body hit bottom."

Sweat pours from my face, my body is shaking, and I feel myself fading, waning into shock. I reach to a tree for support and close my eyes, fighting to remain conscious.

"You're next. Going where you should have all those years ago. Kind of ironic, really, like it's karma or something," he says.

He remains oddly silent for a while. When I open my eyes the fat shadow-giant is staring transfixed at the shaft.

The grayish form of a boy in tattered rags climbs from the mouth of the pit cave. Another follows, and then another, until at least a dozen boys surround the fat shadow-giant. I recognize the ashen faces of Kenny, Paul, and Glen among them, their eyes all locked on their tormentor, their murderer. They step toward him, their circle tightening, and then, as if choreographed, every head turns my way and every eye meets mine. My head is suddenly alive with their voices, and in unison, they give a single nod and say a single word. One command and I obey.

As the fat shadow-giant lifts his gun toward one of the children, I push from the tree with everything I've got left, driving my shoulder into his huge belly. Pain explodes from my leg as I tumble to the ground, and as I let go of my final strand of consciousness, I hear his descent.

I hold the door for Henry and Erica as we enter the restaurant. It's been three weeks since that night at Tom Bossey's house. My leg is mostly healed, although I still limp. The stream of questions has seemed endless since I phoned 911 at three that morning when I came to, lying a few feet from the pit cave. Some people don't believe me, but most do. Certain parts I left out, as you can imagine, but the numbers add up, from my age when I appeared on Broadway in Salem, to the testimony of the two boys they rescued from Tom Bossey's basement.

There were teary reunions. For two families at least, I am a hero.

Today we are celebrating Henry Kinney's retirement and my advancement to president of Kinney Electric. Steve, Becky, Emily, and Cassandra are here, too.

Some things are the same. I still pop a Paxil a day and I'm back to seeing my shrink on Thursday evenings, but there has been a lot of closure. There are still a lot of triggers.

As we all take our seats, I smile at Emily. She leans to me and says, "I love you."

It's been easier to accept this.

I realize I am worth it...most of the time.

AFTERWORD

by Izzy Lee

Everyone okay after reading that last story? No? Yes? Welcome to 2020.

I've known John M. McIlveen (known as "Mac" within our circle) for a few years, and I can't recall a time when I haven't seen him smiling or at least generally cheerful. Although... there was that one time when we were talking about book covers and I pulled out my phone to show him some pretty terribly illustrated covers which had flabbergasted me, and the look he threw me was *are you fucking kidding me??* That was the correct reaction, I promise you.

Anyway, because of that one moment, that flickering of movement behind the happiness curtain, I can see where these stories come from. And no, he's not a lunatic, but a full-fledged human being (as well as a father and husband) who happens to have another side to him. After all, there is no light without darkness, no lotus without at least a little bit of mud.

Let's be honest, people; we all think about getting revenge on someone who's wronged us (or worse) from time to time. For those of you who don't ingest horror on a regular basis (and no, I'm not talking about the last four years of living in the U.S.), create it, or hang out with people who do --- I can tell you that horror people are the best people. We're the kindest, most empathetic people on the planet.

Why? There are theories. One is that we've been through a lot/insert trauma here, and that we tend to treat others kinder, because we can only guess that they, also being human beings, have likely been through a lot as well.

Then there's the catharsis horror offers, the psychological bootcamp we put ourselves through to get a sense of relief from this world. A heightened reality can offer a strange sense of relief from the everyday boredom, stress, and conundrums that this uber fast-paced reality has beset upon us. Those offering an escape consisting of heightened reality can sometimes make a lot of money if they possess talent and a good amount of luck.

Another theory is that creating horror is our therapy, that we get our demons out by expressing them, because we either cannot or will not suppress ourselves. Those that do tend to have issues. All you have to do is look at those that are repressed in any sense. Those unfortunate individuals tend to become villains despite their best intentions, whether they know it or not --- everyone is a hero in their own story.

Mac's stories have an assortment of villains (or heroes, depending how they'd look at it) who may or may not escape comeuppance --- but if they don't, it just may be that we don't get to read that part of their own personal story. Things could (and should) end badly for them. But mostly, the evil ones doing harm to others usually get what they deserve.

Here's the thing --- horror writers and creators see injustice in the world and how so many times that injustice goes unpunished --- and we right that wrong the only way we know how. Otherwise, we may end up in jail alongside those perpetrators due to vigilantism. Likewise for our readers and audiences, consuming horror is a safe way to explore otherwise uncomfortable themes and situations.

If you've never attempted to explore the deepest, darkest depths of horror yourself, I hope you find yourself inspired by reading Mac's stories, which are some very fine examples of the genre indeed.

Izzy Lee
Boston
September 2020

John M. McIlveen is the author of the paranormal suspense novel, *Hannahwhere*, winner of the 2015 Drunken Druid Award (Ireland) and nominated for the 2015 Bram Stoker Award (HWA), and three collections, *A Variable Darkness*, *Inflictions* and *Jerks*.

His forthcoming novel, *Girl Gone North,* nominated for the Wilber and Niso Smith Foundation Award for unpublished manuscripts, will be out in late 2021.

He is a father to five daughters, works at MIT's Lincoln Laboratory, and is CEO and Editor-In-Chief of Haverhill House Publishing. He lives in Haverhill, MA with his wife Roberta Colasanti.

Please visit him on Facebook and at www.johnmcilveen.com and www.haverhillhouse.com